BE GAY DO COMICS!

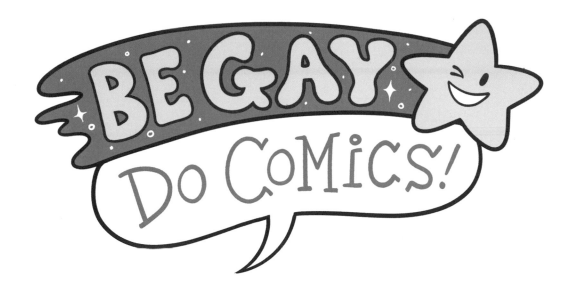

Be Gay, Do Comics:
Queer History, Memoir, and Satire

Editor and Publisher: Matt Bors
Features Editor: Eleri Harris
Associate Editor: Matt Lubchansky
Contributing Editors: Sarah Mirk and Andy Warner
Editorial Assistant: Delta Vasquez
Book Design: Mark Kaufman
Cover and Endpapers: Mady G

thenib.com

Edited for IDW by Justin Eisinger, Alonzo Simon, and Zac Boone
Production assistance by Tara McCrillis

ISBN: 978-1-68405-777-1   25 24 23 22   3 4 5 6
BE GAY, DO COMICS. OCTOBER 2021. THIRD PRINTING.

All Stories © their respective creators.
© 2020 Idea and Design Works, LLC.
The IDW logo is registered in the U.S. Patent and Trademark Office.
IDW Publishing, a division of Idea and Design Works, LLC.
Editorial offices: 2355 Northside Drive, Suite 140, San Diego, CA 92108.
Any similarities to persons living or dead are purely coincidental.
With the exception of artwork used for review purposes, none of
the contents of this publication may be reprinted without the
permission of Idea and Design Works, LLC.

Printed in Korea.

IDW Publishing does not read or accept unsolicited
submissions of ideas, stories, or artwork.

Queer History, Memoir, and Satire from *The Nib*

Contents

Introduction

Without Comics, I Might Not Know I Was Queer.

That might be an exaggeration, but you want these things to really pop, right? I *do* know that without the comics community I'm a part of, it definitely would have taken longer for me to accept myself, come out, and transition. I can't think of a medium where queer voices are more thriving and accepted than the modern independent comics scene. It's obviously not without its problems, but comics provided me a space where I could meet other queer people and where I could read as much queer work as I could possibly ever want.

Comics are the best way I know how to express myself, so the medium even provided me a place (reprinted in the pages of this book, no less!) where I could come out to a lot of people in my life. Comics are accessible in a way that other forms of media could only dream of being. They're not only accessible for the reader, who is presented with a lot of information in an easily digestible way, but for the creator: One person can control the entire narrative in a medium they can publish easily online or cheaply in print. Thus, comics presents amazing opportunities to be heard, and to hear each other, and to make the exact stories that we want and need to tell.

You can trace the phrase "Be Gay, Do Crime" back to the person who popularized it with a meme, Io Ascarium of ABO Comix, a great collective that sells comics made by queer prisoners. And it's a solid ethos to live by as a queer person in these times (and well, always). Queerness has always been transgressive, regardless of its legal status. The world has come seemingly far even in just my lifetime, but I fear the ground will never be as solid as we want, the gains not as permanent as we deserve. For many of us and our siblings, particularly those of color, it's still dangerous to move through the world. We're always one election cycle away from being used as a wedge issue. One public conversation away from one of the identities under the larger LGBTQ+ umbrella being singled out for hatred and sold out for acceptance from the wider straight world. The more queerness is "accepted" by the state and capital, the more vigilant we all have to be. Nike shoes with a pink triangle aren't for us, they're for them. Be gay. Consider who the law was meant to protect and who passed it. Look out for each other instead. So, when our (amazing!) cover artist, Mady G, suggested the title of this book, we knew we had a winner.

We're presented with a lucky opportunity here in independent comics in 2020: make what we want, for who we want. We can tell our stories, remember our history, advocate for our dreams, make each other laugh. Be gay, do comics.

Matt Lubchansky
Associate Editor

1

JOEY ALISON SAYERS

The Final Reveal

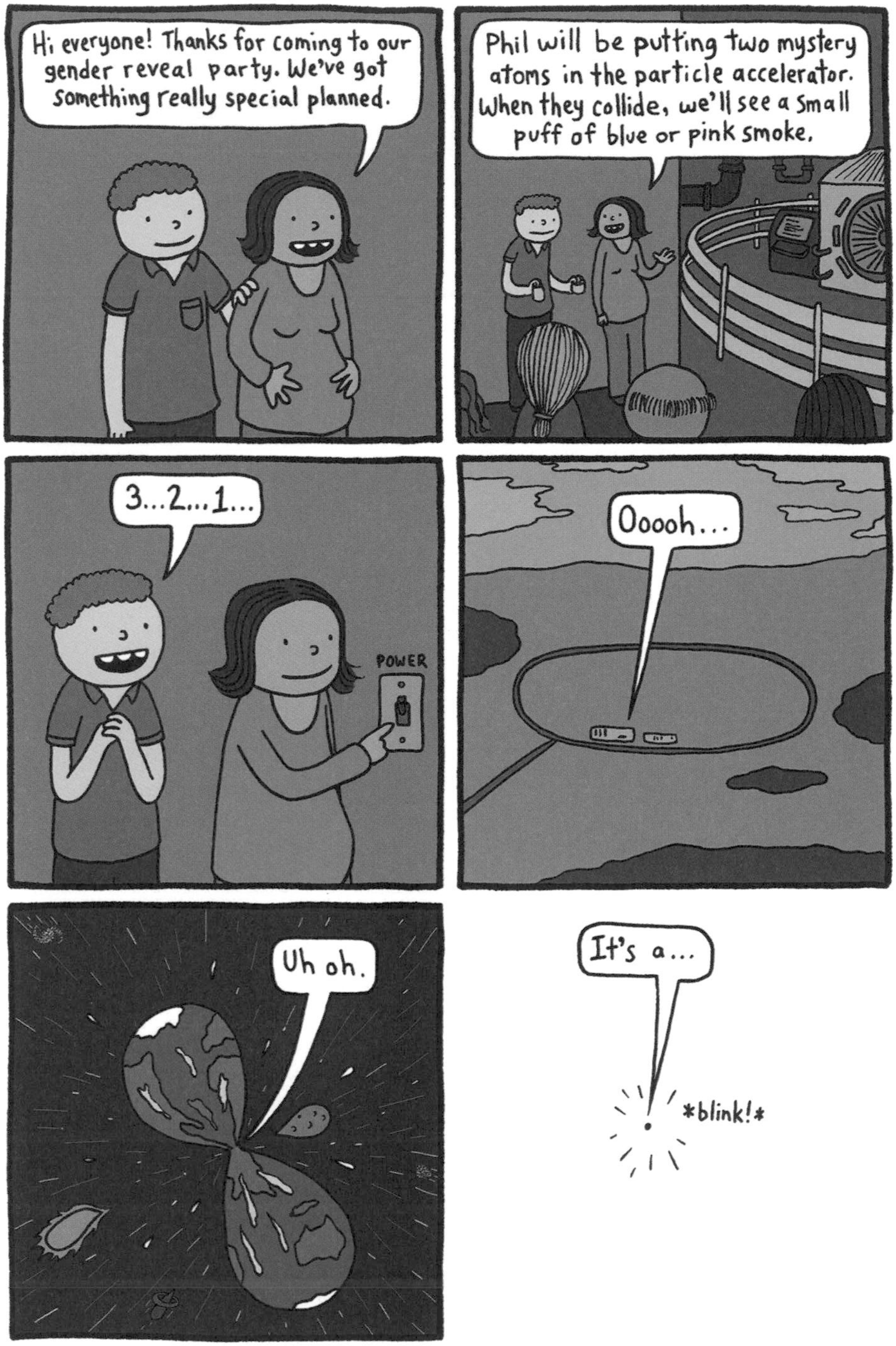
Hi everyone! Thanks for coming to our gender reveal party. We've got something really special planned.
Phil will be putting two mystery atoms in the particle accelerator. When they collide, we'll see a small puff of blue or pink smoke.
3...2...1...
POWER
Ooooh...
Uh oh.
It's a...
blink!

Gender Bent

OOPSIE! AN ARIZONA FATHER PLED GUILTY FOR CAUSING 8 MILLION DOLLARS WORTH OF DAMAGES THANKS TO A GENDER REVEAL PARTY GONE WRONG!

NEED SOME UNIQUE IDEAS FOR YOUR GENDER REVEAL THAT WON'T BURN DOWN 45,000 ACRES OF LAND? WE GOT YOU COVERED!!

RIG A CUSTOM GUILLOTINE TO BEHEAD A DOLL THAT BEARS A COINCIDENTAL RESEMBLANCE TO A POLITICIAN AND THE FAKE BLOOD WILL REVEAL THE GENDER! VIVE LA REVOLUTION, BABY!

COLOR A DOVE EITHER BLUE OR PINK AND RELEASE IT INTO THE SKY! JUST MAKE SURE YOU DO IT IN A CONTAINED ENVIRONMENT, AND NOT OUT IN THE WILDERNESS SOMEWHERE.

CAKES FULL OF CANDY ARE SO PASSE! FILL A CAKE WITH A GOAT'S ORGANS TO PORTEND YOUR HEIR'S GENITALIA!

ESCHEW GENDER REVEALS ALTOGETHER. PISS OFF GRANDMA. WE'RE ALL GONNA DIE, FUCK GENDER.

3

MATT LUBCHANSKY

Brands Love Pride

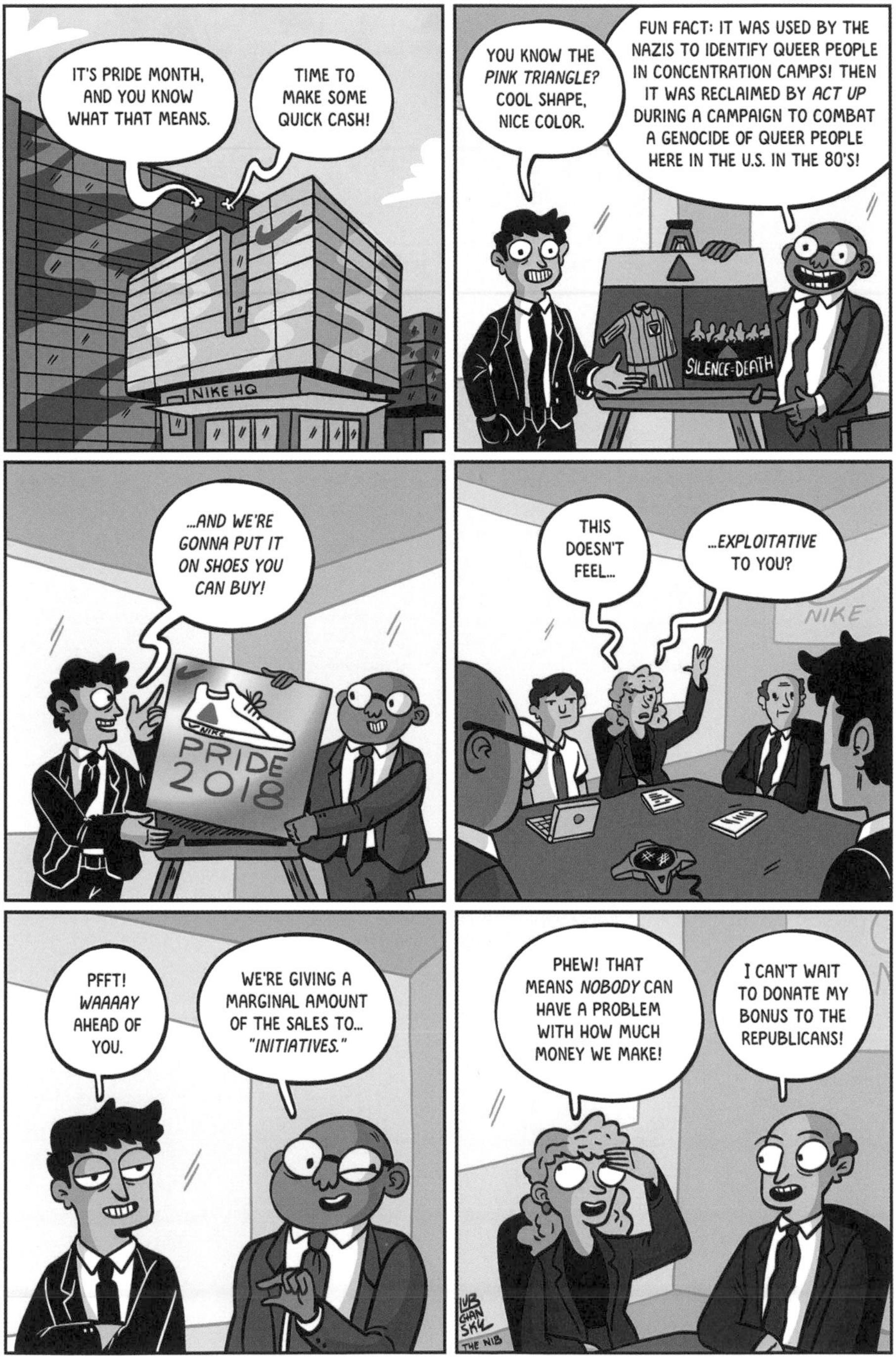
IT'S PRIDE MONTH, AND YOU KNOW WHAT THAT MEANS.
TIME TO MAKE SOME QUICK CASH!
NIKE HQ
YOU KNOW THE *PINK TRIANGLE?* COOL SHAPE, NICE COLOR.
FUN FACT: IT WAS USED BY THE NAZIS TO IDENTIFY QUEER PEOPLE IN CONCENTRATION CAMPS! THEN IT WAS RECLAIMED BY *ACT UP* DURING A CAMPAIGN TO COMBAT A GENOCIDE OF QUEER PEOPLE HERE IN THE U.S. IN THE 80'S!
SILENCE=DEATH
...AND WE'RE GONNA PUT IT ON SHOES YOU CAN BUY!
NIKE
PRIDE 2018
THIS DOESN'T FEEL...
...EXPLOITATIVE TO YOU?
NIKE
PFFT! *WAAAAY* AHEAD OF YOU.
WE'RE GIVING A MARGINAL AMOUNT OF THE SALES TO... *"INITIATIVES."*
PHEW! THAT MEANS *NOBODY* CAN HAVE A PROBLEM WITH HOW MUCH MONEY WE MAKE!
I CAN'T WAIT TO DONATE MY BONUS TO THE REPUBLICANS!
LUBCHANSKY
THE NIB

SASHA VELOUR

Eight Queens

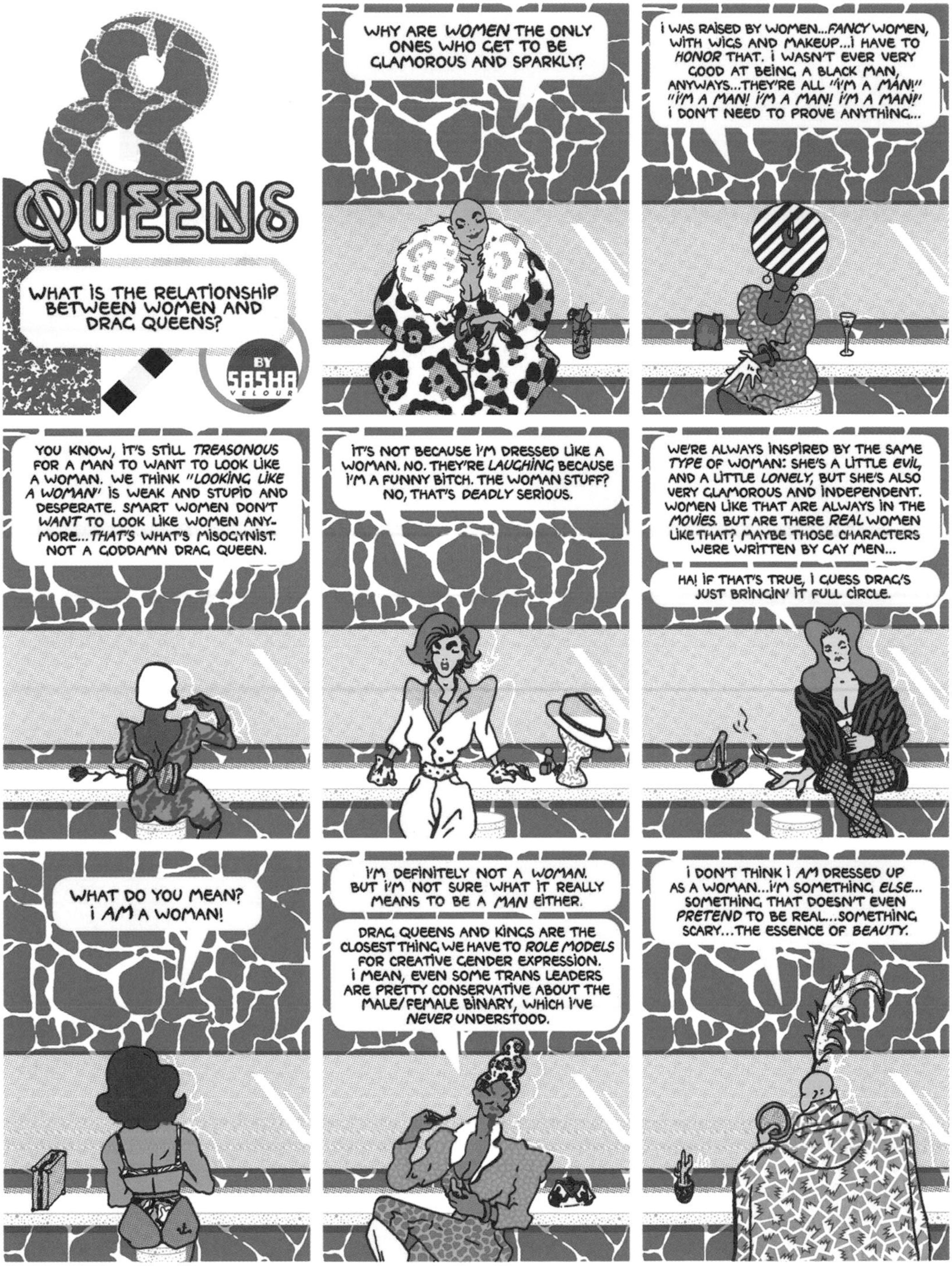
8 QUEENS
WHAT IS THE RELATIONSHIP BETWEEN WOMEN AND DRAG QUEENS?
BY SASHA VELOUR
WHY ARE *WOMEN* THE ONLY ONES WHO GET TO BE GLAMOROUS AND SPARKLY?
I WAS RAISED BY WOMEN...*FANCY* WOMEN, WITH WIGS AND MAKEUP...I HAVE TO *HONOR* THAT. I WASN'T EVER VERY GOOD AT BEING A BLACK MAN, ANYWAYS...THEY'RE ALL *"I'M A MAN!" "I'M A MAN! I'M A MAN! I'M A MAN!"* I DON'T NEED TO PROVE ANYTHING...
YOU KNOW, IT'S STILL *TREASONOUS* FOR A MAN TO WANT TO LOOK LIKE A WOMAN. WE THINK *"LOOKING LIKE A WOMAN"* IS WEAK AND STUPID AND DESPERATE. SMART WOMEN DON'T *WANT* TO LOOK LIKE WOMEN ANY-MORE...*THAT'S* WHAT'S MISOGYNIST. NOT A GODDAMN DRAG QUEEN.
IT'S NOT BECAUSE I'M DRESSED LIKE A WOMAN. NO. THEY'RE *LAUGHING* BECAUSE I'M A FUNNY BITCH. THE WOMAN STUFF? NO, THAT'S *DEADLY* SERIOUS.
WE'RE ALWAYS INSPIRED BY THE SAME *TYPE* OF WOMAN: SHE'S A LITTLE *EVIL*, AND A LITTLE *LONELY*, BUT SHE'S ALSO VERY GLAMOROUS AND INDEPENDENT. WOMEN LIKE THAT ARE ALWAYS IN THE *MOVIES*. BUT ARE THERE *REAL* WOMEN LIKE THAT? MAYBE THOSE CHARACTERS WERE WRITTEN BY GAY MEN...
HA! IF THAT'S TRUE, I GUESS DRAG'S JUST BRINGIN' IT FULL CIRCLE.
WHAT DO YOU MEAN? I *AM* A WOMAN!
I'M DEFINITELY NOT A *WOMAN*. BUT I'M NOT SURE WHAT IT REALLY MEANS TO BE A *MAN* EITHER.
DRAG QUEENS AND KINGS ARE THE CLOSEST THING WE HAVE TO *ROLE MODELS* FOR CREATIVE GENDER EXPRESSION. I MEAN, EVEN SOME TRANS LEADERS ARE PRETTY CONSERVATIVE ABOUT THE MALE/FEMALE BINARY, WHICH I'VE *NEVER* UNDERSTOOD.
I DON'T THINK I *AM* DRESSED UP AS A WOMAN...I'M SOMETHING *ELSE*... SOMETHING THAT DOESN'T EVEN *PRETEND* TO BE REAL...SOMETHING SCARY...THE ESSENCE OF *BEAUTY*.

Astrological Signs As Classic Queer Haircuts

ARIES

SEXY KNOW-IT-ALL QUIFF AND RAT TAIL COMBO

TAURUS

"I STAYED IN BED ALL DAY, ALL I HAD TIME FOR" TOP KNOT

LIBRA

"COULDN'T DECIDE, SO I JUST GOT RID OF IT" BUZZCUT

SCORPIO

TRIES TO MAKE YOU CRY, BUT IS CRYING INSIDE SLICKBACK

GEMINI

FUN BUT SERIOUS IN .02 SECONDS BOB CUT

CANCER

"COOL MOM" RETRO BUN COMBO

SAGITTARIUS

"I FORGOT TO BRUSH MY HAIR AGAIN" MOPTOP

CAPRICORN

"I TRIMMED MY HAIR AND IT'S NOT THAT DIFFERENT, BUT YOU BETTER NOTICE" ANGLED BOB

LEO

SHOWBOAT WITH A FRAGILE EGO MOHAWK

VIRGO

COOL BUT BUSINESS FADE

AQUARIUS

THE "I'M SO UNIQUE BUT HAVE A PRETTY COMMON HAIRCUT" ASYMMETRICAL 'DO

PISCES

SAD POET SHORT HIGH BANG

6

The Life of Gad Beck: Gay. Jewish. Nazi Fighter.

When we think of Queer people and the Holocaust...

It's hard to think of anything but victimization.

But that would be a mistake.

GAD BECK: GAY. JEWISH. NAZI-FIGHTER.

Gad Beck was just ten years old when the Nazis seized power.

Like most Jewish families, the Becks did not have the wealth necessary to flee Germany, even when their passports were still valid.

As a resut, Gad lived most of his early life in Berlin, growing up in the capital of one of the most opressive regimes the world has ever known.

That never stopped Gad.

The attachment he felt to his community was what motivated him to resist the Nazis and find the strength to eventually live a life underground.

Still, the threat was very real.

In 1942, Gad's family received a letter from their Jewish allies in Geneva, warning them of death camps in Eastern Europe.

As the deportation of Berlin's Jewish community picked up pace, Gad grew scared.

He had good reason to be.

But that never stopped Gad.

When his first boyrfriend, Manfred, was seized by the Nazis, Gad responded with a daring rescue.

Disguised as a Hitler Youth, he bluffed his way into where Manfred's family was being held and convinced them to release Manfred into his custody.

Here's some money.

Go to my uncle in Teltow like we discussed, and wait for me.

I'll come as soon as I can.

Gad... My family needs me. If I abandon them, I could never really be free.

Later in life, Gad would say that he "grew up" in those seconds spend watching Manfred walk away.

At the time, Gad could not even begin to imagine what was in store for Manfred.

But he never saw his "first big love" again.

Manfred and his entire family were murdered at Auschwitz.

In 1943, the same year Joseph Goebells declared that all the Jews had been removed from Berlin, Gad helped found CHUG CHALUZI, an underground network of support for Jews living illegally in the city.

Gad spent the rest of the war actively resisting Nazi oppression.

Posing as Swiss diplomats, he and his twin sister became part of a complicated courier system.

Coordinating with fellow resistance movements in Switzerland, they smuggled vital suplies - food, medication, money - into Berlin and covertly distrubuted them to Jewish families living underground.

Despite the danger Gad put himself in as a Jewish resistance organizer in Berlin, he still found time to socialize and eventually came to love again.

It was during his days in the resistance that Gad met and fell in love with Zwi, a fellow member of Chug Chaluzi who became his long-term partner.

As the fight against the Third Reich dragged on, allied bombing only added to the excruciating danger of living underground in Berlin.

BOOM!

Reacting to the overwhelming chaos and confusion that marked the end of the war in 1945, members of Chug Chaluzi and their contacts started taking greater risks...

BANG!

No!

...and Gad and Zwi were eventually caught.

AAAAARRRRGGGHHH!

The Gestapo interrogated Gad by savagely beating Zwi and forcing him to listen.

But he refused to tell them anything of value.

When a bomb hit the Gestapo's makeshift prison, Gad's cell collapsed around him.

Astoundingly, he survived, buried beneath the rubble until a fellow prisoner managed to dig him out.

Gad Beck endured the final days of the war withmultiple broken bones, listening for the sound of machine guns and grenades to end.

Eventually, he and his fellow prisoners were found by Soviet Troops.

Brider, ir zayt fray!

Brothers, you are free!

The Soviets made Gad their "Representative for Jewish Affairs" in Berlin.

But, distrusting their disposition toward the surviving Jews, Gad and a small group of friends decided to leave the city and journey across a ruinous Germany to Munich.

Gad, along with his sister, parents and Zwi ultimately settled in Israel.

There he became a prominent educator and activist, eventually moving mack to Berlin where he remained until his death in 2012.

Nothing stopped Gad from living true to himself.

Today, Nazis are in the streets again.

Sieg Heil!

Fuck you, faggots!

And it can be hard not to tremble.

Because we don't have to imagine what they will do to us if they take enough power.

We already know.

But Gad Beck knew that fear is always the weapon fascists deploy first.

I mustered strength from the individual moments of happiness that I was always able to wring out of life.

No matter how dire the straits.

15

Puerto Rico's LGBT Community is Ready to Kick the Door Down

I SAW MY FIRST REPRESENTATION OF A GAY MAN WATCHING PUERTO RICAN TELEVISION WITH MY GRANDMA IN THE LATE '80s.

ENTRANDO POR LA COCINA

"ENTRANDO POR LA COCINA" WAS ONE OF GRANDMA'S FAVOURITE SHOWS, A COMEDY SKETCH STARRING ALTAGRACIA, A DOMINICAN MAID AND HER FRIENDS.

¡MORÍ FULL!

EXTRA CRISPY.

KKK KKK

ALTAGRACIA   TATO   ENRIQUETA

Guille

IT RAN FROM 1986 UNTIL 2002 AND OF ALL THE RECURRING CHARACTERS NONE WAS MORE BELOVED THAN GUILLE, HER GAY BESTIE.

GUILLE MADE THE SAME ENTRANCE IN EVERY EPISODE. HE BURST INTO THE KITCHEN, OUTRAGEOUSLY DRESSED, CARRYING A SMALL PINK BOOMBOX BLASTING MUSIC.

THE ACTOR, VICTOR ALICEA, WAS A DANCER AS WELL AND HE WOULD PERFORM A SHORT, BUT ENERGETIC ROUTINE.

THEN HE WOULD PROCLAIM:

DESDE BRASIL, LA GRAN POPEYA. BÚSCAME DONDE HAYA UN SOL, DONDE SE ACABE EL MAR...ESE ES EL PUNTO UIIIIIIIII!

<FROM BRAZIL, THE GREAT POPEYA. LOOK FOR ME WHERE THERE'S SUNSHINE, WHERE THE SEA ENDS. THAT'S THE PLACE UIIIIIIII>

PUERTO RICAN VIEWERS ACCEPTED GUILLE AS A PERSON WHO HAPPENED TO BE GAY AND NEVER QUESTIONED HIS FLAMBOYANCE.

GUILLE WAS ALLOWED TO MAKE MISTAKES, GET ANGRY, BE ANNOYING OR BE WISE. THE COMEDY CAME FROM THE SITUATION HE WAS IN, NOT BECAUSE HE WAS GAY.

THE SITCOM ACTUALLY POKED FUN AT HOMOPHOBIA. IN EVERY EPISODE, GUILLE WOULD SWITCH TO MANLY MANNERISMS IN ORDER TO PASS AS STRAIGHT IN FRONT OF LUISITO, WHO LIKED GUILLE AS A BRO.

IT WAS ABSURD! GUILLE DIDN'T CHANGE WARDROBE, HE WOULD BE DRESSED IN SPARKLY BLOUSES AND SHORTS, BUT HE STILL FOOLED LUISITO.

BUT PUERTO RICO IS NOT EXEMPT FROM PERPETUATING PREJUDICES AGAINST GAYS AND QUEERS.

THE CONCEPT OF GENDER IS VERY RIGID AND SLURS ARE UBIQUITOUS IN ARGUMENTS AND CASUAL CONVERSATIONS.

OUR CURRENT ADMINISTRATION CANCELLED PLANS TO IMPLEMENT A CURRICULUM IN PUBLIC SCHOOLS FOCUSING ON GENDER AND EQUALITY. THEY ALSO RETRACTED PROVISIONS FOR TRANS KIDS TO WEAR THE SCHOOL UNIFORM OF THEIR CHOICE.

BUT THE PUERTO RICAN CIVIL CODE HASN'T BEEN UPDATED TO ACCEPT GAY MARRIAGE, AND IT PROBABLY WON'T AS LONG AS THE RELIGIOUS RIGHT RULES OUR HOUSE AND SENATE.

GAY MARRIAGE IS LEGAL BECAUSE U.S. FEDERAL LAWS TAKE PRECEDENCE OVER OUR OWN CONSTITUTION.

STILL THE GAY COMMUNITY IN PUERTO RICO IS CONTINUALLY FIGHTING FOR RIGHTS AND WINNING. RECENTLY, ADOPTION BY GAY PARENTS AND UNMARRIED COUPLES WAS APPROVED, AND THERE ARE NEW LAWS TO PROTECT AGAINST DISCRIMINATION IN THE WORKPLACE BECAUSE OF SEXUAL ORIENTATION.

WHEN I WAS A KID WATCHING "ENTRANDO POR LA COCINA," PEOPLE THOUGHT BEING CALLED A 'LESBIAN' WAS AN INSULT.

BUT BY THE TIME I BECAME A YOUNG ADULT, TEENAGERS WERE OPENLY WEARING RAINBOW PINS ON THEIR UNIFORMS. CHANGE IS SLOW, BUT INEVITABLE.

THE RELIGIOUS RIGHT IS LOCKED IN A TUG OF WAR WITH THE GAY COMMUNITY ON THE ISLAND: THEY'D STUFF EVERYTHING THAT'S QUEER BACK IN THE CLOSET IF THEY COULD.

BUT NO MATTER HOW MANY TIMES THEY TRY, GAY BORICUAS WILL ALWAYS KICK THE DOOR DOWN, PINK BOOMBOX IN HAND, READY TO STEAL THE SPOTLIGHT.

I Came Out Late in Life and That's Okay

HI, I'M 38 AND I ONLY JUST FIGURED OUT I'M QUEER!

LIKE A *LOT!* BIG TIME!

HOW DO I FEEL? OH, YOU KNOW.

RELIEVED. EXCITED.

DEVASTATINGLY EMBARRASSED BY MY OWN IDIOCY.

BUT SERIOUSLY, *WHAT WAS I THINKING?*

I SAID A LOT OF DUMB SHIT WHEN I WAS YOUNGER.

GOD I *WISH* I WAS A LESBIAN.

TOO BAD I'M DEFINITELY ABSOLUTELY 100% STRAIGHT.

IT'S ALMOST LIKE I WAS PLAYING CHICKEN WITH MY OWN QUEER REVELATION.

I THINK I'M PROBABLY IN LOVE WITH HER, BUT WHAT SHOULD I *DO?* I'M STRAIGHT!

IT'D BE REALLY UNFAIR TO SAY ANYTHING TO HER, RIGHT?

AH... ...*WELL*..

I THINK MY FRIENDS PUT THE PIECES TOGETHER BEFORE I DID.

YOU GOING TO THE QUEER MIXER?

OH! I MEAN, I DON'T WANNA INTRUDE...?

IT'S FINE, YOU SHOULD COME.

I NEVER DID GET A CLEAR MOMENT OF REALIZATION. I DIDN'T HAVE A BIG FLASHY *COMING-OUT*. IT'S MORE LIKE I WAS PULLED INTO SEEING THE TRUTH, ONE QUIET LITTLE MOMENT AT A TIME.

UGH, DON'T BOTHER WITH THAT PODCAST, IT'S BORING AND FOR STRAIGHT PEOPLE.

I DUNNO, I DON'T THINK THIS IS SOMETHING CIS PEOPLE REALLY WORRY ABOUT.

I'M SO GLAD YOU'RE HERE, I DIDN'T WANT TO BE THE ONLY QUEER PERSON ON THE TEAM!

CLEARLY, I GOT THERE IN THE END. I WAS LOVINGLY BULLIED OUT OF DENIAL.

I REFRAMED HOW I TALKED ABOUT MYSELF WITH MY FRIENDS. I PUT A RAINBOW FLAG EMOJI ON MY TWITTER BIO. I MENTIONED IT ON A PROFESSIONAL PHONE CALL.

I DON'T USUALLY TALK ABOUT MY PERSONAL LIFE SINCE IT ISN'T YOUR JOB TO WORRY ABOUT IT, BUT AS A QUEER PERSON...

IT'S FELT GOOD TO DO THESE THINGS. IT'S BEEN A **MASSIVE** RELIEF. I FEEL AT HOME IN MY OWN SKIN IN WAYS I NEVER HAVE BEFORE.

BUT I CAN'T STOP THINKING ABOUT HOW MUCH TIME I WASTED BEING STUPID ABOUT THIS.

I'VE NEVER BEEN A PERSON WHO SPENDS A LOT OF ENERGY ON REGRET, BUT SUDDENLY IT'S ON MY MIND ALL OF THE TIME.

THE OPPORTUNITIES I'M NEVER GOING TO GET BACK. THE DOORS THAT FEEL LIKE THEY'RE CLOSED TO ME.

I'LL NEVER BE A TEENAGED LESBIAN EXCITED ABOUT HER FIRST GIRLFRIEND.

I'LL NEVER BE A YOUNG TRANS KID MAKING FRIENDS AT AN ANIME CON.

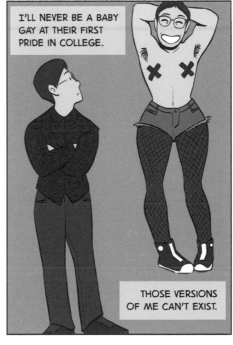

I'LL NEVER BE A BABY GAY AT THEIR FIRST PRIDE IN COLLEGE.

THOSE VERSIONS OF ME CAN'T EXIST.

WHAT WOULD THOSE OTHER ALISONS BE DOING NOW? WOULD THEY BE MARRIED? MAKE COMICS? LIVE IN NEW YORK?

I WONDER IF THEY WOULD HAVE BEEN HAPPIER.

24

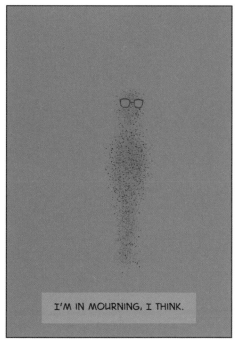

I'M IN MOURNING, I THINK.

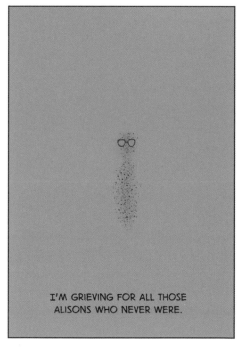

I'M GRIEVING FOR ALL THOSE ALISONS WHO NEVER WERE.

THERE'S A STANDARD NARRATIVE TO THESE THINGS.

KID KNOWS IN THEIR HEART THAT THEY'RE QUEER.

KID EVENTUALLY REACHES A PLACE AND TIME WHERE THEY FEEL COMFORTABLE BEING THEMSELVES.

KID COMES OUT!

EVEN WHEN THAT "KID" IS ACTUALLY AN ADULT, YOU HEAR OVER AND OVER ABOUT HOW THEY'VE "ALWAYS KNOWN."

AND FOR A LOT OF PEOPLE, OF COURSE, THOSE THINGS ARE TRUE.

BUT WHAT ABOUT WHEN YOU MAKE IT TO YOUR THIRTIES MOSTLY BLIND TO YOUR OWN QUEERNESS? WHAT ABOUT WHEN YOUR JOURNEY ISN'T A STEADY MARCH TOWARD OPENNESS AND ACCEPTANCE, BUT A CLUMSY STUMBLE THROUGH "WHAT THE HELL IS EVEN GOING ON WITH ME?"

THERE AREN'T AS MANY OF THOSE KINDS OF STORIES OUT THERE.

BIG CHUNKS OF SOCIETY WANT TO DISMISS QUEERNESS AS "JUST A PHASE," OR FRAME IT AS CORRUPTION OF A "NORMAL" PERSON, AND SO THERE'S PRESSURE ON QUEER PEOPLE TO BE CERTAIN AND UNWAVERING.

STEVEN UNIVERSE DIDN'T MAKE ME TRANS, I'VE *ALWAYS* BEEN THIS WAY!

PEOPLE TEND TO LIKE CLEAN, CLEAR STORIES. WE WANT PEOPLE'S LIVES TO MAKE SENSE, WITH A TIDY CHAIN OF CAUSE AND EFFECT.

WE DON'T LIKE MESS. WE DON'T LIKE "I CAN'T TELL YOU WHY."

I'VE ALWAYS FELT OUT OF STEP WITH SOME OF MY STRAIGHT CIS FRIENDS FOR NOT WANTING CHILDREN, FOR NOT TAKING MY HUSBAND'S NAME, FOR HATING WORDS LIKE "BRIDE" AND "WIFE," FOR NOT DRESSING OR ACTING CERTAIN WAYS.

IT JUST NEVER OCCURRED TO ME THAT MY SEXUALITY OR GENDER HAD ANYTHING TO DO WITH MY FEELINGS ABOUT THESE THINGS.

SO HERE I AM.

38, NEWLY OUT, STILL PINNING DOWN THE DETAILS.

I CAN'T GET THOSE YEARS BACK. ALL I CAN DO IS FORGIVE MYSELF FOR NEEDING TIME.

WHAT ELSE IS GOING TO CHANGE? WHERE WILL I BE IN A YEAR? IN FIVE? IN TEN?

I HAVE NO IDEA. BUT FOR NOW, I'M OKAY WITH NOT KNOWING.

AND I WON'T HAVE TO FIGURE IT OUT ON MY OWN.

Queer Uprisings Before Stonewall

Queer UPRISINGS

HAZEL NEWLEVANT

The Stonewall Riots in 1969 are rightfully remembered as a turning point in the queer liberation movment.

But they were far from the origin of queer organizing or mass resistance. Their legacy was built upon a decade of organizing and similar riots and protests that have been largely forgotten.

Los Angeles, 1959: Cooper Do-Nuts was an all-night doughnut shop frequented by the local queer community, especially queer street-based sex workers.

Police regularly patrolled the area and questioned people. Trans people whose IDs did not match their presentation were arrested for "cross-dressing" or other nuisance crimes.

One night in May, police attempted to arrest five customers. As they protested being loaded into the squad car, others flooded into the street, pelting the cops with whatever was at hand.

As the police called for backup, queer people rioted in the streets. The ensuing melee allowed three of the original detainees to escape.

One of them was John Rechy, who wrote about the experience in his 1963 novel *City of Night*. His immortalization made the Cooper Do-Nuts Riot the first <u>recorded</u> uprising of this kind.

Philadelphia, 1965: Dewey's, a lunch counter and late-night coffeehouse, had served a queer clientele for decades.

But that April, after refusing to serve a rowdy group of gender-nonconforming teens, Dewey's started refusing service to any customers who appeared to be queer or challenged gender conventions.

Customers joined forces with the Janus Society, a local homophile* organization, to protest this policy.

On April 25th, at least 150 protesters were denied service at Dewey's.

*homophile was the term preferred by queer organizations in the '50s and '60s

Three teenagers staged a sit-in and were arrested for disorderly conduct, along with the president of the Janus Society, who was advising them of their rights.

The Dewey's Lunch Counter Sit-In appears to be the first act of civil disobedience protesting anti-trans discrimination.

The Janus Society and supporters demonstrated outside Dewey's, picketing and handing out leaflets.

A week later, on May 2nd, activists staged another sit-in, this time with no arrests. Dewey's subsequently stopped hassling queer patrons.

The Janus Society's newsletter explained their philosophy:

The masculine woman and the feminine man are often looked down upon by the official policy of homophile organizations, but the Janus Society is concerned with the worth of an individual and the manner in which she or he comports himself. What is offensive today we have seen become the style of tomorrow, and even if what is offensive today remains offensive tomorrow to some persons, there is no reason to penalize such non-conformist behavior unless there is direct antisocial behavior connected with it.

San Francisco, 1966: Gene Compton's Cafeteria was a central hangout for trans women in the Tenderloin, the only neighborhood where hotels would rent them rooms.

Employment discrimination and lack of IDs that matched their appearance largely restricted these women to sex work or performance.

The cafeteria was an oasis, away from potentially violent clients, but police could still enter and arrest them at will.

Vanguard, a new organization of queer street youth, started meeting at Compton's. The management didn't appreciate their political attitude or how long they stayed, and began kicking queer customers out.

On July 18th, Vanguard picketed the cafeteria to protest this discrimination. The picket failed to resolve the conflict.

A few weeks later, when a cop grabbed a queen in Compton's, she resisted by throwing coffee in his face.

A dam of righteous anger broke.

By the end of the night, Compton's was trashed, a cop car had its windows smashed out, and a nearby newsstand had been burned to the ground.

In the wake of this collective resistance, San Francisco started to listen to and address the needs of its trans residents.

WE GOT PROGRAMS STARTED FOR TRANSSEXUALS, AND THEN WE BEGAN TO GET THESE PEOPLE IN CONTACT WITH OTHER COMMUNITY SERVICES.

THERE WAS A BIG CHANGE...WE CAN DRESS LIKE WOMEN ALL THE TIME! WE DON'T HAVE TO BE EFFEMINATE LITTLE "HAIR FAIRIES" ANYMORE. WE CAN BE WHO WE ARE INSIDE.

Sgt. Elliot Blackstone

At last, trans people could get ID cards that matched their current presentation and name.

Felicia Elizondo

[ELLIOT BLACKSTONE] WAS INSTRUMENTAL TO GETTING LAWS ABOUT CROSSDRESSING CHANGED AND THE LIKE.

THE FEDERAL GOVERNMENT PAID FOR MY EDUCATION... I GOT TO GO THROUGH THE NEIGHBORHOOD YOUTH CORPS TO GET MY EDUCATION AS A CLERK TYPIST.

Suzan Cooke

Amanda St. Jayme

Stonewall was not the start of queer mass resistance. It was the first time activists were able to publicize a riot's importance and organize a successful public commemoration: the first Pride marches.

The idea that Stonewall was unique or that change was inevitable obscures the effort, planning, and bravery that got us to that point. We deserve to remember our legacy of resistance.

The Response
Visbility Has Its Rewards

For The Nib's *The Response* feature, we ask our roster of contributors a single question and have them each answer it. For Pride month in 2018, we asked six trans contributors about their process of transition. They told us about what the word meant to them, important moments in their journeys, and the impact of others' expectations.

I STARTED TO PRESENT QUITE MASCULINE AS A TEEN. I HADN'T REALIZED BEFORE THAT IT WAS POSSIBLE TO FEEL SO CONFIDENT.

I'D HAVE WHAT I MENTALLY REFERRED TO AS "BOY DAYS" AND "GIRL DAYS". IT WAS EMPOWERING, BUT SCARY. WAS THIS OK?

AT COLLEGE, IN A NEW CITY SURROUNDED BY NEW PEOPLE, A STRANGER ASKED ME:

IT WAS AS THOUGH A LIGHT HAD BEEN SWITCHED ON.

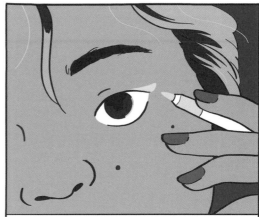

SINCE THEN, I'VE FELT MORE AT HOME IN MY BODY, REGARDLESS OF HOW I DRESS IT.

OOH! TELL ME WHAT IT WAS LIKE TO TRANS-ITION GENDERS, THAT SOUNDS SO MAGICAL.

GAWD, I DUNNO?? LIKE, I NEVER REALLY TRANSITIONED FROM A THING INTO ANOTHER THING??

NO, NO, I MEAN LIKE, HOW DID YOU COME OUT TO YOUR PARENTS? DID YOUR BOSS FREAK WHEN YOU GOT BOOBS? WHERE'S THE TRAINING MONTAGE OF YOUR EYELINER WINGS??

HM... WELL, UM...

36

... I GUESS MY MOM BOUGHT ME MY FIRST GIRL CLOTHES AT LIKE... 10? I THINK I STARTED TUCKING AROUND 16? I MUST HAVE FREAKED OUT A DOZEN BOSSES. BUT I DIDN'T CHANGE MY DOCUMENTS UNTIL MY 30s. SOMEWHERE ALONG THE WAY I STARTED CONSCIOUSLY USING PRONOUNS & HAD SURGERY & HRT AND STUFF, BUT MY WINGS HAVE **ALWAYS** BEEN SHARP AND I STILL DON'T HAVE BOOBS — THIS BRA IS PADDED...

WAIT, NO... I WANT A BUTTERFLY CHRYSALIS MOMENT TO INSPIRE ME IN THESE DARK TIMES. WHY DO YOU EVEN CALL YOURSELF 'TRANS' IF YOU NEVER EVEN **TRANSFORMED?**

—YOU'RE ACTUALLY THE ONE WHO PICKED THAT WORD. I WOULD'A CHOSEN SOMETHING COOLER.

I'VE SPENT THE LAST COUPLE YEARS THINKING NONSTOP ABOUT MY GENDER. AND THE THING THAT KEEPS SURFACING, OVER AND OVER AND OVER, IS:

...IS THIS REAL?

NON-BINARY? IT'S A PHASE.

YOU LOOK RIDICULOUS

NONE OF THE REAL QUEER PEOPLE ARE GOING TO BELIEVE YOU

I RECENTLY CAME OUT TO EVERYONE IN MY LIFE AND PUBLICLY CHANGED MY PRONOUNS, COMBINING MY THREE MOST ANXIETY-INDUCING ACTIVITIES: TALKING ON THE PHONE, TALKING ABOUT MY EMOTIONS, AND ASKING PEOPLE TO DO ANYTHING FOR ME.

THERE'S NO GODDAMNED WAY I'D BE PUTTING MYSELF THROUGH THIS IF IT WASN'T REAL.

~RING~ ~RING~

38

TOP SURGERY IS RESHAPING THE CHEST TO LOOK MORE MASCULINE.

PART OF ME FEELS LIKE TOP SURGERY IS RIGHT FOR ME AND THE OTHER PART OF ME ISN'T SO SURE.

MY BODY IS CONSTANTLY CHANGING IN SHAPE AND SIZE, AND THAT'S SOMETHING I LOVE ABOUT IT.

MAYBE ONE DAY I CAN PASS ON THE BINDER I WON'T NEED ANYMORE,

BUT FOR NOW I'M HAPPY AS IS.

2000 - WHEN I FIRST CAME OUT, TRANS CULTURE WAS ALL ABOUT PASSING. INVISIBILITY WAS THE END GOAL.

YOU DID A COMIC ABOUT TRANS STUFF? WON'T PEOPLE *SUSPECT??*

I HAVE A COMIC ABOUT A MANATEE. DO PEOPLE SUSPECT I'M A MANATEE?

2008 - I BEGAN WORK ON MY BOOK *TRANSPOSES*, A NON-FICTION COMIC ABOUT QUEER TRANS GUYS, BUT I STRUGGLED WITH COMING OUT OFFICIALLY IN PUBLIC.

READERS ARE GOING TO WANT TO KNOW YOUR RELATIONSHIP TO THE MATERIAL.

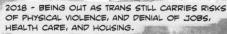

MY EDITOR

2014 - INSPIRED BY THE OPENNESS OF YOUNGER TRANS FOLK, I GOT BOLDER ABOUT COMING OUT.

UGH, WHAT'S UP WITH THIS "CHELSEA" MANNING FREAK.

I'M TRANS AND YOU DIDN'T HAVE ANY PROBLEMS WITH ME BEFORE NOW.

2018 - BEING OUT AS TRANS STILL CARRIES RISKS OF PHYSICAL VIOLENCE, AND DENIAL OF JOBS, HEALTH CARE, AND HOUSING.

BUT VISIBILITY ALSO HAS ITS REWARDS:

OUR 8-YEAR-OLD SON IS TRANS. DO YOU HAVE ANY AGE-APPROPRIATE COMICS FEATURING TRANS GUYS?

40

I know what this is. I know what I am. I am transgender, but not binary; **I am a person *in* transition.**

queer

transgender

transition

dysphoria

Oh.

That's me.

things I learned at 14

Though it took me years to find the strength I knew I *needed* to do this.

ok...

ok ♥

Since the first time I bound my chest I have been transitioning.

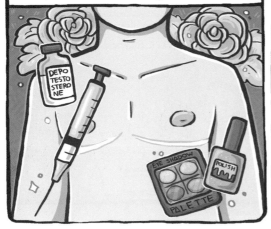

With each step I have refined the aperture of my gender and slowly come to understand myself as ever-evolving.

DEPO TESTO STERO NE

EYE SHADOW

POLISH

PALETTE

they

The process is far from over but I'm glad to be on this journey. I'm glad to be living this; I'm *glad* I'm doing this.

The Undercut

I've always had beautiful hair.

It is dark and shiny and straight and easy to run a brush through,

unlikely to tangle.

My boyfriends have always liked it long.

When I was 22, I sat by a creek in Vermont, still covered in sawdust from my day job, and cut off my long, beautiful hair.

I felt pretty queer, but "queer" wasn't my word yet.

41

I remember the heady days of that first short cut. It felt giddy to be someone who women lingered on. I was thin and pretty and young and still exhilaratingly invisible to men.

I wanted to be both seen and unseen and I didn't know that was what I wanted.

HI.

Years later, I would realize that itchy feeling was what power felt like.

I cut my hair, and I had absolute power over how I was seen.

The next time I cut my hair was the day after I agreed to marry a man.

Was I rebelling against my upcoming admission into the hallowed halls of perceived heterosexuality?

I got married in a china doll haircut. It was the worst haircut of my life.

I love my husband. I do not like my wedding pictures.

My hair looks wrong. I look wrong.

Queerness looks like many things. I am queer no matter what I look like.

I still crave a short-hand, a signal as clear as a rosary.

I want to decouple my queerness from my style. I also want to look gay as hell.

I've never had a coming out conversation because I don't like talking about queerness with straight people.

I started being treated as queer when I shaved my first undercut.

I felt more queer with an undercut than I did waking up next to the woman who taught me how to make myself come.

UM, HI?

I let it grow out last winter as I wondered whether I deserved to be queer, to have a style that projected more than I really was.

45

Stages of growing OUT an UNDERCUT

I CAN'T POSSIBLY LOOK LIKE THIS

DENIAL

YOU'VE GOT TO BE KIDDING ME!!

ANGER

AUGHHHH

PLEASE BE KINDA CUTE SOMEDAY...

BARGAINING

DEPRESSION

ACCEPTANCE

...

I want to rebel against the idea of normative queer beauty. I love having the shorthand to normative queer beauty.

YOU'RE SO SOFT!

I love it when I rub my hand against my shaved head and I love it when my lovers do.

There is no meaning to this, except when there is. It is just hair, except when it's not.

It is just a sharp razor, cut close to my skin, letting me know that I am okay and I am beautiful.

I shaved another chunk out of my hair today, currently happy and comfortable with my queerness.
I like it.
It looks good.
It looks queer.
It looks like me, for now.

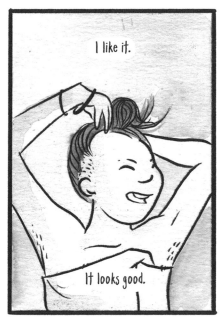

How Do You Translate Non-Binary?

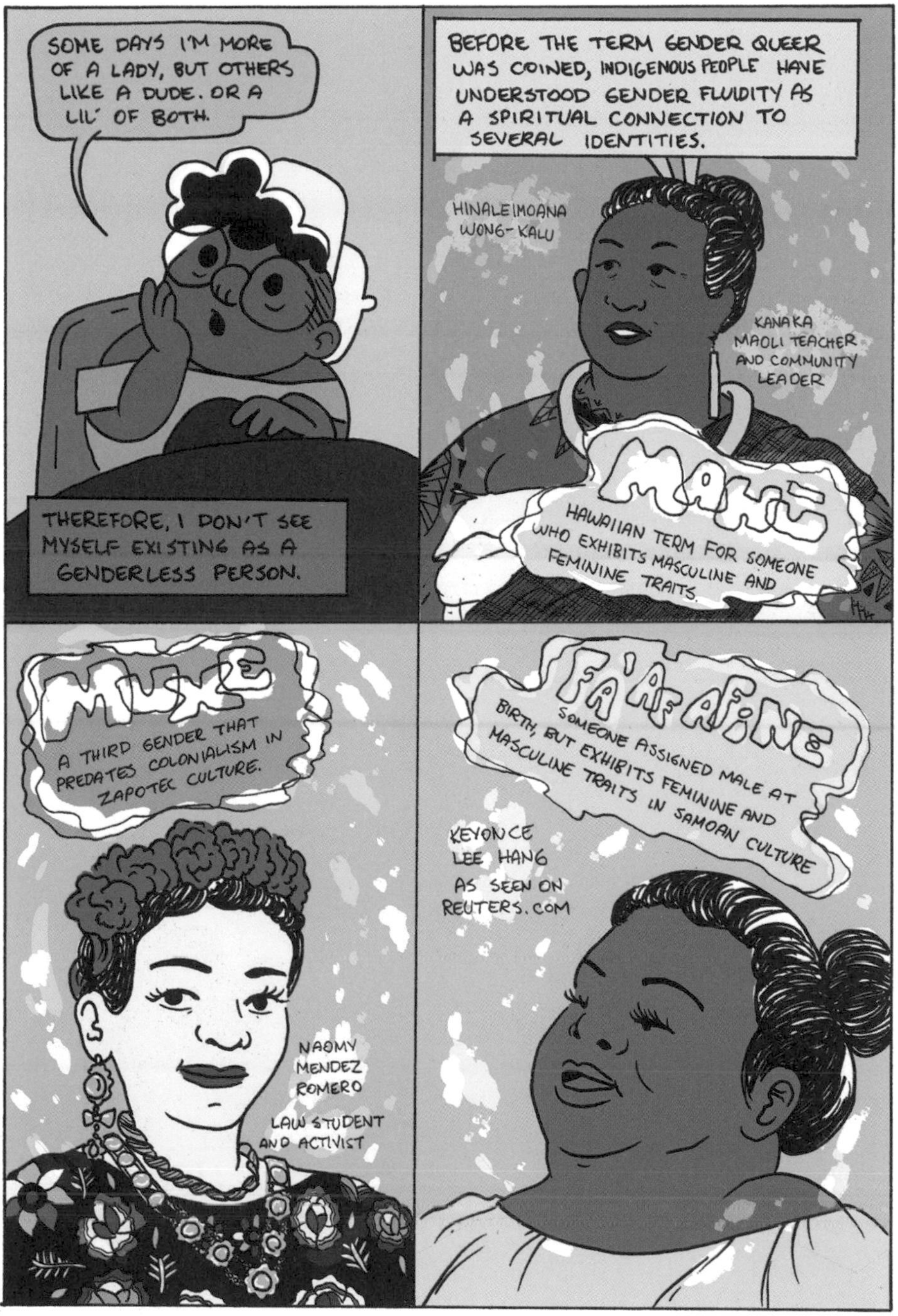
SOME DAYS I'M MORE OF A LADY, BUT OTHERS LIKE A DUDE. OR A LIL' OF BOTH.
THEREFORE, I DON'T SEE MYSELF EXISTING AS A GENDERLESS PERSON.
BEFORE THE TERM GENDER QUEER WAS COINED, INDIGENOUS PEOPLE HAVE UNDERSTOOD GENDER FLUIDITY AS A SPIRITUAL CONNECTION TO SEVERAL IDENTITIES.
HINALEIMOANA WONG-KALU
KANAKA MAOLI TEACHER AND COMMUNITY LEADER
MAHŪ
HAWAIIAN TERM FOR SOMEONE WHO EXHIBITS MASCULINE AND FEMININE TRAITS.
MUXE
A THIRD GENDER THAT PREDATES COLONIALISM IN ZAPOTEC CULTURE.
NAOMY MENDEZ ROMERO
LAW STUDENT AND ACTIVIST
FA'AFAFINE
SOMEONE ASSIGNED MALE AT BIRTH, BUT EXHIBITS FEMININE AND MASCULINE TRAITS IN SAMOAN CULTURE
KEYONCE LEE HANG
AS SEEN ON REUTERS.COM

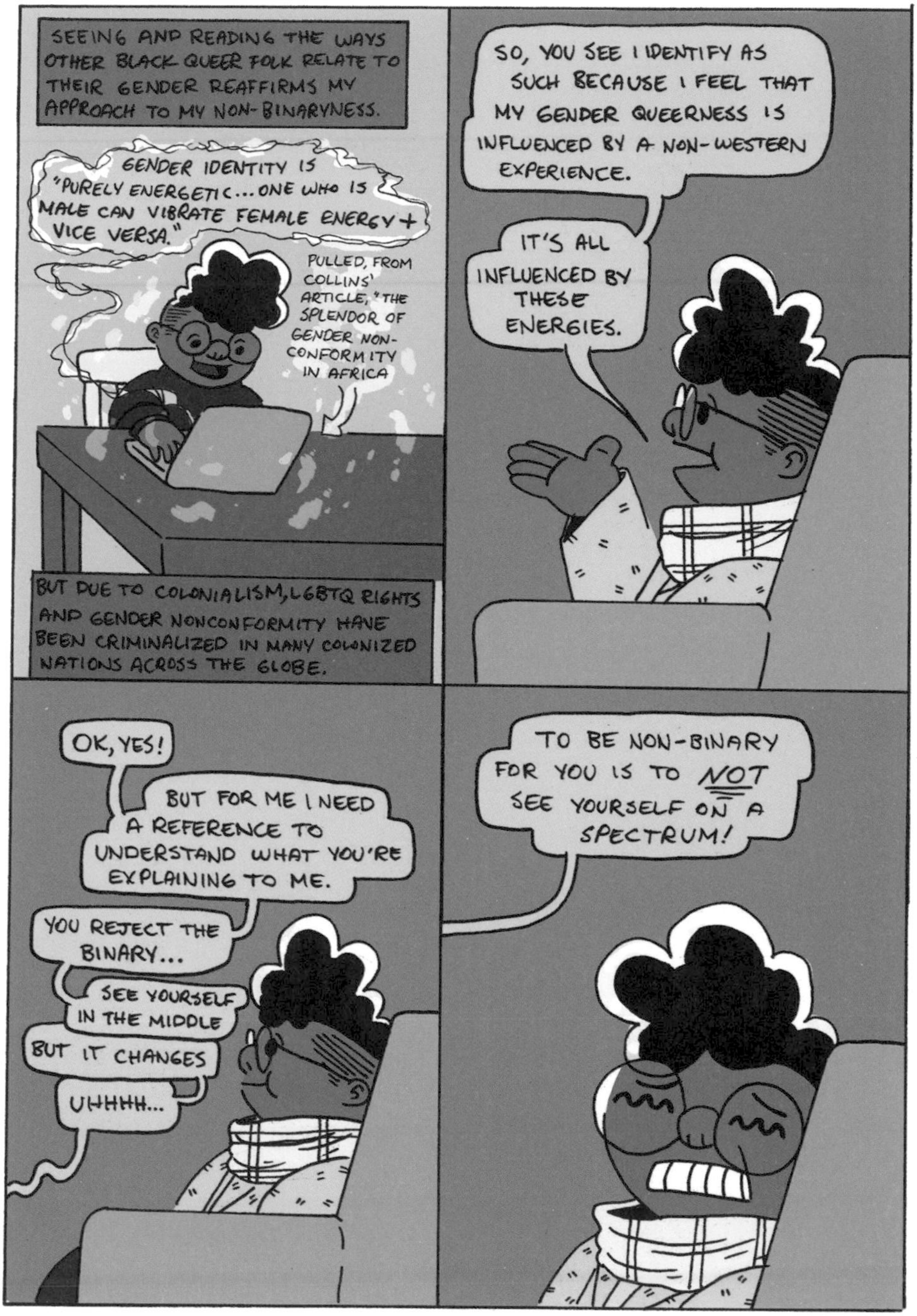
SEEING AND READING THE WAYS OTHER BLACK QUEER FOLK RELATE TO THEIR GENDER REAFFIRMS MY APPROACH TO MY NON-BINARYNESS.
GENDER IDENTITY IS "PURELY ENERGETIC... ONE WHO IS MALE CAN VIBRATE FEMALE ENERGY + VICE VERSA."
PULLED, FROM COLLINS' ARTICLE, "THE SPLENDOR OF GENDER NON-CONFORMITY IN AFRICA
BUT DUE TO COLONIALISM, LGBTQ RIGHTS AND GENDER NONCONFORMITY HAVE BEEN CRIMINALIZED IN MANY COLONIZED NATIONS ACROSS THE GLOBE.
SO, YOU SEE I IDENTIFY AS SUCH BECAUSE I FEEL THAT MY GENDER QUEERNESS IS INFLUENCED BY A NON-WESTERN EXPERIENCE.
IT'S ALL INFLUENCED BY THESE ENERGIES.
OK, YES!
BUT FOR ME I NEED A REFERENCE TO UNDERSTAND WHAT YOU'RE EXPLAINING TO ME.
YOU REJECT THE BINARY...
SEE YOURSELF IN THE MIDDLE
BUT IT CHANGES
UHHHH...
TO BE NON-BINARY FOR YOU IS TO NOT SEE YOURSELF ON A SPECTRUM!

Queerativity!

ELECTION NIGHT IS TECHNICALLY OUR ANNIVERSARY NIGHT. WE HOOKED UP THE NIGHT OBAMA WAS ELECTED AND THE 2016 ELECTION MARKED EIGHT BEAUTIFUL YEARS OF LIVING TOGETHER.

ELECTION NIGHT

NOVEMBER 8th, 2016

I WENT TO BED EARLY THAT NIGHT. I HAD A SICK FEELING IN THE PIT OF MY STOMACH AND, HONESTLY, I DIDN'T WANT TO SEE, HEAR, OR EVEN THINK ABOUT THE NEWS.

EVENTUALLY, SHE SLIPPED INTO BED. SHE DIDN'T NEED TO SAY A WORD...INSTEAD WE SPENT THE NIGHT TOGETHER AND CRIED.

THE NEXT MORNING, I WOKE UP TO A BRAND-NEW DAY AND HER SMILING FACE. WITH MY MORNING TEA I MADE A RESOLUTION TO MYSELF TO...

Stay Queerative, no matter what!

So what does it mean to be queerative?

IT'S NOT JUST A COMBINATION OF BEING QUEER AND CREATIVE. IT'S A MENTALITY I'VE KEPT FOR THE PAST FEW YEARS TO STAY THE COURSE.

UNFORTUNATELY, IT DOES NOT COME WITH A TRAINING MONTAGE, BUT IF IT DID IT WOULD LOOK A LITTLE SOMETHING LIKE THIS:

HERE ARE SOME RULES I FOLLOW TO STAY QUEERATIVE:

WHEN THE GOING GOT TOUGH, MY TOUGH SELF KNEW IT NEEDED TO TAKE A BREAK.

I NEVER FELT GUILTY FOR INDULGING OTHER HOBBIES OR HABITS. IN FACT, THEY HELPED ME GROW CLOSER TO MY FRIENDS.

I WENT OUT AND PARTICIPATED IN MY LOCAL QUEER COMMUNITY. VOLUNTEER WORK AND ORGANIZING DONATION DRIVES WAS NOT HARD TO FIND.

PROJECT Q

MY FAVORITE WAS LEARNING PROPER SELF-CARE. IT'S NOT JUST REWARDING MYSELF FOR A JOB WELL DONE, IT'S BEING ABLE TO REMEMBER I'M JUST ONE PERSON AND I CAN'T FIX EVERYTHING.

THERAPY

FINALLY, A WORD OF CAUTION. BEWARE ANYONE WHO TELLS YOU THAT STRUGGLING MAKES THE BEST ART. THEY'RE NOT BEING QUEERATIVE, THEY'RE TRYING TO MAKE PAIN SOUND LIKE AN OPPORTUNITY.

ULTIMATELY, WE'RE STILL HERE. WHETHER OR NOT YOU'VE REALIZED IT, YOU'VE ALREADY BEEN QUEERATIVE THIS WHOLE TIME AND WE THANK YOU FOR THAT.

DELTA VASQUEZ

Seeing Others

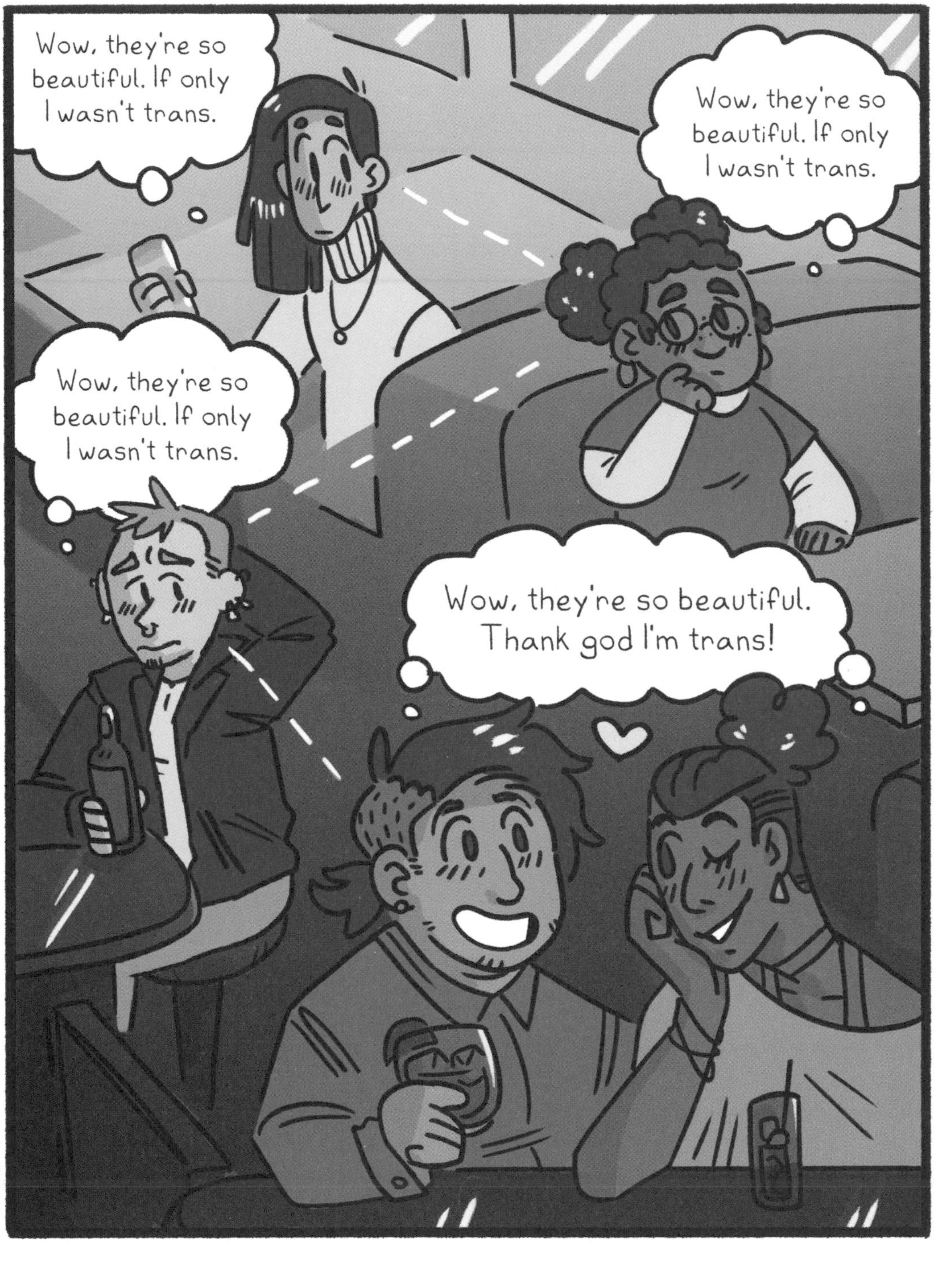

Wow, they're so beautiful. If only I wasn't trans.
Wow, they're so beautiful. If only I wasn't trans.
Wow, they're so beautiful. If only I wasn't trans.
Wow, they're so beautiful. Thank god I'm trans!

Queerness Has Always Been Part of Life in the Middle East

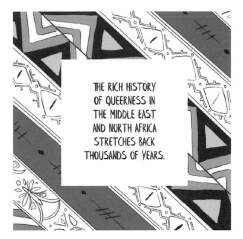

THE RICH HISTORY OF QUEERNESS IN THE MIDDLE EAST AND NORTH AFRICA STRETCHES BACK THOUSANDS OF YEARS.

MANY PEOPLE ASSUME THAT THIS REGION AND THE ISLAMIC CULTURES WITHIN IT, HAVE ALWAYS BEEN INTESENLY HOMOPHOBIC.

BUT THEY'RE WRONG.

IN ANCIENT TIMES, MESOPOTAMIA, SUMERIA, PHOENICIA, AND VARIOUS CULTURES IN THE LEVANT WERE OFTEN VERY OPEN ABOUT SEXUALITY. QUEERNESS AND POLYAMORY WERE A WAY OF LIFE.

ONE OF THE OLDEST AND MOST FAMOUS STORIES KNOWN IN HUMANITY THAT AROSE FROM THIS REGION, THE EPIC OF GILGAMESH, IS FAMOUSLY VERY GAY. (READ IT FOR YOURSELF AND SEE!)

55

THERE ARE MANY LEGENDS AND HISTORICAL ACCOUNTS OF QUEERNESS IN ANCIENT EGYPT AS WELL. ONE OF THE MOST FAMOUS IS OF KHNUMHOTEP AND NIANKHKHNUM, TWO ROYAL ATTENDANTS WHO ARE COMMONLY BELIEVED TO HAVE BEEN IN LOVE.

WHEN THE PHOENICIANS FOUNDED CARTHAGE, THEY CARRIED THE CULTURAL ACCEPTANCE OF QUEERNESS OVERSEAS. FUTURE BISHOP ST. AUGUSTINE WROTE IN THE 4TH CENTURY ABOUT NUMEROUS "LOVE AFFAIRS," WHICH ARE BELIEVED TO BE "OVERHEATED ACCOUNT{S} OF... HOMOSEXUALITY."*

*STEPHEN GREENBLATT, THE NEW YORKER, 2017

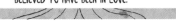

FOR EXAMPLE, HAMILCAR BARCA, A CARTHIGINIAN RULER AND FATHER OF THE FAMOUS HANNIBAL, IS ALSO BELIEVED TO HAVE BEEN IN HOMOSEXUAL RELATIONS SHIPS. HISTORICAL ACCOUNTS POINT TO HIM HAVING A ROMANCE WITH HASDRUBAL THE FAIR.

ANCIENT BERBER KINGDOMS AND COMMUNITIES, INCLUDING NUMIDIA AND MAURETANIA -- LOCATED IN MODERN-DAY ALGERIA, TUNISIA, AND MOROCCO -- ARE NOTED BY HISTORIANS TO HAVE HAD A SIMILAR ATTITUDE TO QUEERNESS AS WELL.

IN GENERAL, THERE WERE VERY FEW SEXUAL LAWS IN PLACE WITHIN ALL OF THESE AREAS, AND THEY WERE MOSTLY ABOUT PREVENTING HARM -- DON'T HURT OR COERCE ANYONE, AND SOMETIMES DON'T HAVE SEX ON CERTAIN HOLIDAYS.

THAT'S ABOUT IT.

THOSE LAWS WEREN'T ABOUT CRIMINALIZING SOMEONE'S IDENTITY, OR PREVENTING EXPRESSION; THEY WERE THERE TO HELP PREVENT HARM TO OTHERS.

ONE'S PREFERENCES OR IDENTITY (EXEMPTING STATUS SOMETIMES) HAD NOTHING TO DO WITH IT.

MODERN CRITICS OFTEN ASSUME THAT QUEERNESS WAS OUTLAWED BY ISLAM, BUT MANY EXPERTS SUCH AS MAAJID NAWAS OF QUILLIUM INSTEAD POINT TO IDEAS AND LAWS INTRODUCED DURING THE PERIOD OF EUROPEAN COLONIALISM AS THE SOURCE OF INTOLERANCE TO QUEERNESS.

INTOLERANCE TOWARDS QUEERNESS IN CHRISTIANITY -- ALSO FORMED IN THE MIDDLE EAST -- HAS A SIMILAR STORY ON A DIFFERENT TIMELINE.

THIS MENTALITY BEGAN TO APPEAR IN THE MIDDLE AGES, IN VARYING EUROPEAN INTERPRETATIONS OF THE BIBLE.

THE QUR'AN IS QUITE SEX-POSITIVE; MANY TEACHINGS SUGGEST THAT SEX GOES HAND-IN-HAND WITH SPIRITUALITY, AND CERTAIN ASPECTS OF SEXUALITY ARE REFERRED TO AS "BLESSINGS."

AND THE TEXT'S CASUAL TONE TOWARDS SEXUAL IDENTITY -- INCLUDING QUEERNESS -- CAN SOMETIMES COME AS A SURPRISE.

THE MUSLIM WORLD CONTAINS A VAST NUMBER OF QUEER POETRY, STORIES, AND LEGENDS WRITTEN IN ARABIC, FARSI, AND TURKISH, FROM THE DAWN OF ISLAM ALL THE WAY UNTIL NOW.

IN THE 13TH CENTURY, JALAL AD-DIN MUHAMMAD RUMI, KNOWN BEST AS SIMPLY RUMI, WROTE SO PASSIONATELY ABOUT HIS SPIRITUAL INSTRUCTOR SHAMS AL-TABRIZI THAT MANY THEORIZE THAT THE TWO WERE DEEPLY IN LOVE.

EVEN PAST THE GOLDEN AGE, THERE ARE MANY ACCOUNTS FROM EUROPEAN WRITERS AND TRAVELLERS UP UNTIL THE 19TH CENTURY THAT EXPRESS AMAZEMENT AT THE SEX-POSITIVITY AND QUEER-ACCEPTING COMPONENTS OF ISLAM.

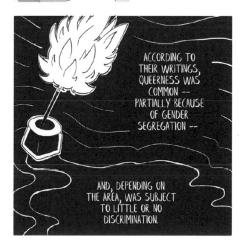

ACCORDING TO THEIR WRITINGS, QUEERNESS WAS COMMON -- PARTIALLY BECAUSE OF GENDER SEGREGATION --

AND, DEPENDING ON THE AREA, WAS SUBJECT TO LITTLE OR NO DISCRIMINATION.

CRIMINALIZATION OF QUEERNESS GAINED MOMENTUM IN THE LATE 1800'S, AS EUROPEAN FORCES WERE CLOSING IN ON THE OTTOMAN EMPIRE.

EUROPEAN ATTITUDES ABOUT QUEERNESS AS "AGAINST NATURE" BEGAN TO RIPPLE THROUGHOUT THE MIDDLE EAST AND NORTH AFRICA.

AS A RESULT, QUEERNESS BECAME WIDELY PERSECUTED, AND 150 YEARS LATER, THE WEST DENIGRATES AND MOCKS THE VERY AREAS THAT IT IMPRESSED HOMOPHOBIA INTO.

HOWEVER, THE SITUATION IS CHANGING FOR THE BETTER. HOMOSEXUALITY HAS BEEN AT LEAST PARTIALLY DECRIMINALIZED IN...

TURKEY

CYPRUS

JORDAN

PALESTINE

KUWAIT

BAHRAIN

OF COURSE, QUEERNESS IS STILL STIGMATIZED AND PERSECTED. THERE ARE MULTIPLE CASES EVERY DAY OF QUEER PEOPLE IN THE REGION BEING HURT, HARASSED, DENIGRATED, AND ERASED.

more Progressiv Mosques

WE EXIS

BUT STRIDES ARE BEING MADE QUICKLY IN THE MODERN WORLD FOR THE RETURN TO ACCEPTANCE. A GROWING NUMBER IN THE MIDDLE EAST AND NORTH AFRICA ARE CALLING FOR DECRIMINALIZING AND DESTIGMATIZING.

AND ONLINE COMMUNITIES OF THIS INTERSECTION OF IDENTITY ARE GROWING,

CONNECTING, AND WORKING TIRELESSLY TOWARDS CHANGE.

THOUSANDS OF YEARS OF OUR CULTURES IN THIS REGION WERE TORN ASUNDER BY 150 YEARS OF COLONIALISM.

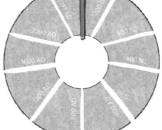

BUT 150 YEARS IS LIKE TWO SECONDS, IN COMPARISON TO OUR VAST AMOUNT OF TIME ACCEPTING AND PRACTICING QUEERNESS.

I LIKE TO THINK ABOUT HOW MY ANCESTORS --
MY GREAT-GRANDPARENTS, AND THEIR PARENTS,
AND THEIR PARENTS' PARENTS -- COULD HAVE BEEN
AS ACCEPTING OF QUEERNESS AND POLYAMORY,
IF NOT OF THOSE IDENTITIES THEMSELVES.

AND THOSE
THOUGHTS
BRING ME A
NEW CONFIDENCE
IN MY
IDENTITY AS
A QUEER MUSLIM,
WHO IN
THE PAST
HAS HAD
CONFLICTING
FEELINGS
ABOUT
CONSOLIDATING
THE TWO.

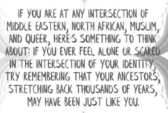

IF YOU ARE AT ANY INTERSECTION OF
MIDDLE EASTERN, NORTH AFRICAN, MUSLIM,
AND QUEER, HERE'S SOMETHING TO THINK
ABOUT: IF YOU EVER FEEL ALONE OR SCARED
IN THE INTERSECTION OF YOUR IDENTITY,
TRY REMEMBERING THAT YOUR ANCESTORS,
STRETCHING BACK THOUSANDS OF YEARS,
MAY HAVE BEEN JUST LIKE YOU.

Dancing With Pride

LAST YEAR I SIGNED UP FOR FOLK DANCING CLASSES HELD AT A SENIOR CENTER.

I ARRIVED AT MY FIRST LESSON WEARING A PRONOUN BADGE, DETERMINED NOT TO LET MY GENDER BE ASSUMED.

60

Welcome everyone! Let's go around the circle and say our names— I'm Lyn.

OUR TEACHER, IN HER 70s!

Pamela

Charlie

Barb

I STEELED MY NERVES AS MY TURN APPROACHED . . .

My name is Maia and I use the gender neutral pronouns e, em, eir—here's an example sentence: Ask em what e wants in eir tea.

MY INTRODUCTION WAS MET WITH POLITE CONFUSION— A MUCH GENTLER RESPONCE THAN WHAT MANY GENDER NONCONFORMING PEOPLE IN THIS COUNTRY RECEIVE.

?

IN THE FIRST NINE MONTHS OF CLASSES EVERY DANCE WE LEARNED WAS GENDER NEUTRAL

DANCED WHILE HOLDING HANDS

IN ONE BIG CIRCLE.

I ENJOY FOLK DANCING SPECIFICALLY FOR THIS REASON.

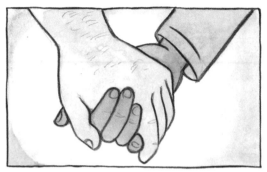

WHEN THE GENDER BINARY DID INTRUDE I WAS STRANGELY UNPREPARED.

AS THE THREE VISIBLY MALE DANCERS MOVED TO THE FRONT OF THE LINE

I HAD A SILENT GENDER-INDUCED CRISIS.

What do I do, what do I do, what do I do...

The longer I wait the harder it's going to be to speak up, Shit, Shit, Shit

On this step the men will yell "Teh, Teh" and the women will respond "li, li, li, li" —

I have to either speak up or else sit this dance out.

I took a deep breath...

And made a choice.

I'm going to join the men.

DESPITE MY EFFORTS

I'M FAIRLY SURE MY FELLOW DANCERS STILL SEE AND UNDERSTAND ME AS A FEMALE PERSON.

ASK ABOUT MY PRONOUNS
E EM EIR
THEY THEM
SHE HER
SHE THEY
HE
ALL THE MORE REASON TO BE A LIVING EXAMPLE
XE XER
THAT GENDER DIVISIONS
ARE FLUID.

NO ONE SAID ANYTHING UNTIL THE END OF CLASS

THE FOLLOWING WEEK WE DID THIS DANCE AGAIN.

BREAKING DOWN
THE BINARY
ONE STEP
AT A TIME.

Gender Isn't Binary and Neither is Anatomy

When I was a kid, the doctors told my parents to tell me that I'd had cancer in my ovaries.

Pidgeon Pagonis →

That would explain everything

"Why I had a scar across my belly."

Something special about me is I'm a cancer survivor!

SHOW + TELL

"Why I had to go to the doctor a lot. Why I didn't get my period."

"I was terrified that my cancer would come back."

Androgen Insensitivity Syndrome (AIS) symptoms:
No period

little or no pubic hair

an enlarged clitoris.

"Then when I'm 18, I'm taking this psychology class..."

Huh.

Hey, mom, I know this is weird, but in class we were talking about something called AIS. Have you heard of that?

Yes, that's what you have.

Shocked, Pidgeon got their medical records. The paperwork showed they were born with XY chromosomes and had multiple surgeries as a child to remove undescended gonads, reduce their clitoris, and enlarge their vagina.

I've never had cancer in my life.

ound
r X and Dr
rents were co
tient has to continu
tests are inconclusive, on
Blood tests were ordered
PSEUDO-MALE HERMAPHRODITE
Dr X and Dr. Y were consult
the repeated test has show
ANDROGEN INSENSITIVITY
SYNDROME. On March thirt
should be consulted bef
Dr. Z ordered two Psyche
in instance of mor
health and t
accuraci
r X

"It really hit home that I was called a hermaphrodite. There's not many things in this world ridiculed as much as hermaphrodites.

People think they're weird, disgusting, and gross, like you're a monster."

How am I going to tell my boyfriend?

Everything fell apart. In my worldview at that time, there's men and women. And that's it. I have XY chromosomes, that means I'm a man.

If a baby has testes,
a penis, and XY
chromosomes,
doctors classify as male.
If a baby has a vulva,
womb, and XX
chromosomes,
it's classified as female.

But there's a lot of
variation in
human anatomy.
About one in every 1,700
people have a
different configuration
of internal and
external parts.
They're intersex.

There's a wide diversity
of variations among
intersex people.

Has testes,
a penis, and
XX chromosomes.

Has a uterus,
no vagina, and
XX chromosomes

Sometimes intersex people
need surgery for a medical
reason—like to help them
pee more easily or to
reduce cancer risk.
But, for 50 years, doctors
defaulted to performing
surgery on intersex kids
for purely cosmetic
reasons, to create
"normal-looking" genitalia.

"Two common goals of these cosmetic "normalizing" surgeries on children's genitals are to enable heterosexual penetrative intercourse, and to help the child conform to gender and sexual norms and expectations."

—2017 Human Rights Watch and InterAct report

Medical norms are evolving and nowdays, intersex children and their parents can often talk to teams of specialists and learn about non-surgical options. But still, no clinic has firmly banned medically unnecessary surgeries on intersex kids.

In 2018, intersex advocacy group InterAct campaigned for an intersex rights resolution in California that condemed cosmetic genital surgery on kids.

These surgeries should be performed only with informed consent.

A baby cannot provide that consent.

California State Senator Scott Wiener

The resolution passed but the legislature didn't go as far as actually banning the surgery. A 2019 bill aimed at doing was stalled by doctors' opposition.

Our concern is that the approach in this bill may be being overly prescriptive and not give families and medical professionals the ability to take the specifics of each case into account.

Janus Norman, California Medical Association senior vice president for governmental relations

People are very uncomfortable with this kind of difference because it unsettles binaries around sex and gender.

InterAct Staff Attorney Sylvan Fraser

Well-meaning folks who oppose us think that children will be bullied for growing up with sex traits that we think of as different.

In other cases, we treat bullying by treating the community. We don't treat it by doing surgery on someone who we think of as 'not normal.'

In college, Pidgeon joined an intersex support group, came out as nonbinary, and eventually became an activist and media-maker.

In 2018, Pidgeon returned to Lurie Hospital in Chicago, where surgeries were performed on them as a kid. This time, Pidgeon wasn't a patient but a protester.

We want an apology, reparations, and an end to unnecessary surgery!

I wish I had grown up untouched and with the ability to make a decision on my own someday.

At the end of the day, it's never right, I believe, to not tell a patient the truth about their bodies.

KENDRA WELLS

Pronoun Panic

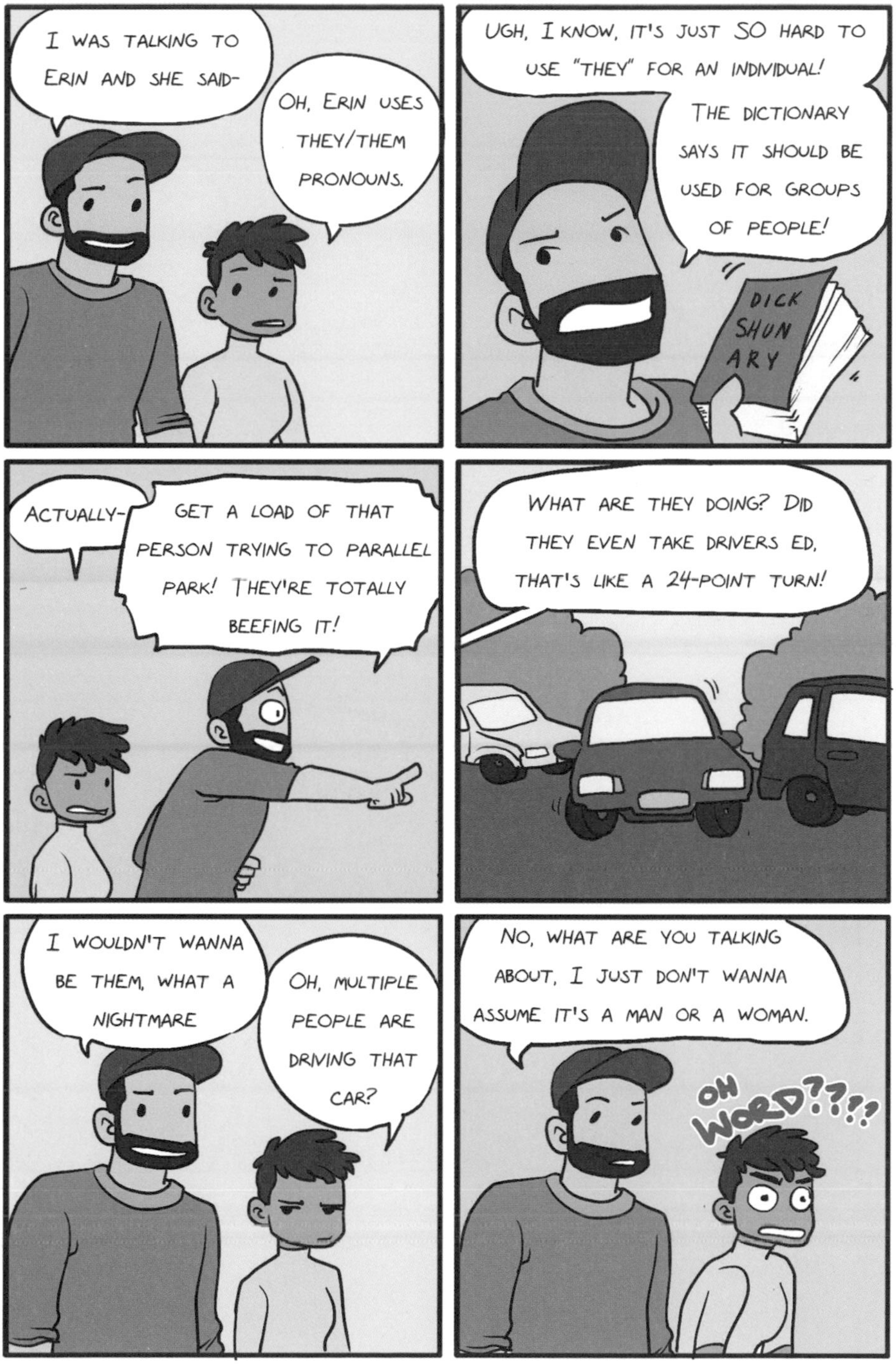
I WAS TALKING TO ERIN AND SHE SAID-
OH, ERIN USES THEY/THEM PRONOUNS.
UGH, I KNOW, IT'S JUST SO HARD TO USE "THEY" FOR AN INDIVIDUAL!
THE DICTIONARY SAYS IT SHOULD BE USED FOR GROUPS OF PEOPLE!
DICK SHUN ARY
ACTUALLY-
GET A LOAD OF THAT PERSON TRYING TO PARALLEL PARK! THEY'RE TOTALLY BEEFING IT!
WHAT ARE THEY DOING? DID THEY EVEN TAKE DRIVERS ED, THAT'S LIKE A 24-POINT TURN!
I WOULDN'T WANNA BE THEM, WHAT A NIGHTMARE
OH, MULTIPLE PEOPLE ARE DRIVING THAT CAR?
NO, WHAT ARE YOU TALKING ABOUT, I JUST DON'T WANNA ASSUME IT'S A MAN OR A WOMAN.
OH WORD??!?!

Just Another Day at the Newspaper

76

JOEY ALISON SAYERS

I'd be an Okay Mom

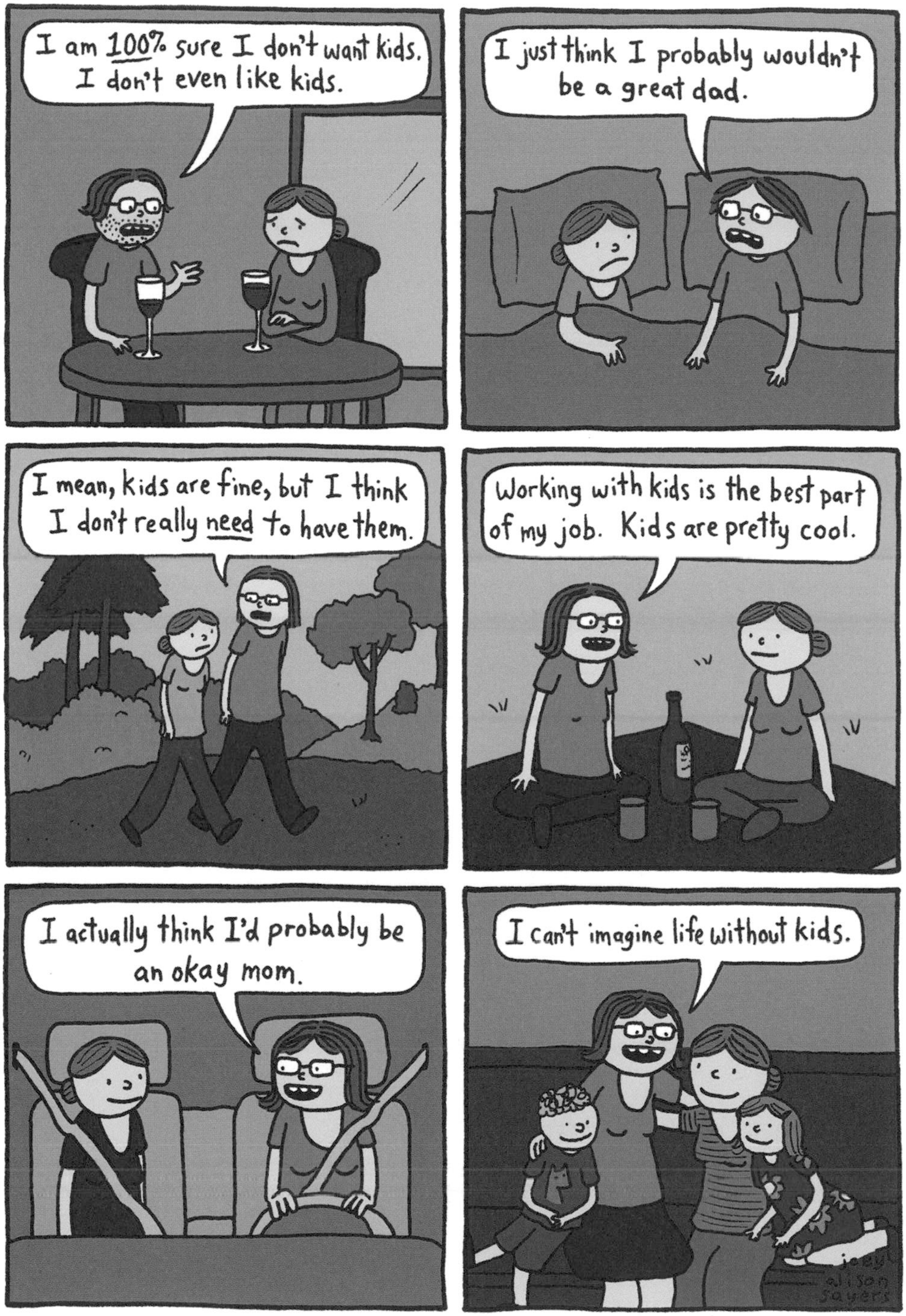
I am 100% sure I don't want kids. I don't even like kids.
I just think I probably wouldn't be a great dad.
I mean, kids are fine, but I think I don't really need to have them.
Working with kids is the best part of my job. Kids are pretty cool.
I actually think I'd probably be an okay mom.
I can't imagine life without kids.
joey alison sayers

Just a Joke:
Where Alt-Right Guys Get Their Start

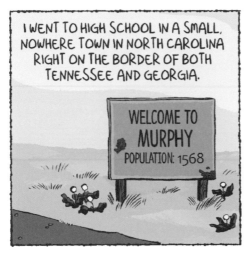

I WENT TO HIGH SCHOOL IN A SMALL, NOWHERE TOWN IN NORTH CAROLINA RIGHT ON THE BORDER OF BOTH TENNESSEE AND GEORGIA.

WELCOME TO
MURPHY
POPULATION: 1568

IN MURPHY, THREE THINGS MATTERED: FOOTBALL, JESUS, AND THAT ONE MCDONALD'S EVERYBODY WENT TO AFTER SCHOOL.

I WAS LUCKY ENOUGH TO FIND THE ONLY OTHER QUEER ARTIST IN TOWN. (WE ALWAYS GOT NUGGETS TOGETHER.)

HER FAMILY ALSO HAPPENED TO BE THE ONLY JEWISH ONE.

BULLIES USED TO DRAW SWASTIKAS ON ALL OF OUR THINGS TO "GET A RISE OUT OF US".

THEY LIKED SEEING HOW UPSET WE GOT.

THE FACULTY NEVER DID ANYTHING ABOUT IT.

IT'S JUST A JOKE! THEY'RE TAKING IT TOO SERIOUSLY.

THIS "GAG" KEPT GOING UNTIL WE GRADUATED.

JOSH

7 HRS

my FxxKING Hell. These SJWs don't know anything about the first ammendment. Censoring Swastikas is the REAL facism! people should be allowed to say what they want. It doesn't matter what.

NOW THE SAME GUY DEFENDS IT ONLINE.

BUT I HEARD AT SOME POINT, IT STOPPED BEING A JOKE TO HIM TOO.

The Dream of a Gay Separatist Town

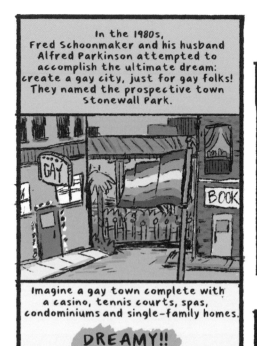

In the 1980s, Fred Schoonmaker and his husband Alfred Parkinson attempted to accomplish the ultimate dream: create a gay city, just for gay folks! They named the prospective town Stonewall Park.

Imagine a gay town complete with a casino, tennis courts, spas, condominiums and single-family homes.

DREAMY!!

You get tired of all the daily jokes, the humiliation. Stonewall Park is telling the world we exist! That we have feelings! That we deserve equality! Stonewall Park is our living symbol to the world that we will no longer live in fear!

Alfred

Fred

"The Ghost Town as Gay Mecca" Washington Post. December 9th 1986

LGBTQ people have always wanted a place to play, fuck, fall in love, cultivate friendships, and be ourselves.

I don't need to spell out all the reasons why Fred and Alfred wanted a separate town as an interracial gay couple in the 1980s.

They faced racism, homophobia, discrimination because of AIDS and—never forget—sodomy was illegal in some states until 200-fucking-3.

Fred and Alfred wanted what we all want: A place to just...BE.

Their friend Stormy quoted Alfred warning Fred:

"Well, if you're ever going to find a place like that, you're going to have to build it *yourself*."

Quote from Marguerita "Stormy" Caldwell interview by Dennis McBride March 26th, 2005

LGBTQ people have often dreamed of establishing separatist spaces. In the 1970s, the Los Angeles Gay Liberation Front's "Stonewall Nation" project advocated moving hundreds of people to a tiny town called Alpine Nation and taking over the county.

"It'd result in a gay government, a gay civil service...the world's first gay university...the world's first museum of gay arts, sciences and history..."

Carl Wittman

However, due to homophobia and lack of support, it never materialized.

81

We Are Everywhere: A Historical Sourcebook of Gay and Lesbian Politics Edited by Mark Blasius and Shane Phelan. New York, Routledge 1997

Also in the 70s, four men founded the Radical Faeries: an anti-establishment, environmentalist, sex-positive movement that rejects assimilation in favor of rural living.

While never actually forming their own towns, Radical Faeries still exist today in intentional communities called Sanctuaries.

Fred and Alfred first tried to build Stonewall Park in Silver Springs, Nevada.

I can't believe that under these circumstances with regard to AIDS that someone is trying to bring this into our community... bringing the homosexual "death style" to Reno would be a blight on our community!

Janine Hansen of the anti-gay Pro-Family Christian Coalition

Reno Gazette-Journal December 20, 1985

Facing homophobic opposition, the couple tried again in the ghost town of Rhyolite, Nevada.

However, they again met with fierce opposition from nearby residents.

This is redneck country. When they get to the Nye County line, they cease being gays.

They turn into queers.

Nye County Commissioner Bob Revert

Death Valley Gateway Gazette October 10, 1986

SAVE OUR CHILDREN FROM AIDS

Snipers shot up the home they'd built in an old train car. Fred and Alfred were driven out.

Fred and Alfred tried one last time. Using money he'd inherited after his mother died, Fred bought an abandoned ranch.

But Nevadans circulated a petition with signatures opposed Stonewall Park. Out of resources and support, the two moved on.

In 1987, dying from AIDS, Fred was still plotting a separatist community in the form of a Gay Summer Camp.

"We are assured the sodomy law will be enforced...This will come in legal form during the day and there is every possibility of danger at night."

Fred died that May. Alfred, also infected with AIDS, moved to San Francisco until he passed away.

MS 1990-15 (Fred Schoonmaker Papers), Museum of GLBT History in San Francisco, CA.

Fred and Alfred never built their dream. But other queer people have. Places exist like A-Camp—a summer camp for lesbian, bisexual, transgender and queer folks to get away from it all. And Idyll Dandy Arts—a queer and trans intentional community in rural Tennessee.

I think about Fred and Alfred a lot.

About how they never reached their dreams. About how they opened themselves up to racism and homophobia trying to loudly, publicly and proudly build their town. About how they exhausted all their money, energy and resources trying for an impossible dream before both dying of AIDS.

So in these spaces, where I feel myself and others thriving, being our beautiful flamboyant selves without fear or persecution, living and loving each other wildly, I feel the two of them thriving too, existing without fear.

Am I Queer Enough?

Since I didn't start identifying as pansexual until later in life –

My relationship with my own queer identity hasn't come easy.

QUEER

I constantly wonder – Do I deserve to use the term? Am I 'Queer Enough'?

84

It's easy to view queerness as a badge of adversity.

If I didn't deal with as much hardship, does that make me less queer?

I've only recently started feeling like I belong in queer spaces.

Even so, I wouldn't feel at ease if I didn't paint my nails first. They're my little queer passports.

And it turns out, I'm not the only one who needs a passport.

I knew I was queer from, like, grade school...

LISA: FEMME BISEXUAL CIS WOMAN.

But once she started dating boys, it was as though Lisa had lost all her queer cred.

Like she was a punk band doing a Coke commercial.

Queer women refuse to date her, accusing her of just being curious, or just "trying on" being queer.

They boast about not dating bisexual girls.

This constant exclusion makes Lisa feel like an impostor in her own queerness.

I've also spoken with trans friends who suffer from the same kinds of gatekeeping.

In some spaces I would feel less queer or non-conforming just because my appearance tends to lean to the more masculine side of the spectrum.

ALEX: TRANS MAN

Can you imagine finally feeling comfortable in your own body, only to then feel uncomfortable in your supposedly 'safe spaces'?

I love fashion of all kinds, but I feel immense pressure to only dress in a subdued masculine way to be gendered correctly at all.

Being non-binary, it's tricky to be taken seriously while expressing my authentic self at the same time.

MADY (MY PARTNER): AGENDER. DREW THIS COMIC

Perhaps if queer representation in media was more diverse, we might more easily reject the boundaries imposed on us.

Rather than making queerness an identity that is founded within an extremely discrete and bounded location, searching for commonality extends queerness outwards.

DR. HANNAH MCCANN: LECTURER IN GENDER STUDIES AT THE UNIVERSITY OF MELBOURNE.

I don't know if I'll ever feel like I'm queer enough.

But I also never used to think I'd look forward to trying a new nail color, so who knows?

Freedom, Joy and Power:
The History of the Rainbow Flag

In 1978, an artist and activist named Gilbert Baker hand-dyed and stitched two flags in the attic of the Gay Community Center in San Francisco with a group of thirty volunteers.

They broke into a laundromat at night

SORRY!

to rinse the dye from the fabrics.

88

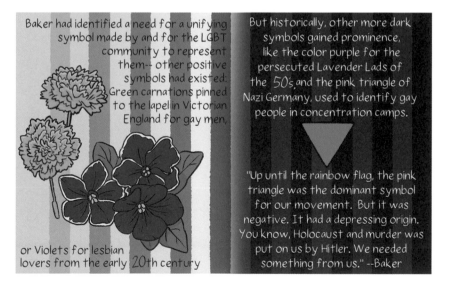

Baker had identified a need for a unifying symbol made by and for the LGBT community to represent them-- other positive symbols had existed: Green carnations pinned to the lapel in Victorian England for gay men,

or Violets for lesbian lovers from the early 20th century

But historically, other more dark symbols gained prominence, like the color purple for the persecuted Lavender Lads of the 50's, and the pink triangle of Nazi Germany, used to identify gay people in concentration camps.

"Up until the rainbow flag, the pink triangle was the dominant symbol for our movement. But it was negative. It had a depressing origin. You know, Holocaust and murder was put on us by Hitler. We needed something from us." --Baker

The rainbow flag first flew in the Gay Freedom Day Parade celebration in San Francisco on June 25, 1978.

"We needed something to express our joy, our beauty, our power. And the rainbow did that."
--Baker

The original eight colors of the flag represent:

SEX
LIFE
HEALING
SUNLIGHT
NATURE
MAGIC / ART
SERENITY
SPIRIT

The pink stripe was soon removed due to pink flag-making fabric being unavailable. The turquoise and indigo stripes were combined into one blue stripe (now representing harmony) to keep the number of stripes even.

When Harvey Milk, California's first openly gay city supervisor, was assassinated on November 27 the same year the rainbow flag debuted, demand rose exponentially.

In 1989, the flag recieved nationwide attention when John Stout successfully sued his landlords over infringement of his right to fly the flag from his apartment balcony.

The Pride flag has now risen to international prominence and represents the incredible diversity of the LGBT community.

There is no single correct way to be LGBT, but an entire spectrum of identities and orientations that make the community as vibrant and lively as it is.

While the rainbow flag still stands for the entire community, sub-groups have developed their own flags to represent their distinct identities.

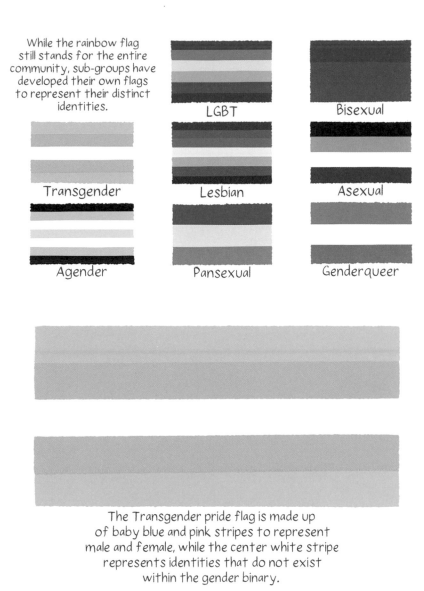

LGBT

Bisexual

Transgender

Lesbian

Asexual

Agender

Pansexual

Genderqueer

The Transgender pride flag is made up of baby blue and pink stripes to represent male and female, while the center white stripe represents identities that do not exist within the gender binary.

In the Bisexual pride flag, the pink stripe represents attraction to the same sex, blue represents attraction to the opposite sex, and the middle purple stripe represents where those two intersect.

Nowadays, the pride flag is so ubiquitous

that even the rainbow itself is seen as a symbol of belonging to the LGBT community.

To LGBT individuals who have been rejected by their families and peers, the flag is an especially important reminder that they belong, and that there are people like them who have survived and thrived.

Gilbert Baker passed away in 2017, but his contribution to the LGBT community's rich history will love on forever as something that helps remind us that we are a family.

"Flags are about proclaiming power... that visibility is key to our success and to our justice." -- Baker

Birth Control is About More than Just Birth

After some soul-searching over the past few years, I realized I'm

ASEXUAL!

no interest in sex

does not experience attraction

But being asexual doesn't negate my sexual organs or need for healthcare.

Like pap smears.

People shove things in their vagina for *pleasure*?!

I had an ovarian cyst scare in high school, and in adulthood I regularly get debilitating menstrual cramps, so recently I sought out birth control as a superior option to downing ibuprofen and suffering every month.

Because birth control isn't just for avoiding pregnancy!

Doctors also prescribe the pill to reduce or help prevent:

Acne
- Bone thinning
- Anemic iron deficiency
- Breast & ovarian cysts
- Endometrial & ovarian cancers
- Serious infections in the ovaries, fallopian tubes, & uterus
- Menstrual cramps & heavy period flow
- PMS

94

Under the Affordable Care Act, the Obama Administration hoped to broadly expand access to contraception by making it a mandatory health insurance benefit, but it stirred controversy and sparked lawsuits from corporations, colleges, and religious affiliates and organizations, such as the Little Sisters of the Poor.

Birth control has continually been opposed to by those who believe its use promotes sexual promiscuity in youth, specifically teenagers.

SLURP ♡

smooch ♡

(though this did not apply to me)

But studies have proven there is no link between a greater access to oral contraception and an increase in sexual behavior.

A 2014 study showed abortion rates dropped 26% from 2008...

...But it isn't clear if increased contraception usage or a decline in access to abortions is the cause of the drop.

My doctor warned me pills were more likely to be intercepted by conservative pharmacists, so she recommended an IUD or implanon implant that would last at least three years.

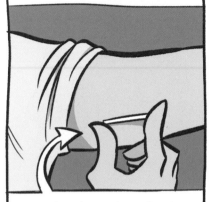

I had no desire to go digging around in my hooha again, so I chose the arm implant.

The Nexplanon arm implant pumps out a low, regular dose (about 68mg) of the hormone etonogestrel throughout the bloodstream, stopping ovaries from releasing eggs and preventing sperm from reaching them.

STOP

STOP

But I was scared to insert something in my body to change it forever—or at least for three years.

Now we just want to numb your arm.

You'll feel a little burning, like someone pinching you, but it'll be brief.

"Once numb, the Introducer is worked very carefully under the skin.

When it's fully in, the introducer unlocks and leaves behind the implant."

KA-K!! CHNK!!

Sounds like a stapler!

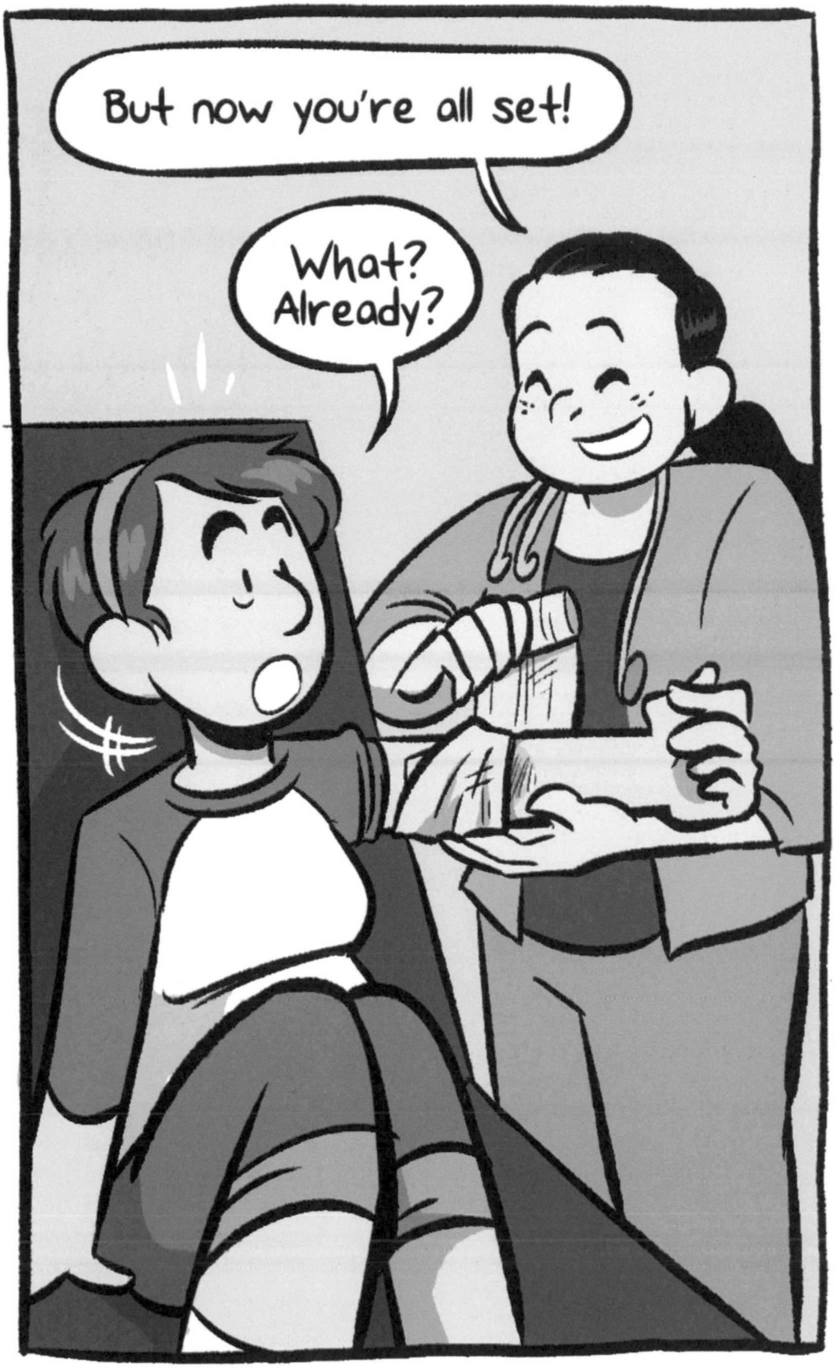
But now you're all set!
What? Already?

After the election, Planned Parenthood noted a 900 percent increase in implant and IUD appointments. Many women feared if Trump kept his promise to repeal the ACA, they would not be able to afford contraception out-of-pocket.

Birth control pills can cost anywhere from $4 to $55 a month, with IUDs costing anywhere between $600 and $1000!

On October 6, 2017, the Trump administration rolled back the requirement that employer-provided health insurance policies cover birth control methods.

Health policy analysts argue that the ruling creates a huge loophole for employers to claim an exemption so they don't have to provide birth control coverage, forcing employees to pay the full cost out of pocket.

It's not about promiscuity—limiting access to birth control for religious and monetary motives is an attack on public health.

BIRTH CONTROL GIVES ME CONTROL OF MY OWN BODY!

(...but that control should've been mine in the first place.)

Dating a Trans Person Changed My Partner's Life

99

I DON'T KNOW HOW LONG IT WOULD HAVE TAKEN FOR ME TO THROW GENDER NORMS INTO THE TRASH ON MY OWN, BUT BEING IN THIS RELATIONSHIP HAS MADE ME A MORE CURIOUS, UNDERSTANDING, AND EMPATHETIC PERSON.

MY PARTNER

ME

IT'S HELPED TEACH ME TO STEP OUTSIDE OF MY OWN EXPERIENCE, AND EVEN RE-EXAMINE THE ASSUMPTIONS I HAD ABOUT MYSELF.

OTHER FRIENDS*, BOTH TRANS AND CIS, TOLD ME SIMILAR STORIES ABOUT THEIR TRANS-INCLUSIVE RELATIONSHIPS...

MY EX TOLD ME ONCE THAT HE ADMIRED THE LEVEL OF SELF-CONFRONTATION NECESSARY IN MY TRANSITION.

*APPEARANCES CHANGED FOR ANONYMITY

I THINK THAT SELF-CONFRONTATION BECAME A PRACTICE IN ALL AREAS OF MY LIFE, BUT ESPECIALLY IN MY LOVE LIFE- I HAVE HEALTHIER, MORE COMMUNICATIVE RELATIONSHIPS, AND I ENGAGE WITH THE PEOPLE I LOVE ON A PERSON TO PERSON LEVEL WITHOUT MAKING ASSUMPTIONS BASED ON GENDER...

... ALSO, MY SEX LIFE IS WAY BETTER NOW THAT I RELATE TO MY BODY, HAHA!

IT'S AN EXCELLENT FEELING TO BE 100% YOURSELF AND HAVE SOMEONE LOVE 100% OF YOU.

PEOPLE WHO SAY [THEY WOULDN'T DATE A TRANS PERSON] DON'T SEEM REALLY READY FOR THAT COMMITMENT IN GENERAL.

THERE WAS THE RELIEF OF KNOWING THAT IF [MY PARTNER] STILL LOVED ME BEYOND THIS, WHICH AT THE TIME WAS MY CLOSEST GUARDED SECRET, I FELT LIKE WE COULD WEATHER ANYTHING THAT CAME OUR WAY.

IF SHE LOVED THIS TRUEST PART OF ME, THEN I COULD FINALLY SHOW HER EVERYTHING.

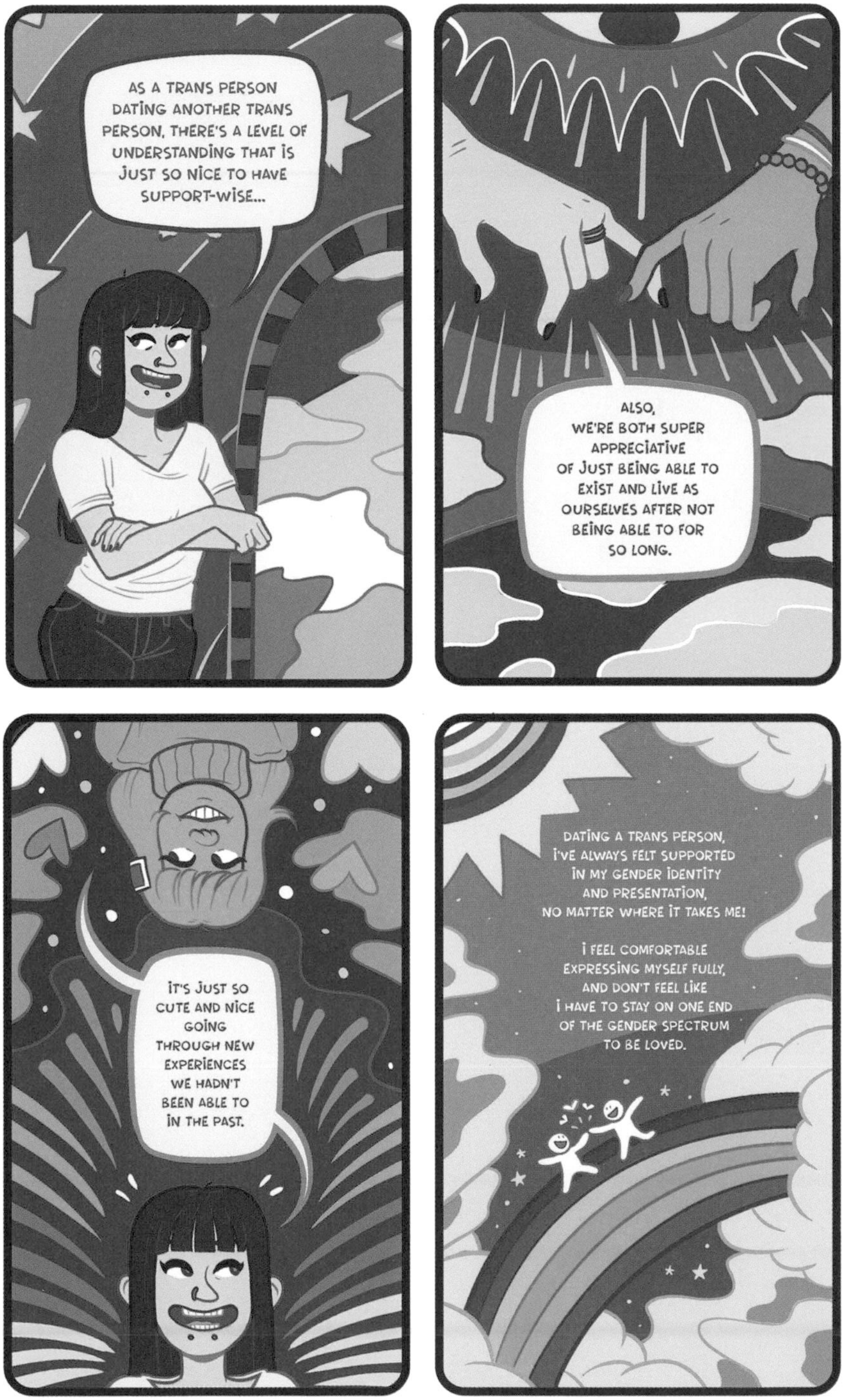
AS A TRANS PERSON DATING ANOTHER TRANS PERSON, THERE'S A LEVEL OF UNDERSTANDING THAT IS JUST SO NICE TO HAVE SUPPORT-WISE...
ALSO, WE'RE BOTH SUPER APPRECIATIVE OF JUST BEING ABLE TO EXIST AND LIVE AS OURSELVES AFTER NOT BEING ABLE TO FOR SO LONG.
IT'S JUST SO CUTE AND NICE GOING THROUGH NEW EXPERIENCES WE HADN'T BEEN ABLE TO IN THE PAST.
DATING A TRANS PERSON, I'VE ALWAYS FELT SUPPORTED IN MY GENDER IDENTITY AND PRESENTATION, NO MATTER WHERE IT TAKES ME!
I FEEL COMFORTABLE EXPRESSING MYSELF FULLY, AND DON'T FEEL LIKE I HAVE TO STAY ON ONE END OF THE GENDER SPECTRUM TO BE LOVED.

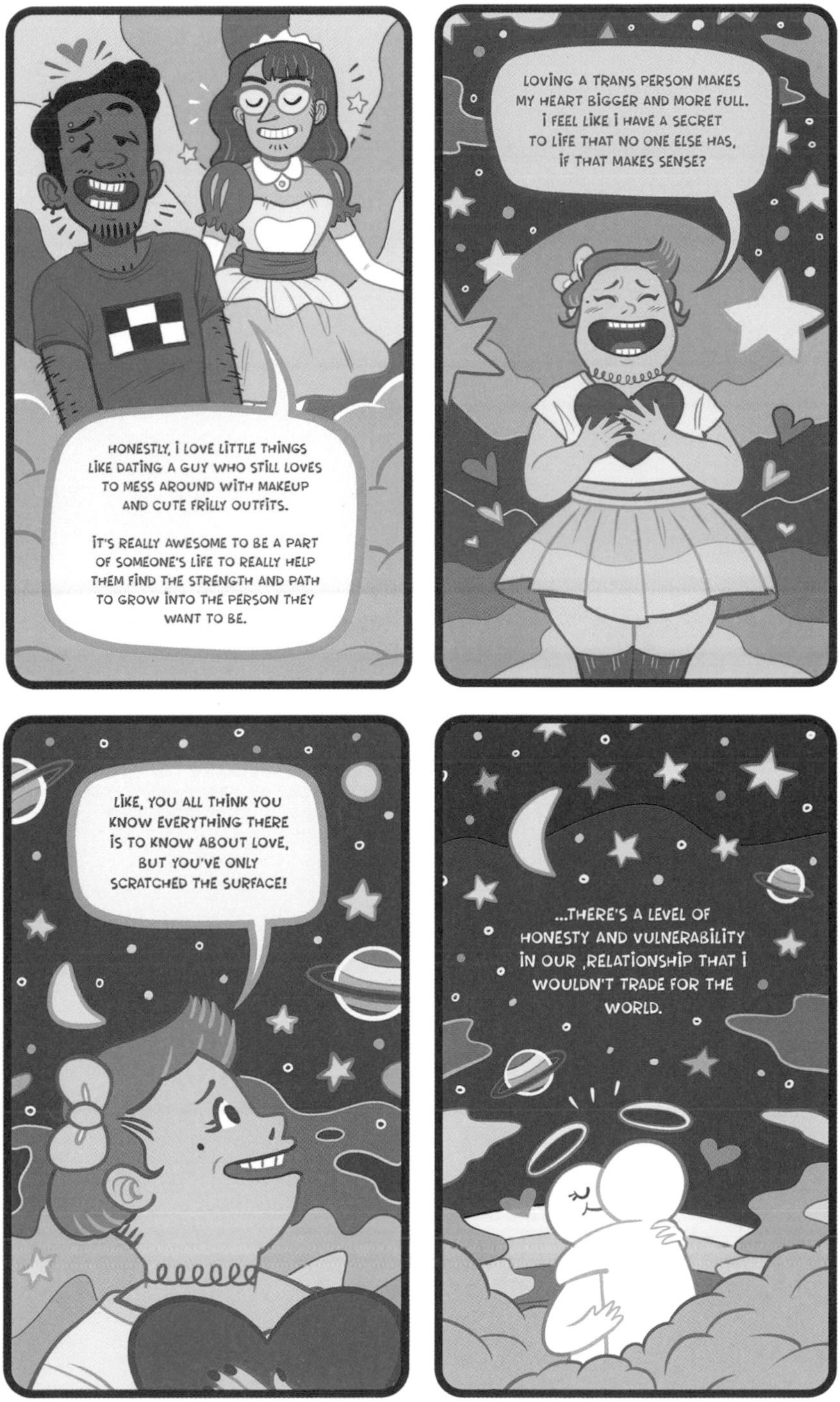
HONESTLY, I LOVE LITTLE THINGS LIKE DATING A GUY WHO STILL LOVES TO MESS AROUND WITH MAKEUP AND CUTE FRILLY OUTFITS.
IT'S REALLY AWESOME TO BE A PART OF SOMEONE'S LIFE TO REALLY HELP THEM FIND THE STRENGTH AND PATH TO GROW INTO THE PERSON THEY WANT TO BE.
LOVING A TRANS PERSON MAKES MY HEART BIGGER AND MORE FULL. I FEEL LIKE I HAVE A SECRET TO LIFE THAT NO ONE ELSE HAS, IF THAT MAKES SENSE?
LIKE, YOU ALL THINK YOU KNOW EVERYTHING THERE IS TO KNOW ABOUT LOVE, BUT YOU'VE ONLY SCRATCHED THE SURFACE!
...THERE'S A LEVEL OF HONESTY AND VULNERABILITY IN OUR ,RELATIONSHIP THAT I WOULDN'T TRADE FOR THE WORLD.

Decolonizing Queerness in the Philippines

ACROSS THE USA, CITIES CELEBRATE PRIDE AT THE END OF JUNE– THE DATE COMMEMORATES THE STONEWALL RIOTS, WHICH WERE LED BY TRANS AND GENDERQUEER PEOPLE OF COLOR.

AT THE TIME OF STONEWALL, THESE IDENTITIES WEREN'T NECESSARILY CALLED THAT. MANY PEOPLE EMBRACED THE IDENTITY OF DRAG QUEEN.

THE LANGUAGE WE USE TO DESCRIBE GENDER AND SEXUALITY IS ALWAYS EVOLVING AND IS DEEPLY ROOTED IN CULTURE.

104

OTHER COUNTRIES HAVE THEIR OWN WORDS, OF COURSE.

THESE WORDS ARE OFTEN USED TO HUMILIATE AND SHAME LGBTQI PEOPLE, ESPECIALLY THOSE WITH FEMME CHARACTERISTICS.

ACCORDING TO THE SURVEY "THE GLOBAL DIVIDE ON HOMOSEXUALITY" CONDUCTED IN 2013 BY THE US-BASED PEW RESEARCH CENTER, THE PHILIPPINES IS ONE OF THE MOST GAY-FRIENDLY COUNTRIES IN THE WORLD AND IS THE MOST GAY-FRIENDLY COUNTRY IN ASIA.

I am heartened to know the percentage of adult Pilipinos who believe gay people should have rights goes up every year. This is largely influenced by Western shifts in culture and acceptance.

Philippine culture, like many countries around the world, is inextricably linked to the USA by colonialism and imperialism. In turn, our homophobic and transphobic beliefs were born from colonization.

BAKLA
<FAGGOT>

IN FACT, MANY WOULD ARGUE THAT HOMOPHOBIA ITSELF IS A TOOL OF COLONIAL OPPRESSION. HOMOPHOBIA DID NOT EXIST IN MOST PRE-COLONIAL CULTURES OF THE PHILIPPINES.

BABAYLAN, typically a femme priestess of any gender

TRIBES AND MICRO-NATIONS THAT MADE UP WHAT WE NOW CALL THE PHILIPPINE ISLANDS EMBRACED THE BAKLA IDENTITY. IT IS AN UMBRELLA IDENTITY THAT IS BEYOND GAY, LESBIAN, TRANS, OR EVEN DRAG QUEEN.

IT CANNOT BE TRANSLATED ACCURATELY INTO ENGLISH.

IT IS SIMILAR TO THE CONCEPT OF TWO-SPIRIT IDENTITY IN THE PAN-INDIGENOUS GROUPS OF NORTH AMERICA OR THE HIJRA IDENTITY IN INDIA.

Hijras

Celebrated Crow Two Spirit (bade) Osh-Tisch

THESE IDENTITIES WERE ONCE REVERED AND THOSE WHO EMBODIED THESE TRAITS WERE GIVEN LEADERSHIP ROLES IN SOCIETY.

Itneg shaman, diviner, spirit guide

WE'WHA Zuni potter, weaver, leader

BAYBAYIN IS ONE OF OUR PRE-COLONIAL INDIGENOUS WRITING SYSTEMS. THE PHILIPPINE GOVERNMENT IS NOW TRYING TO REINSTATE IT AS A NATIONAL ALPHABET.

BAKLA:

KA the symbol for unity and freedom.

BA is the symbol for the feminine.

LA the symbol for the masculine.

THIS RETURN TO OUR WRITING SYSTEM IS ALSO A RETURN TO OUR CULTURAL PSYCHOLOGY AND THE NAMES FOR IDENTITIES THAT WERE LOST FOR SO LONG. THAT IS LIFE-SAVING FOR MANY PEOPLE WHO COME OUT TO THEIR FAMILIES.

WHEN WE REVERSE THE SYMBOLS FOR BAKLA, WE GET THE WORD LAKBAY, THE TAGALOG WORD FOR JOURNEY.

This set of symbols not only humanizes queer and trans identities, but it supports and uplifts them as well, in ways that the limitations of *homosexual* cannot.

Lakbay is a journey you take away from your usual environment to understand yourself ... meeting new people opens your eyes to see yourself in other ways.

Omehra Sigahne
author of
BABAYLAN ALIVE
(with co-author
Diwata Olympia-Nguyen)

Bakla is the inward journey to wholeness where you find that you are complete within yourself, and this wholeness is what you share ... For modern Filipinos, discovering the mere existence of baybayin is like discovering a missing piece of their cultural identity.

Pat Pat

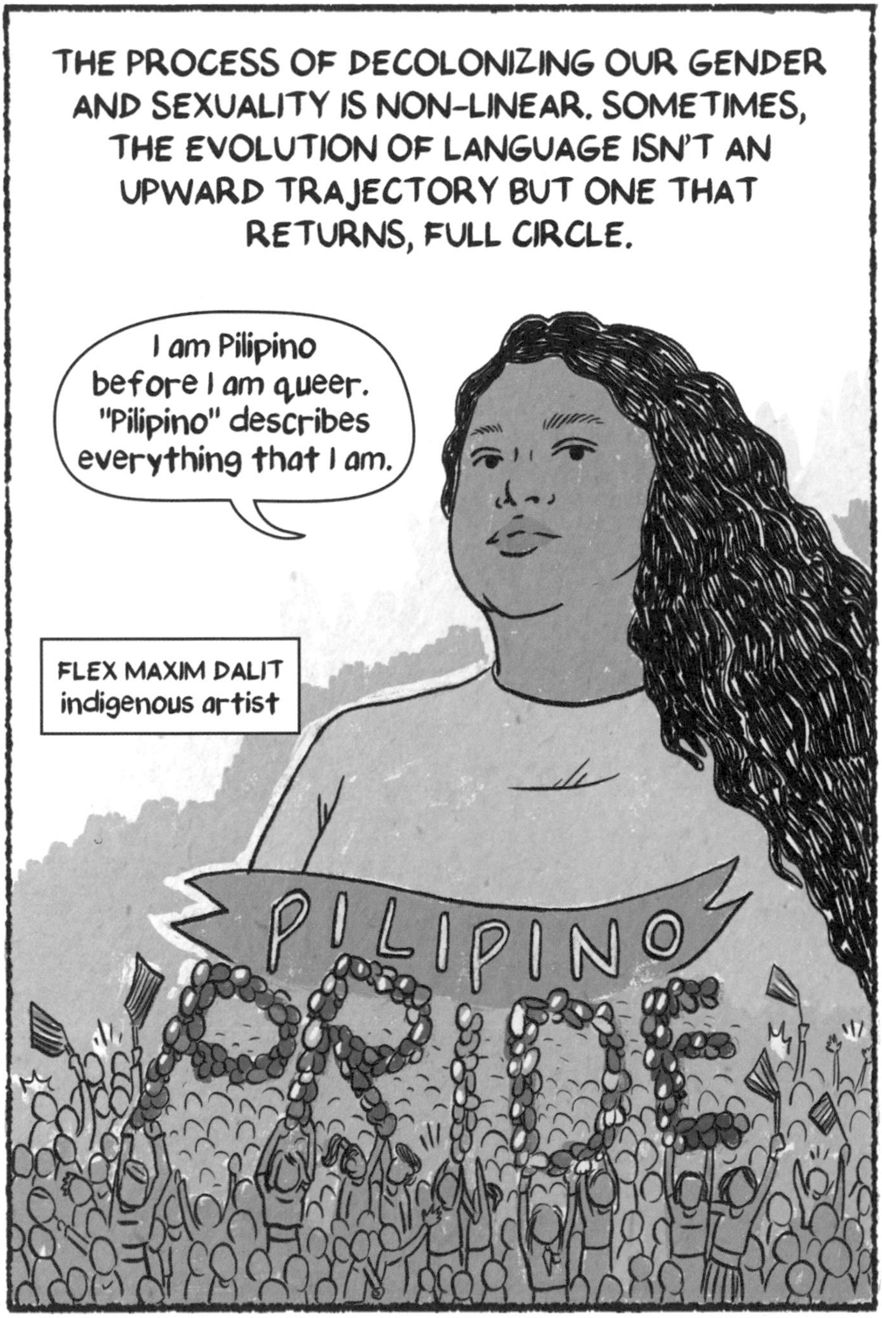
THE PROCESS OF DECOLONIZING OUR GENDER AND SEXUALITY IS NON-LINEAR. SOMETIMES, THE EVOLUTION OF LANGUAGE ISN'T AN UPWARD TRAJECTORY BUT ONE THAT RETURNS, FULL CIRCLE.
I am Pilipino before I am queer. "Pilipino" describes everything that I am.
FLEX MAXIM DALIT
indigenous artist
PILIPINO
PRIDE

When You're Invisible in Pop Culture

SO I GUESS WE SHOULD DIVE RIGHT IN!

YEAH. GROWING UP, OTHERNESS WAS PORTRAYED IN A LOT OF FILMS BUT IT WAS VAGUE. "BE YOURSELF, BUT ONLY IF YOURSELF IS THIS VERSION!" TODAY, FILMS AND TV FEEL SO MUCH MORE SPECIFIC!

DEFINITELY! I HEAR THE TERM "QUEERBAITING" GETTING USED A LOT TO REFER TO FILMS FROM THE 80'S OR 90'S BY QUEER KIDS WHO HAD TO IDENTIFY THEMSELVES AS THE OUTCAST EVEN IF THE CHARACTER THEMSELVES WASN'T GAY.

ABSOLUTELY. AND CHARACTERS WHO WERE OPENLY QUEER WERE EITHER WRITTEN OFF AS A **JOKE** OR **DEMONIZED.**

109

ONE PERSON I IDENTIFIED WITH A LOT AS A TEEN WAS JANIS IAN FROM MEAN GIRLS, A GOTH WHO WAS MADE FUN OF FOR SUPPOSEDLY BEING GAY (WHICH WAS NEVER ACTUALLY CONFIRMED).

OH YES!! THIS IS SO TRUE, OR EVEN AS KIDS THE "QUEER" CHARACTERS WERE USUALLY DISNEY VILLAINS LIKE JAFAR, SCAR, OR—MY FAVORITE—URSULA. PAINTING QUEERNESS AS SOMETHING THAT WAS DEEMED ALMOST EVIL.

WHAT ARE SOME MOVIES THAT REALLY SPOKE TO YOU GROWING UP AND HOW DO YOU SEE THAT CHANGING?

HAHA, I WAS ABOUT TO ASK YOU THE SAME THING! "MULAN" WAS A HUGE ONE FOR ME. I USED TO LISTEN TO "REFLECTION" DAILY. IT WAS THE FIRST INSTANCE I SAW OF SOMEONE BEING ABLE TO LOVE YOU REGARDLESS OF THE GENDER YOU PRESENTED AS; WITH LI SHANG AND MULAN (WHO ALSO PRESENTED AS PING)'S RELATIONSHIP.

SAGE: BUT NOW, WITH THE UPCOMING LIVE-ACTION REMAKE SUPPOSEDLY ERASES LI SHANG'S IMPLIED INTEREST IN MULAN WHILE SHE PRESENTS AS A MAN. IT FEELS LIKE A STEP BACKWARDS FOR MULAN SPECIFICALLY.

BIANCA: THAT'S REALLY IRRITATING.

IT REALLY IS! "TOM BOY" (2012) TOUCHED ME IN A WAY NO OTHER FILM HAD. I WATCHED IT IN COLLEGE AND REGARDLESS OF THE MAIN CHARACTER EXPLORING THEIR GENDER, THEY'RE LOVED.

PEOPLE KEEP SAYING "DEAR SIMON" IS A FILM WE NEEDED THIS YEAR, BUT WE'VE ALWAYS NEEDED FILMS LIKE THIS! QUEER FOLKS HAVE ALWAYS BEEN HERE AND LEARNING AT A YOUNG AGE THAT YOUR FEELINGS ARE NORMAL IS SO, SO IMPORTANT.

I ALSO FEEL LIKE MORE MODERN MEDIA HAS BEEN BETTER ABOUT LETTING WOMEN HAVE THEIR SPACE, BEING MORE REBELLIOUS, AND PORTRAYING THE ROCKY RELATIONSHIPS PRESENT IN FAMILIES. LIKE 2017'S LADYBIRD!

YES LADYBIRD WAS SOOO PIVOTAL TO ME. I'VE HONESTLY NEVER SEEN SUCH A CANDID MOVIE ABOUT A MOTHER DAUGHTER RELATIONSHIP THAT DIDN'T OVER-DEMONIZE THE MOTHER.

I GET TIRED OF THAT TROPE BECAUSE, GROWING UP, MY OWN RELATIONSHIP WITH MY OWN MOTHER WAS HARD BUT SHE WORKED SO HARD TO RAISE THREE KIDS ON HER OWN I HAVE EMPATHY FOR HER.

YESSS! I FEEL LIKE THE CLOSEST THING WE HAD TO THAT GROWING UP WAS "A GOOFY MOVIE". I TOOK THAT FILM FOR GRANTED AT THE TIME. I WAS GROWING UP WITH A SINGLE MOM WHO DIDN'T REALLY GET ME.

EVEN THEN, WE ONLY GET THE BRIEFEST IDEA OF WHAT GOOFY WAS GOING THROUGH, WORKING DIFFERENT JOBS (PHOTOGRAPHER, FACTORY WORKER, ETC.) TO SUPPORT HIS SON AND KINDLE THE FRIENDSHIP GOOFY AND HIS FATHER SEEMED TO HAVE!

BUT MAX IN THAT MOVIE DIDN'T REALLY HAVE AN "OTHERNESS" ELEMENT TO HIS STORY LIKE LADYBIRD. HE HAD CLOSE FRIENDS AND WASN'T REALLY CONSIDERED WEIRD BY HIS PEERS.

TRUE. MORE THAN ANYTHING, I APPRECIATE FILMS THAT OFFER A PARENT'S PERSPECTIVE VERSUS JUST A "YOU DON'T KNOW ME DOOR SLAM" BECAUSE OUR PARENTS ARE PEOPLE TOO, PROBABLY SOFT-HEARTED LIKE US, HARDENED BY THEIR PARENTS.

WHAT'RE SOME MOVIES THAT REALLY STUCK WITH YOU GROWING UP? DO YOU FEEL MORE SEEN IN MODERN MOVIES COMPARED TO THE ONES YOU GREW UP WITH?

HONESTLY I'M ON THE FENCE I SEE MYSELF HERE AND THERE BUT I'VE YET TO SEE A FULL VERSION OF MYSELF. THAT'S WHY I WRITE COMICS.

I WOULD SEE MYSELF AS THE OUTCAST IN JOHN HUGHES MOVIES LIKE "PRETTY IN PINK". I RELATE TO ANDIE, GROWING UP POOR, HAVING A PARENT THAT DEALT WITH DEPRESSION, EVEN CLINGY MALE FRIENDS WHO PROJECTED THE PERFECT WOMAN ON TO ME. BUT I'M NOT WHITE NOR WOULD I FALL FOR BLAINE!!

MORE RECENTLY, I ALSO FOUND MYSELF IN MOONLIGHT. SOME OF THE QUIETER MOMENTS WHERE WE WATCH CHRION GROW UP WERE SINCERE AND BEAUTIFUL. BUT I DIDN'T FEEL FULLY REPRESENTED BY THE FILM OTHER THAN US SHARING A RACE. OFTEN I FEEL LIKE I HAVE TO PIECE MYSELF TOGETHER THROUGH FILM AND TV.

THE MOST SUCCESSFUL VERSION OF MYSELF I'VE SEEN WAS IN CHEWING GUM, WHICH CAME OUT IN 2015.

OOOH, CHEWING GUM IS SO GOOD. ESPECIALLY IN ITS PORTRAYAL OF GROWING UP POOR.

I GREW UP POOR, RELIGIOUS, AWKWARD, AND BLACK. SO CHEWING GUM NAILS IT ON THE HEAD FOR ME!!

I HATE THIS "POOR LITTLE NEGRO" STEREOTYPE. I WAS HAPPY, DESPITE MY FAMILY'S MEANS. CHEWING GUM CREATOR MICHELA COLE TALKS ABOUT HOW SHE DIDN'T WANT HER APARTMENT COMPLEX TO LOOK SAD BUT TO SHOW THE COMMUNITY ASPECT, AND I LOVED THAT!

THAT'S AMAZING! YEAH, I FEEL LIKE OFTEN PORTRAYALS OF POOR FAMILIES ARE USUALLY MISERABLE. UNLESS THEY'RE MIDDLE CLASS, IN WHICH CASE EVERYTHING IS CONSIDERED "NORMAL" AND "RELATABLE."

I JUST WANT OTHERNESS TO BE NORMALIZED. NOT EVERY BLACK GIRL STORY IS PRECIOUS. HOW OFTEN DO WE GET TO SEE BLACK WOMEN FALL IN LOVE ON SCREEN IN A MAJOR MOTION PICTURE? ALMOST NEVER?

ABSOLUTELY!

WHAT ARE YOUR HOPES FOR OUR MEDIA?

A BIG THING FOR ME IS JUST HAVING A SINCERE NONBINARY CHARACTER ON SCREEN. I CANNOT THINK OF A SINGLE NONBINARY CHARACTER FROM A FILM OTHER THAN BENEDICT CUMBERBATCH'S JOKE CHARACTER IN "ZOOLANDER 2".

YIKES.

ALSO, TRANS STORIES THAT AREN'T ABOUT TRANSITIONING AND WHOSE IDENTITIES AREN'T USED AS SOME TWIST OR ACT OF BETRAYAL. JUST GIVE ME SOMEONE WHO'S TRANS AND LIVING THEIR LIFE. THEY CAN HAVE CONFLICT, SURE BUT GOING BACK TO WHAT YOU SAID, THERE JUST NEEDS TO BE MORE THAN ONE NARRATIVE FOR THESE CHARACTERS!

I GUESS FOR NOW WE CAN CONTINUE TO HOPE!

FINGERS CROSSED!

"That's all folks"

Nothing is Wrong With Me

AS A 13-YEAR-OLD EVANGELICAL CHRISTIAN, I ASSUMED MY LACK OF INTEREST IN SEX WAS A SIGN OF MY INHERENT MORAL PURITY.

80s SEX POP IDOL SAMANTHA FOX

NAUGHTY GIRLS NEED LOVE, TOO

DISGUSTING.

I KNEW THE WORD "ASEXUAL" FROM BIOLOGY CLASS. BUT I WAS NOT A HYDRA, SO IT DIDN'T APPLY TO ME.

WE'RE AROMANTIC, TOO!

Hydra is a genus of small, fresh-water animals. Hydra reproduce asexually by producing buds in the body wall, which grow to be miniature adults and simply break away when they are mature. When a hydra is well fed, a new bud can form

I BELIEVED THE CULTURAL NARRATIVE THAT MEN ONLY WANT SEX, AND WOMEN ARE GATEKEEPERS WHO CORRAL MALE SEXUAL IMPULSE.

TWO THINGS HAPPENED TO KNOCK ME OFF MY PURITY PEDESTAL.

FIRST, I BROKE UP WITH CHRISTIANITY.

JUDAISM
ISLAM
HINDUISM
BUDDHISM
CONFUSCIANISM
BAHA'I
SHINTO
ZOROAST
TAOIS
SIKH

YoungLife

NOW, THE STATE OF TEXAS *REQUIRES* ME TO TEACH YOU ABOUT THESE OTHER RELIGIONS ...

BUT PLEASE UNDERSTAND THAT DOES *NOT* MAKE THEM TRUE, AND I AM *NOT* TRYING TO CONVERT YOU TO ANY OF THEM.

IF I'D BEEN BORN IN INDIA INSTEAD OF AMERICA, I'D PROBABLY BE HINDU INSTEAD OF CHRISTIAN.

THIS IS ALL JUST AN ACCIDENT OF BIRTH.

SECOND, I DISCOVERED OTHER GIRLS MY AGE WERE HAVING SEX. BECAUSE *THEY* WANTED TO.

SO THEN I PUT SYRUP ON HIS STOMACH AND LICKED IT OFF!

GIGGLE!

OH MY GOD!

IF EVEN ONE OF MY HEALTH CLASSES HAD MENTIONED ASEXUALITY AS A POSSIBLE ORIENTATION, I MIGHT HAVE UNDERSTOOD THE DISCONNECT BETWEEN ME AND MY PEERS.

HEALTH STUDIES for the CISNORMATIVE HETEROSEXUAL

BUT NONE OF THEM DID. NOT IN JUNIOR HIGH. NOT IN HIGH SCHOOL. NOT IN COLLEGE.

IN COLLEGE I SOUGHT OTHER EXPLANATIONS FOR WHAT MADE ME DIFFERENT. SOMETHING ABOUT QUEERNESS SEEMED TO FIT.

MAYBE I'M A LESBIAN. MAYBE *THAT'S* WHY I DON'T WANT TO HAVE SEX WITH GUYS.

ONE SLIGHT PROBLEM.

I DIDN'T FIND MYSELF WANTING TO HAVE SEX WITH WOMEN, EITHER.

None of my health classes had mentioned the existence of trans people, either, so I had to work out that part of my identity by trial and error.

I'm not a butch lesbian! I'm a guy!

The problem the whole time has been that I'm attracted to men, but as a gay man!

Surely it was the body dysphoria that made me not want sex!

LOU SULLIVAN

Louis Graydon Sullivan was an American transgender man, one of the first to publically identify as gay.

I knew several trans guys who said their sex drives increased after they started hormone therapy.

T made me really horny!

I don't see how it could make me any hornier than I already am!

I know, right??

Eh, my sex drive didn't change. I guess I'm a dud.

Doctors may prescribe small doses of testosterone to women with flagging sex drives (though such use is considered off-label).

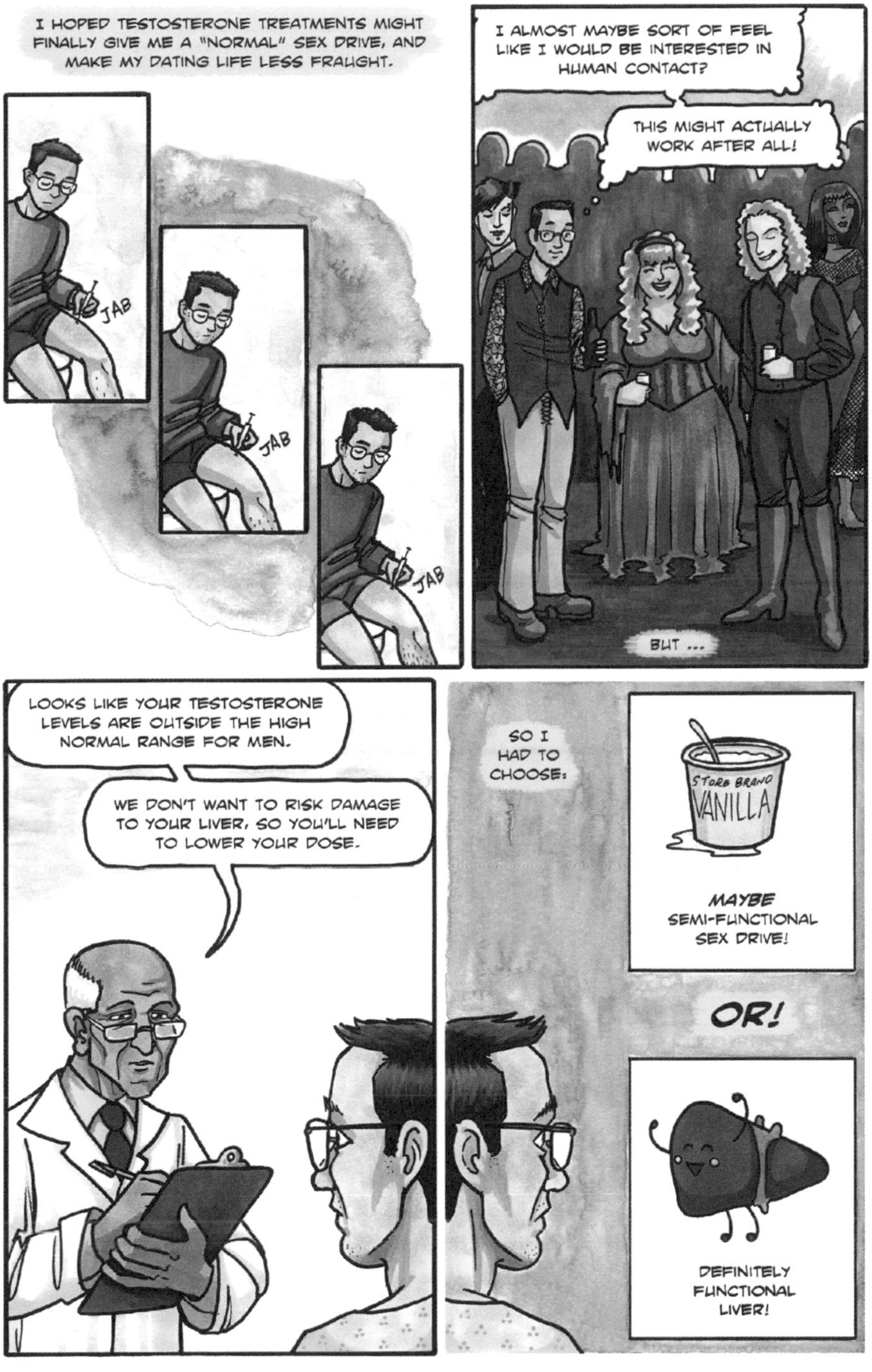
I HOPED TESTOSTERONE TREATMENTS MIGHT FINALLY GIVE ME A "NORMAL" SEX DRIVE, AND MAKE MY DATING LIFE LESS FRAUGHT.
JAB
JAB
JAB
I ALMOST MAYBE SORT OF FEEL LIKE I WOULD BE INTERESTED IN HUMAN CONTACT?
THIS MIGHT ACTUALLY WORK AFTER ALL!
BUT ...
LOOKS LIKE YOUR TESTOSTERONE LEVELS ARE OUTSIDE THE HIGH NORMAL RANGE FOR MEN.
WE DON'T WANT TO RISK DAMAGE TO YOUR LIVER, SO YOU'LL NEED TO LOWER YOUR DOSE.
SO I HAD TO CHOOSE:
STORE BRAND VANILLA
MAYBE SEMI-FUNCTIONAL SEX DRIVE!
OR!
DEFINITELY FUNCTIONAL LIVER!

I, TOO, WAS TURNING OUT TO BE A DUD.

RAINBOW BOOKS AND MORE!

MEAT INSPECTO[R]

ROMANTICALLY ATTRACTED TO MEN, AND LIVING AS A MAN, BUT UNABLE TO RELATE TO THE HYPERSEXUALIZED GAY MALE WORLD.

MALE SOCIALIZATION, WHETHER STRAIGHT OR QUEER, ATTACHES A GREAT DEAL OF IMPORTANCE TO BEING A SEXUAL DYNAMO.

ANYTIME, ANYWHERE, BEHBEH!

IN GAY MALE CULTURE, NOT BEING OVERT ABOUT YOUR SEXUAL DESIRES MAY BE SEEN AS SELF-REPRESSION THAT NEEDS TO BE OVERCOME (PUN INTENDED).

OUR SOCIETY DOESN'T ALLOW MEN TO BE UNINTERESTED IN SEX, AND THERE'S A MULTI-BILLION DOLLAR INDUSTRY TO SHOW FOR IT.

SPANISH FLY

AXE

VIAGRA

EXTEN[Z]

I FINALLY DECIDED TO BRING UP MY LACK OF INTEREST IN SEX WITH MY NEW TRANS-FRIENDLY DOCTOR.

IF YOU HAD A SEX DRIVE AND LOST IT, THEN SOME OF THOSE DRUGS MIGHT HELP.

BUT IF YOU NEVER HAD ONE TO BEGIN WITH, THEY AREN'T LIKELY TO WORK.

IF IT'S REALLY BOTHERING YOU, WE CAN TALK.

BUT IF IT'S NOT BOTHERING YOU, THEN THERE'S NOTHING TO FIX.

AND THE TRUTH IS, IT *WASN'T* BOTHERING ME. IT WAS ONLY BOTHERING OTHER PEOPLE.

YOU'RE JUST REPRESSING YOURSELF

YOU'RE BEING CRUEL TO PEOPLE YOU DATE

HOW DO YOU *REALLY* KNOW YOU'RE ASEXUAL

YOU JUST NEED TO TRY HARDER TO BE NORMAL

TRYING HARD TO BE A NORMAL/STRAIGHT/CIS PERSON HADN'T WORKED OUT, THOUGH.

HE'S CUTE. WHY AM I NOT INTO THIS?

AND TRYING TO BE A NORMAL SEXUAL PERSON WASN'T FARING MUCH BETTER.

119

I DON'T WANT TO SUGGEST I'VE NEVER BEEN SEXUALLY ATTRACTED TO SOMEONE.

BUT I *HAVE* TO FEEL A STRONG EMOTIONAL CONNECTION FIRST.

AND IT'S JUST EXTREMELY RARE FOR ME TO FEEL THAT CONNECTION WITH SOMEONE.

Sex-Repulsed

BASICALLY NEVER GONNA HAVE A ONE-NIGHT-STAND, IS WHAT I'M SAYING.

Sensualist

Asexual

Touch Averse

Libidoist

Sex-Averse

No...idoist

Sex-Ne...

Gray Asexual

Demisexual

UNFORTUNATELY, IT'S VERY DIFFICULT TO EXPLAIN THIS TO SOMEONE YOU JUST MET.

"HEY! I THINK MAYBE I LIKE YOU, BUT I DON'T KNOW IF I'LL EVER WANT TO SLEEP WITH YOU?"

UGH, SO PRESUMPTUOUS.

"CAN WE NOT-DATE FIRST TO SEE IF WE GET ALONG AS FRIENDS?"

POSSIBLY INSULTING? HMM.

I'LL LET YOU KNOW IF I EVER FIGURE OUT HOW TO HANDLE THIS ONE GRACEFULLY.

BUT THERE ARE DEFINITELY OTHER ACE TRANS GUYS OUT THERE, AND ACE TRANS WOMEN, CIS FOLKS, AND NONBINARY PEOPLE.

Asexual

THERE ARE VERY SEXUAL TRANS, CIS, AND NONBINARY FOLKS.

Allosexual

THERE ARE PEOPLE OF ALL LEVELS OF SEXUAL DESIRE REGARDLESS OF BIOLOGY.

TRYING TOO HARD TO FIT SOMEONE ELSE'S EXPECTATIONS OF WHAT YOUR SEX DRIVE SHOULD BE WILL JUST MAKE YOU MISERABLE.

SO, SAMANTHA FOX, I APOLOGIZE ON BEHALF OF MY 13-YEAR-OLD SELF.

GO GET ALL THE NAUGHTY LOVE YOU NEED.

MY VERSION OF THE SONG JUST HAS SLIGHTLY DIFFERENT LYRICS.

ACE TRANS BOYS NEED LOVE, TOO

Off the Rack

IT'S WELL-KNOWN THAT HIGH HEELS WERE INVENTED FOR MEN. MAKEUP TOO.

QUITE A MANLY SHADE, I DARESY!

PROOF THAT OUR CONCEPTION OF MASCULINE OR FEMININE PRESENTATIONS ARE ALWAYS IN FLUX, THOUGH THEY MAY SEEM UNSHAKEABLE FROM OUR FIXED PLACES IN HISTORY.

CHECK OUT THE *MACHO MAN* OVER HERE.

OH, A PEASANT!

YOU'D *LOOOVE* MY HERMITAGE.

121

AND WE'VE BEEN TOLD FOR A WHILE – BY THE FASHION INDUSTRY AND MEDIA, THAT THIS IS WHAT THE GENDERLESS FUTURE LOOKS LIKE:

BUT IS THAT POSSIBLE? DO WE EVEN WANT IT?

MATT_L   greetings from the future lol

IMAGINE, IN YOUR MIND'S EYE: WHAT DOES AN ANDROGYNOUS PERSON LOOKS LIKE?

I DON'T KNOW WHAT YOU SEE, BUT WHAT CURRENT FASHION TRENDS AND MEDIA DO IS CLEAR TO ME:

wow

so brave

AND IT'S CLEAR IT'S NOT ME.

IT'S TRUE THAT THE POLES OF BINARY GENDER EXPRESSION ARE ALWAYS SHIFTING (AND ALONG WITH THEM, THE ENTIRE SPECTRUM). THERE'S BEEN TIMES WHERE THEY'RE CLOSER THAN OTHERS, ESPECIALLY AMONGST THE WEALTHY.

THANK GOD WE AREN'T WEARING SLIGHTLY LESS CLOTHING, LIKE A PEASANT!

BUT THE POWER HAS ALWAYS FLOWED IN ONE DIRECTION.

OK, you can have pants now. Please stop complaining.

PEOPLE PERCEIVED AS MALE HAVE ALWAYS BEEN PUNISHED AS TRAITORS FOR EMBRACING THE FEMININE, NO MATTER WHAT THAT MEANS IN THE SPECIFIC – WHILE CIS PEOPLE ARE OFTEN REWARDED FOR "TAKING RISKS" WHEN THEY PLAY WITH THEIR PRESENTATIONS.

I DON'T THINK I'VE BOUGHT ANY MEN'S CLOTHES SINCE TRANSITIONING. THE OPTIONS AREN'T GREAT FOR A PERSON MY SIZE. BUT ANY FEMININE-PRESENTING PERSON THAT ISN'T SKINNY – CIS OR TRANS – KNOWS THAT ALREADY.

EVERY TIME I'M IN A SHOE STORE, I HAVE SOME VERSION OF THIS EXCHANGE:

I'D LIKE THIS SHOE!

OH...WE ONLY CARRY THOSE IN *WOMEN'S* SIZES.

THE REAL GENDERLESS FUTURE IN FASHION TO ME? ALL THE CLOTHING, MADE FOR ALL SHAPES AND SIZES.

HEY LOOK! THE FUTURE!

THE FUTURE HOPEFULLY WILL BE LESS GENDERED IN ITS POWER DYNAMICS THAN NOW, BUT THAT SPECTRUM OF EXPRESSION MAY NOT EVER BE EXCISED FROM THE HUMAN PSYCHE.

I'M GONNA LOOK *SO GOOD* AT MY 35TH BIRTHDAY PARTY.

ABOUT THAT,

123

IT'S CERTAINLY NOT GOING ANYWHERE FOR NOW. AND THAT'S OK! EVERY SPECTRUM HAS ITS ENDPOINTS AND PLENTY OF PEOPLE, BINARY TRANS FOLKS INCLUDED, FIND THE DISTINCTION A NECESSARY AND EVEN JOYFUL ONE.

BUT SOMETIMES?

I JUST WANT TO BUY SOME GODDAMNED SHOES!

Great Moments in Pride History

JUNE IS PRIDE MONTH, WHERE WE CELEBRATE THE PEOPLE OF THE LGBT COMMUNITY. LET'S TAKE A LOOK AT SOME MAJOR MILESTONES IN LGBT HISTORY IN THE UNITED STATES!

IN 1924, THE FIRST HOMOSEXUAL RIGHTS GROUP IN AMERICA WAS FOUNDED BY WWI VETERAN HENRY GERBER. THEY ALSO PUBLISHED THE FIRST RECORDED GAY RIGHTS NEWSLETTER!

IN 1950, GAY ACTIVIST HARRY HAY FORMS THE MATTACHINE SOCIETY, ONE OF THE FIRST GAY RIGHTS GROUPS IN THE U.S.

IN 1969, NYC GAY BAR THE STONEWALL INN WAS RAIDED BY POLICE. MARSHA P. JOHNSON AND SYLVIA RIVERA, TWO TRANS WOMEN OF COLOR, ARE TWO OF THE PROMINENT FIGURES WHO TOOK A STAND AND HELPED SPARK THE GAY CIVIL RIGHTS MOVEMENT.

IN 2015, GAY MARRIAGE BECOMES LEGAL! STRAIGHT PEOPLE AND CAPITALISTS BEGIN TO TAKE NOTE.

FROM THEN ON, CORPORATIONS REALIZED THAT GAY PEOPLE BUY STUFF TOO, AND THAT SPONSORING PRIDE IS PROFITABLE! LOVE WINS!

124

The Trans Discourse Minefield

These voices might be loud, or featured in prominent media, but they're not necessarily right or true.

My experien

LISTEN TO ME!

So, seek out positive voices,

Personally, my life has improved immeasurably since I transitioned over a decade ago. It didn't solve all of my problems, but it helped me make improvements I was previously unable to.

Seek out the facts,

The truth is that the positive effects are numerous and regrets are extremely uncommon*

study #172

*bit.ly/trans_studies

And remember, there is only one expert on what is right for you: YOU.

Trust yourself, trust your heart, and do what you need to become your true, authentic self.

(And the expert on everything else is, of course: ME.)

jas

A Covert Gaze at Conservative Gays

127

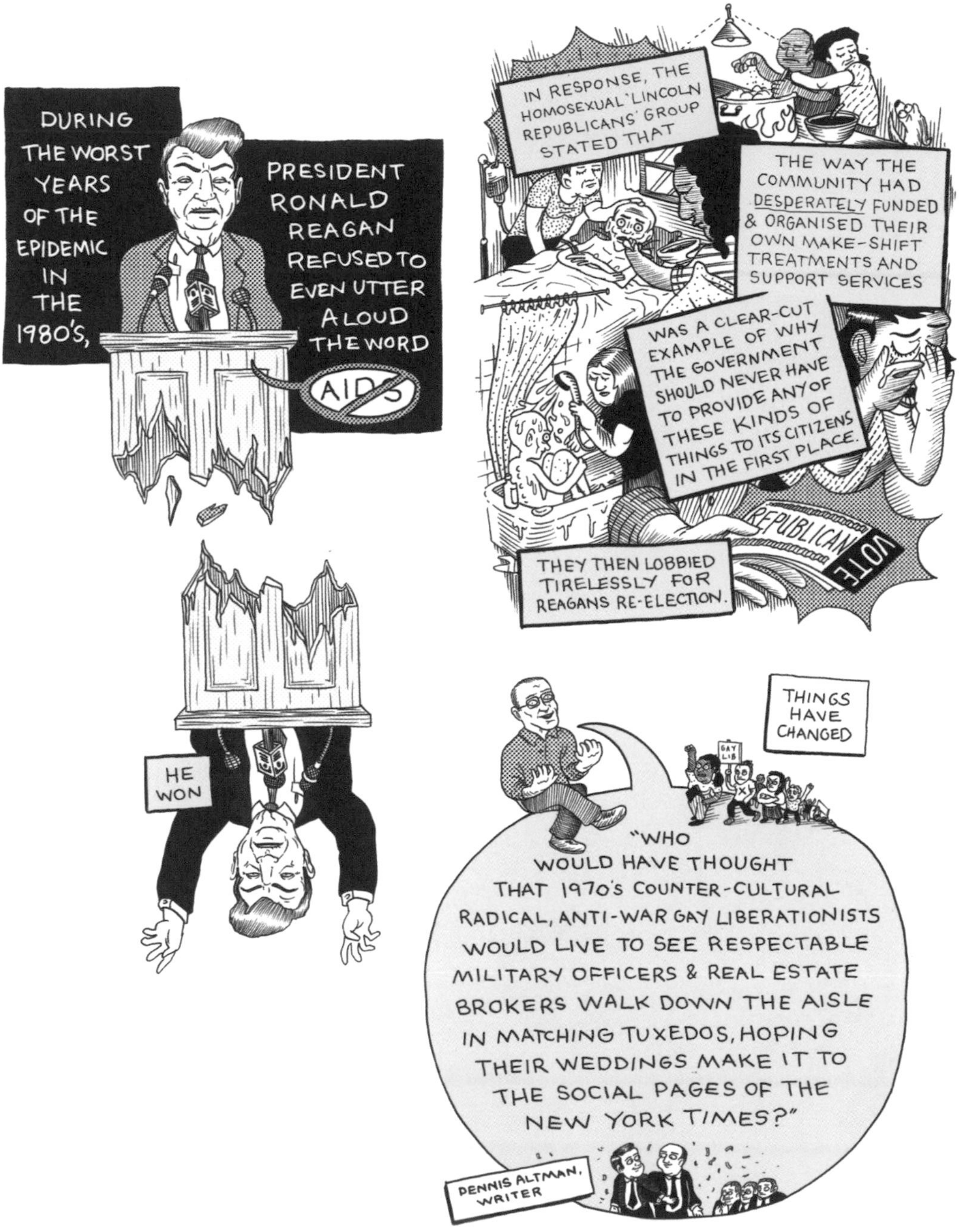

DURING THE WORST YEARS OF THE EPIDEMIC IN THE 1980'S,
PRESIDENT RONALD REAGAN REFUSED TO EVEN UTTER ALOUD THE WORD
AIDS
IN RESPONSE, THE HOMOSEXUAL 'LINCOLN REPUBLICANS' GROUP STATED THAT
THE WAY THE COMMUNITY HAD DESPERATELY FUNDED & ORGANISED THEIR OWN MAKE-SHIFT TREATMENTS AND SUPPORT SERVICES
WAS A CLEAR-CUT EXAMPLE OF WHY THE GOVERNMENT SHOULD NEVER HAVE TO PROVIDE ANY OF THESE KINDS OF THINGS TO ITS CITIZENS IN THE FIRST PLACE.
THEY THEN LOBBIED TIRELESSLY FOR REAGANS RE-ELECTION.
REPUBLICAN
VOTE
HE WON
THINGS HAVE CHANGED
GAY LIB
"WHO WOULD HAVE THOUGHT THAT 1970'S COUNTER-CULTURAL RADICAL, ANTI-WAR GAY LIBERATIONISTS WOULD LIVE TO SEE RESPECTABLE MILITARY OFFICERS & REAL ESTATE BROKERS WALK DOWN THE AISLE IN MATCHING TUXEDOS, HOPING THEIR WEDDINGS MAKE IT TO THE SOCIAL PAGES OF THE NEW YORK TIMES?"
DENNIS ALTMAN, WRITER

CONSERVATIVE STRANDS OF HOMO POLITICS ARE ABLE TO EXIST TODAY BECAUSE OF THE HUGE STRIDES TOWARDS EQUALITY THAT HAVE TAKEN PLACE OVER THE LAST 50 YEARS.

AND ALSO BECAUSE OF THE WAY THAT THE INTERNET HAS FLATTENED THE WORLD & MADE FRINGE POLITICS EFFORTLESS TO ACCESS & NAVIGATE;

IT'S MUCH EASIER TO FIND YOUR NICHE SUBCULTURE

EXPOSED ONLY TO THAT WAY OF THINKING.

ONE SUCH GROUP THAT DOES A LOT OF ONLINE ORGANISING, ARE THE

Pink Pistols
Pick on someone your own calibre.

- A HUGE, DECENTRALISED GROUP OF LGBTIQ+ GUN ADVOCATES.

THEY NOW BOAST 45 CHAPTERS AROUND THE U.S.A.

THANKS TO A MASSIVE UPTURN IN INTEREST SINCE THE ORLANDO SHOOTING EARLIER THIS YEAR.

THEIR LOGO IS A PINK TRIANGLE: THE MARKER USED TO IDENTIFY QUEER PEOPLE WHO WERE SYSTEMATICALLY KILLED IN THE NAZI HOLOCAUST.

WHETHER OR NOT YOU AGREE WITH THE WAY IN WHICH THEIR POLITICS MANIFEST — IT'S HARD NOT TO EMPATHISE WITH THEM.

"I DON'T FEEL SAFE IN THESE STREETS. NEVER HAVE."

WOMAN AT 'PINK PISTOLS' L.A. MEETUP, SEPTEMBER '16

TECH BILLIONAIRE & PROUD HOMOSEXUAL PETER THIEL OPPOSES TAXES

& IS INTERESTED IN AVOIDING "THE INEVITABILITY OF THE DEATH OF EVERY INDIVIDUAL"...

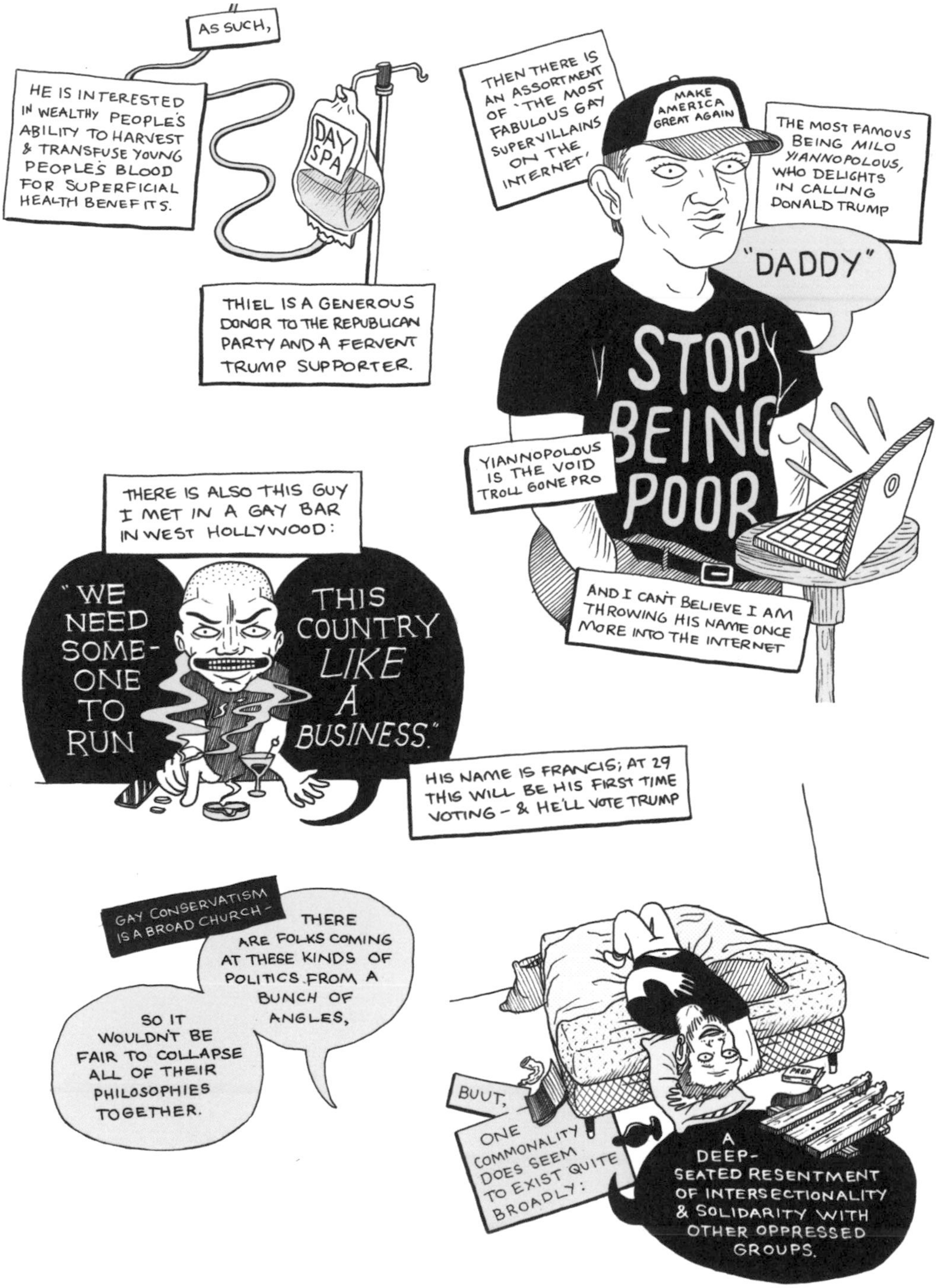

AS SUCH,
HE IS INTERESTED IN WEALTHY PEOPLE'S ABILITY TO HARVEST & TRANSFUSE YOUNG PEOPLE'S BLOOD FOR SUPERFICIAL HEALTH BENEFITS.
DAY SPA
THIEL IS A GENEROUS DONOR TO THE REPUBLICAN PARTY AND A FERVENT TRUMP SUPPORTER.
THEN THERE IS AN ASSORTMENT OF "THE MOST FABULOUS GAY SUPERVILLAINS ON THE INTERNET,"
MAKE AMERICA GREAT AGAIN
THE MOST FAMOUS BEING MILO YIANNOPOLOUS, WHO DELIGHTS IN CALLING DONALD TRUMP
"DADDY"
STOP BEING POOR
YIANNOPOLOUS IS THE VOID TROLL GONE PRO
AND I CAN'T BELIEVE I AM THROWING HIS NAME ONCE MORE INTO THE INTERNET
THERE IS ALSO THIS GUY I MET IN A GAY BAR IN WEST HOLLYWOOD:
"WE NEED SOMEONE TO RUN
THIS COUNTRY LIKE A BUSINESS."
HIS NAME IS FRANCIS; AT 29 THIS WILL BE HIS FIRST TIME VOTING – & HE'LL VOTE TRUMP
GAY CONSERVATISM IS A BROAD CHURCH –
THERE ARE FOLKS COMING AT THESE KINDS OF POLITICS FROM A BUNCH OF ANGLES,
SO IT WOULDN'T BE FAIR TO COLLAPSE ALL OF THEIR PHILOSOPHIES TOGETHER.
BUUT,
ONE COMMONALITY DOES SEEM TO EXIST QUITE BROADLY:
A DEEP-SEATED RESENTMENT OF INTERSECTIONALITY & SOLIDARITY WITH OTHER OPPRESSED GROUPS.

130

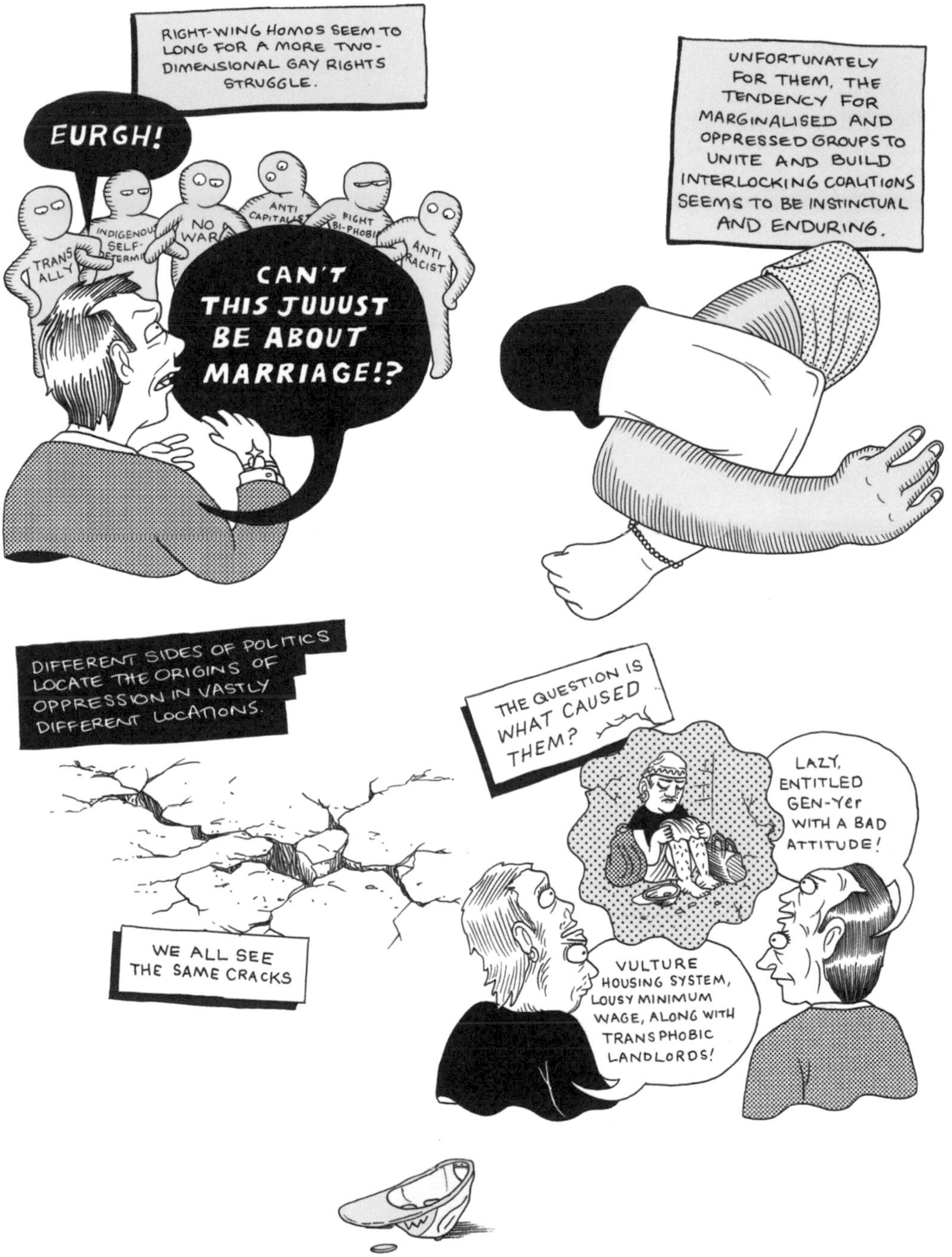
RIGHT-WING HOMOS SEEM TO LONG FOR A MORE TWO-DIMENSIONAL GAY RIGHTS STRUGGLE.
EURGH!
TRANS ALLY
INDIGENOU SELF-DETERMI
NO WAR
ANTI CAPITALIS
FIGHT BI-PHOBI
ANTI RACIST
CAN'T THIS JUUUST BE ABOUT MARRIAGE!?
UNFORTUNATELY FOR THEM, THE TENDENCY FOR MARGINALISED AND OPPRESSED GROUPS TO UNITE AND BUILD INTERLOCKING COALITIONS SEEMS TO BE INSTINCTUAL AND ENDURING.
DIFFERENT SIDES OF POLITICS LOCATE THE ORIGINS OF OPPRESSION IN VASTLY DIFFERENT LOCATIONS.
WE ALL SEE THE SAME CRACKS
THE QUESTION IS WHAT CAUSED THEM?
LAZY, ENTITLED GEN-Yer WITH A BAD ATTITUDE!
VULTURE HOUSING SYSTEM, LOUSY MINIMUM WAGE, ALONG WITH TRANSPHOBIC LANDLORDS!

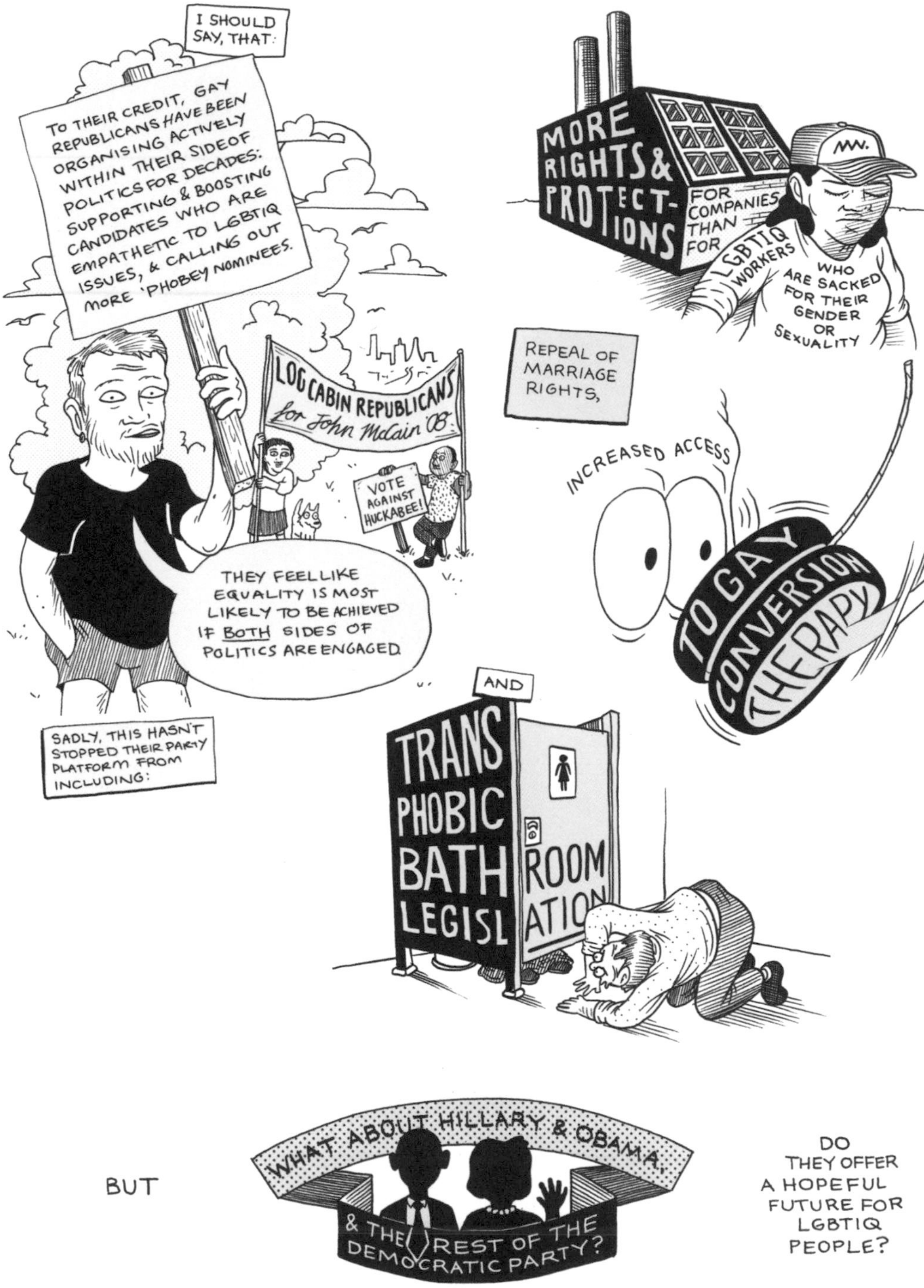

I SHOULD SAY, THAT:
TO THEIR CREDIT, GAY REPUBLICANS HAVE BEEN ORGANISING ACTIVELY WITHIN THEIR SIDE OF POLITICS FOR DECADES: SUPPORTING & BOOSTING CANDIDATES WHO ARE EMPATHETIC TO LGBTIQ ISSUES, & CALLING OUT MORE 'PHOBEY NOMINEES.
LOG CABIN REPUBLICANS for John McCain '08
VOTE AGAINST HUCKABEE!
THEY FEEL LIKE EQUALITY IS MOST LIKELY TO BE ACHIEVED IF BOTH SIDES OF POLITICS ARE ENGAGED
SADLY, THIS HASN'T STOPPED THEIR PARTY PLATFORM FROM INCLUDING:
MORE RIGHTS & PROTECT-IONS FOR COMPANIES THAN FOR LGBTIQ WORKERS WHO ARE SACKED FOR THEIR GENDER OR SEXUALITY
REPEAL OF MARRIAGE RIGHTS,
INCREASED ACCESS TO GAY CONVERSION THERAPY
AND
TRANS PHOBIC BATH ROOM LEGISL ATION
BUT
WHAT ABOUT HILLARY & OBAMA, & THE REST OF THE DEMOCRATIC PARTY?
DO THEY OFFER A HOPEFUL FUTURE FOR LGBTIQ PEOPLE?

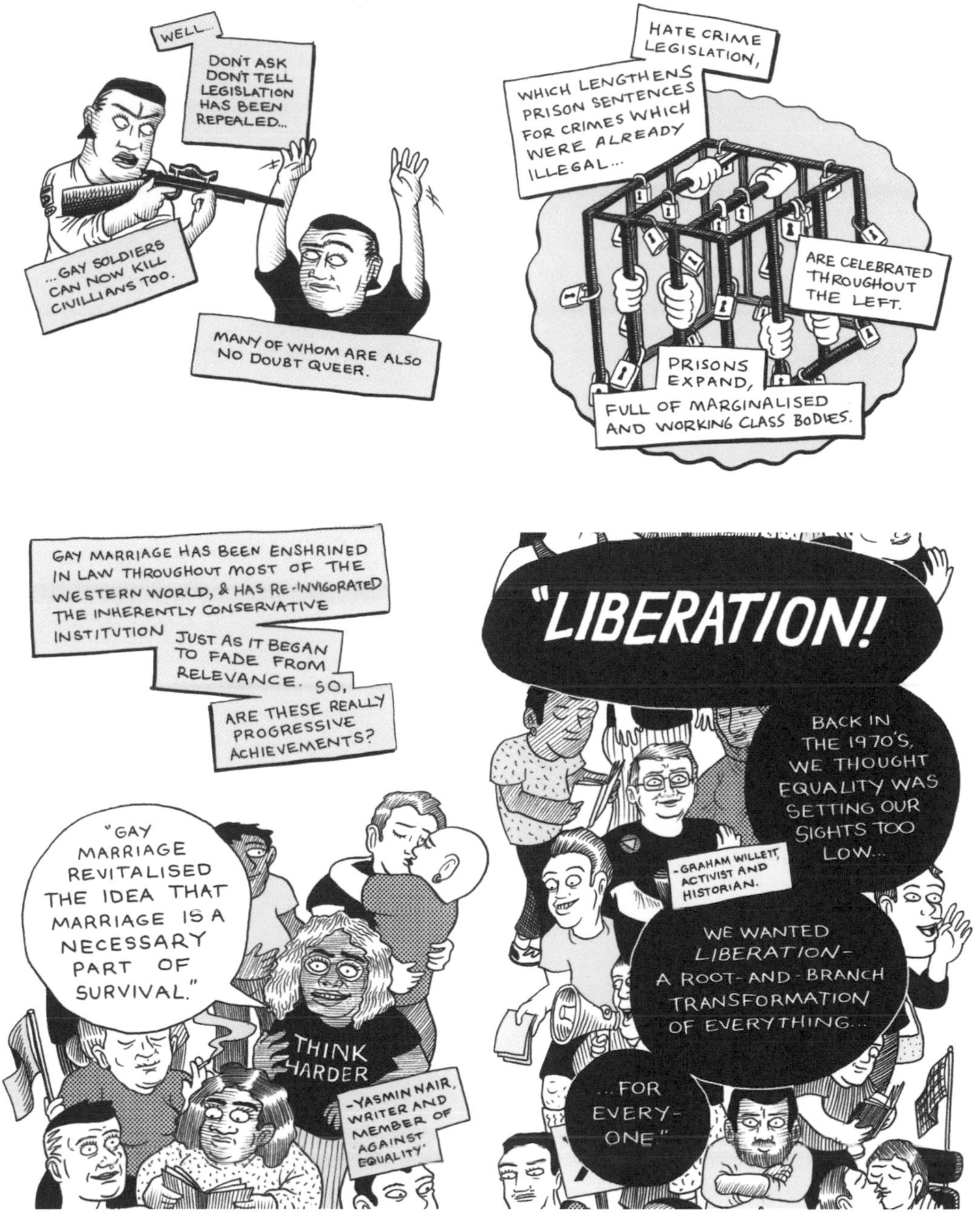
WELL...
DON'T ASK DON'T TELL LEGISLATION HAS BEEN REPEALED...
...GAY SOLDIERS CAN NOW KILL CIVILLIANS TOO.
MANY OF WHOM ARE ALSO NO DOUBT QUEER.
HATE CRIME LEGISLATION,
WHICH LENGTHENS PRISON SENTENCES FOR CRIMES WHICH WERE ALREADY ILLEGAL...
ARE CELEBRATED THROUGHOUT THE LEFT.
PRISONS EXPAND,
FULL OF MARGINALISED AND WORKING CLASS BODIES.
GAY MARRIAGE HAS BEEN ENSHRINED IN LAW THROUGHOUT MOST OF THE WESTERN WORLD, & HAS RE-INVIGORATED THE INHERENTLY CONSERVATIVE INSTITUTION
JUST AS IT BEGAN TO FADE FROM RELEVANCE. SO,
ARE THESE REALLY PROGRESSIVE ACHIEVEMENTS?
"GAY MARRIAGE REVITALISED THE IDEA THAT MARRIAGE IS A NECESSARY PART OF SURVIVAL."
THINK HARDER
-YASMIN NAIR, WRITER AND MEMBER OF AGAINST EQUALITY.
"LIBERATION!
BACK IN THE 1970'S, WE THOUGHT EQUALITY WAS SETTING OUR SIGHTS TOO LOW...
-GRAHAM WILLETT, ACTIVIST AND HISTORIAN.
WE WANTED LIBERATION- A ROOT-AND-BRANCH TRANSFORMATION OF EVERYTHING...
...FOR EVERY-ONE."

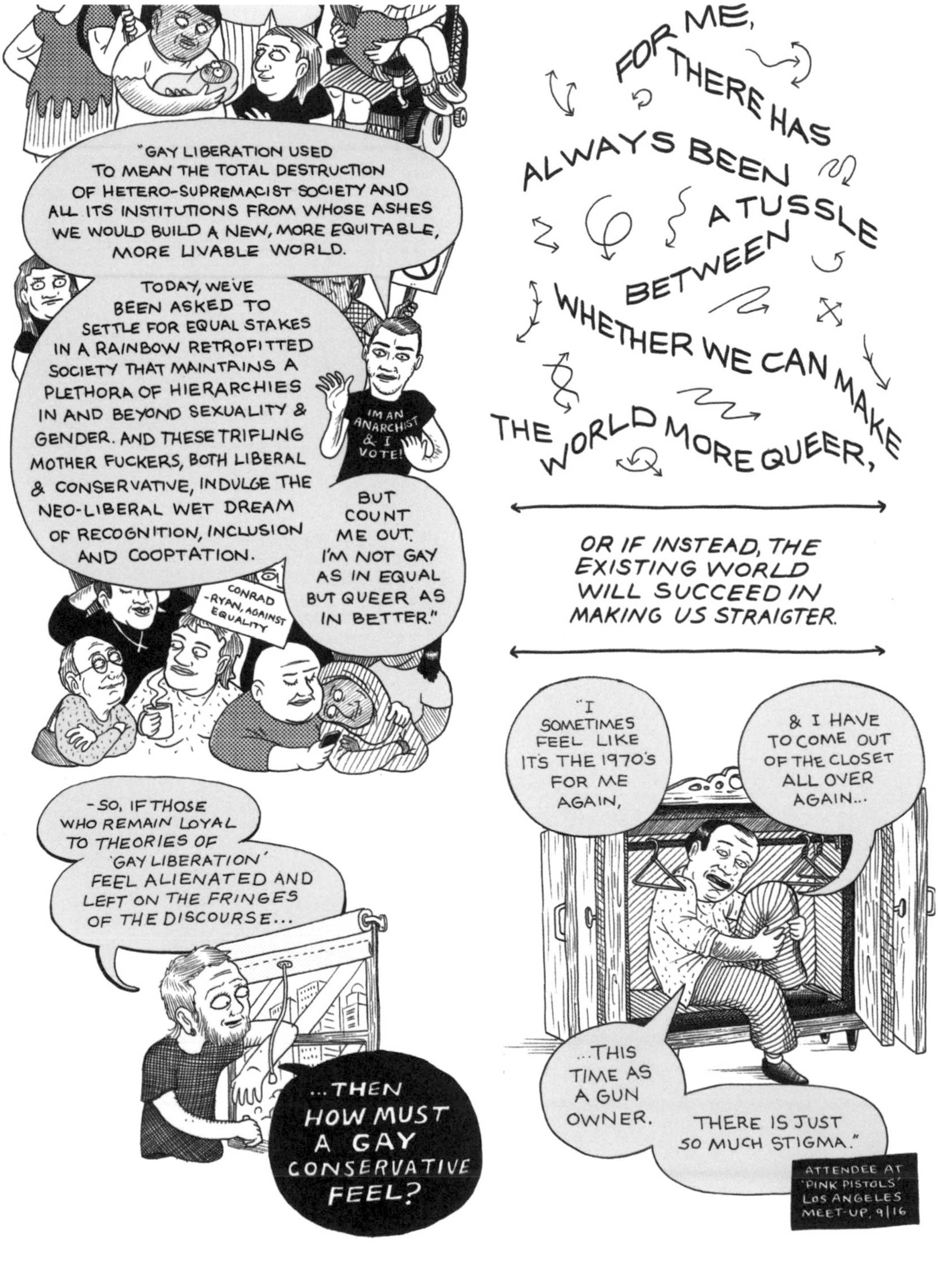
"GAY LIBERATION USED TO MEAN THE TOTAL DESTRUCTION OF HETERO-SUPREMACIST SOCIETY AND ALL ITS INSTITUTIONS FROM WHOSE ASHES WE WOULD BUILD A NEW, MORE EQUITABLE, MORE LIVABLE WORLD.
TODAY, WE'VE BEEN ASKED TO SETTLE FOR EQUAL STAKES IN A RAINBOW RETROFITTED SOCIETY THAT MAINTAINS A PLETHORA OF HIERARCHIES IN AND BEYOND SEXUALITY & GENDER. AND THESE TRIFLING MOTHER FUCKERS, BOTH LIBERAL & CONSERVATIVE, INDULGE THE NEO-LIBERAL WET DREAM OF RECOGNITION, INCLUSION AND COOPTATION.
BUT COUNT ME OUT. I'M NOT GAY AS IN EQUAL BUT QUEER AS IN BETTER."
I'M AN ANARCHIST & I VOTE!
CONRAD -RYAN, AGAINST EQUALITY
-SO, IF THOSE WHO REMAIN LOYAL TO THEORIES OF 'GAY LIBERATION' FEEL ALIENATED AND LEFT ON THE FRINGES OF THE DISCOURSE...
...THEN HOW MUST A GAY CONSERVATIVE FEEL?
FOR ME, THERE HAS ALWAYS BEEN A TUSSLE BETWEEN WHETHER WE CAN MAKE THE WORLD MORE QUEER,
OR IF INSTEAD, THE EXISTING WORLD WILL SUCCEED IN MAKING US STRAIGTER.
"I SOMETIMES FEEL LIKE IT'S THE 1970'S FOR ME AGAIN,
& I HAVE TO COME OUT OF THE CLOSET ALL OVER AGAIN...
...THIS TIME AS A GUN OWNER.
THERE IS JUST SO MUCH STIGMA."
ATTENDEE AT 'PINK PISTOLS' LOS ANGELES MEET-UP, 9/16

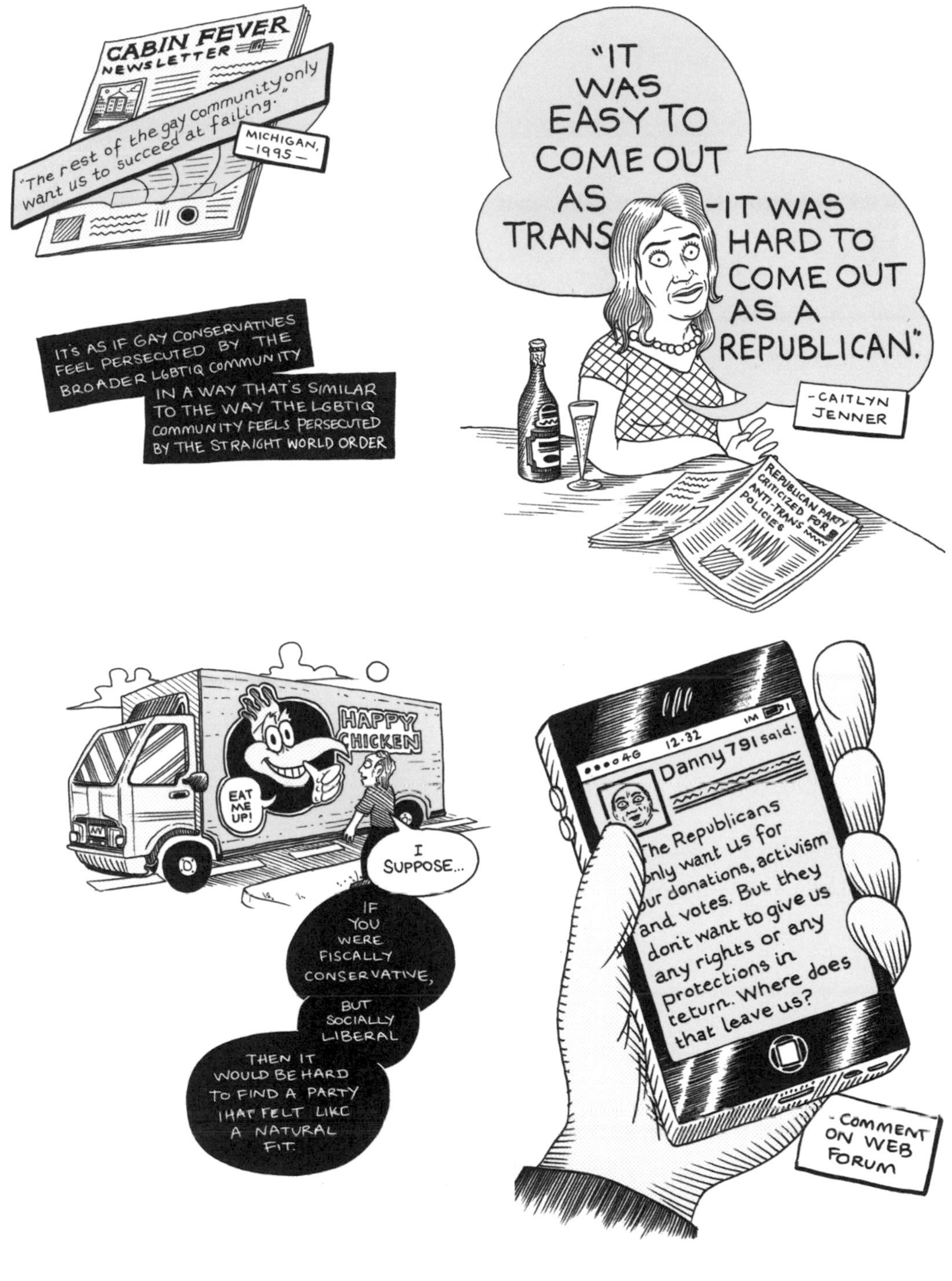
CABIN FEVER
NEWSLETTER
"The rest of the gay community only want us to succeed at failing."
MICHIGAN, —1995—
IT'S AS IF GAY CONSERVATIVES FEEL PERSECUTED BY THE BROADER LGBTIQ COMMUNITY
IN A WAY THAT'S SIMILAR TO THE WAY THE LGBTIQ COMMUNITY FEELS PERSECUTED BY THE STRAIGHT WORLD ORDER
"IT WAS EASY TO COME OUT AS TRANS -IT WAS HARD TO COME OUT AS A REPUBLICAN."
-CAITLYN JENNER
REPUBLICAN PARTY CRITICIZED FOR ANTI-TRANS POLICIES
HAPPY CHICKEN
EAT ME UP!
I SUPPOSE...
IF YOU WERE FISCALLY CONSERVATIVE,
BUT SOCIALLY LIBERAL
THEN IT WOULD BE HARD TO FIND A PARTY THAT FELT LIKE A NATURAL FIT.
12:32
4G
Danny791 said:
The Republicans only want us for our donations, activism and votes. But they don't want to give us any rights or any protections in return. Where does that leave us?
-COMMENT ON WEB FORUM

WELL...
I GUESS IT LEAVES YOU

SOLIDARITY

STANDING OUT IN THE COLD,

STUCK SMACK BANG IN BETWN

OF TWO DISPARATE PHILOSOPHIES

SHRUG

BUT, AS ALL QUEERS KNOW,

& AS ANDRÉ GIRE SAID ON THE BACK COVER OF A 1994 ISSUE OF TEXAN GAY CONSERVATIVE NEWSLETTER

THE 'METROPLEX MESSENGER';

"It is better to be hated for what you are, than to be loved for what you are not."

TRUMP

The Homophobic Hysteria
of the Lavender Scare

THE RED SCARE, SENATOR JOSEPH MCCARTHY'S COLD WAR CRUSADE TO RID THE GOVERNMENT OF ALL ITS SUPPOSED COMMUNIST SPIES, IS A STAPLE OF AMERICAN HISTORY TEXTBOOKS WORLD WIDE.

THE ONLY GOOD COMMU... DEA...

BETTER DEAD THAN RED

WHAT'S USUALLY NEGLECTED IS THE

THE LAVENDER SCARE

AN EVENT VITAL TO THE UNDERSTANDING OF QUEER HISTORY.

137

IN 1950, THE STATE DEPARTMENT UNDERSECRETARY JOHN PEURIFOY TOLD TO CONGRESS THAT, WHILE NO COMMUNISTS HAD BEEN FOUND TO BE IN THEIR EMPLOY—

THEY HAD FORCED OUT 91 HOMOSEXUALS.

HIS TESTIMONY WAS MEANT TO DEFLATE THE HARM SEN. MCCARTHY'S RED SCARE WAS INFLICTING UPON THE STATE DEPARTMENT.

BUT IT BACKFIRED SPECTACULARLY.

THE NOTION OF A LIMP WRISTED, "LAVENDER" BUREAUCRATIC CLASS OF EMASCULATED SEX PERVERTS TAKING OVER AMERICA QUICKLY BECAME A DEFINING FACET OF THE POSTWAR MORAL PANIC.

WHILE THE COMMUNIST VILLAINS OF THE RED SCARE WERE LARGELY JUST FANTASIES OF MCCARTHY'S DEMAGOGUERY—

THERE ACTUALLY WERE A SIGNIFICANT NUMBER OF GAYS AND LESBIANS LIVING AND WORKING IN WASHINGTON D.C. AT THE TIME...

...REAL PEOPLE WHO WOULD SUFFER IMMENSELY AS A RESULT OF THE LAVENDER SCARE.

THE NEW DEAL LAUNCHED THE FEDERAL GOVERNMENT ON A TRAJECTORY OF RAPID EXPANSION—

—WHICH CONTINUED THROUGHOUT WORLD WAR II AND THE POSTWAR PERIOD.

S HIGHEST STANDARD OF LIVING

There's no way like the American Way!

THE FEDERAL GOVERNMENT HAD PROGRESSIVE, GENDER-NEUTRAL HIRING PRACTICES, AND THE TACITLY ACCEPTANCED GAY MEN IN CLERICAL CAREERS—

THIS MADE D. C. AN ENTICING DESTINATION FOR YOUNG GAYS AND LESBIANS,

WITH A VIBRANT AND OPENLY ESTABLISHED SOCIAL NETWORK—

—D.C.'S QUEER SCENE EASILY ADOPTED THE STEADY INFLUX OF NEWCOMERS INTO THE COMMUNITY.

BUS STOP

IT FLOURISHED THROUGHOUT THE '30S AND '40S.

TRANSIT

THE PROBLEM OF PERSONAL ACCEPTANCE OF ONESELF AS GAY SEEMS A GREATER PROBLEM NOW THAN IT USED TO BE.

I CAN HONESTLY SAY THAT I NEVER KNEW WHAT "THE CLOSET" WAS, FOR THERE WAS NEVER A TIME WHEN I OR MY FRIENDS WERE NOT OUT OT IT.

WASHINGTONIAN POET HAVILAND FERRIS

BUT THE POSITION OF QUEER PEOPLE IS ALWAYS TENUOUS. IN 1948, PRESIDENT TRUMAN SIGNED THE MILLER SEXUAL PSYCHOPATH LAW.

SUBLIMINAL ACUTE HOMOSEXUAL

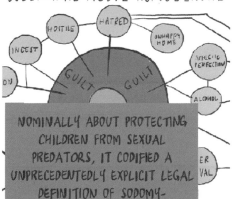

NOMINALLY ABOUT PROTECTING CHILDREN FROM SEXUAL PREDATORS, IT CODIFIED A UNPRECEDENTEDLY EXPLICIT LEGAL DEFINITION OF SODOMY—

UNSURPRISINGLY, THE LAW WAS USED AGAINST MORE MARGINALIZED MEMBERS OF THE COMMUNITY FIRST.

—MAKING IT EASIER TO POLICE "TRANSGRESSIVE" SEX.

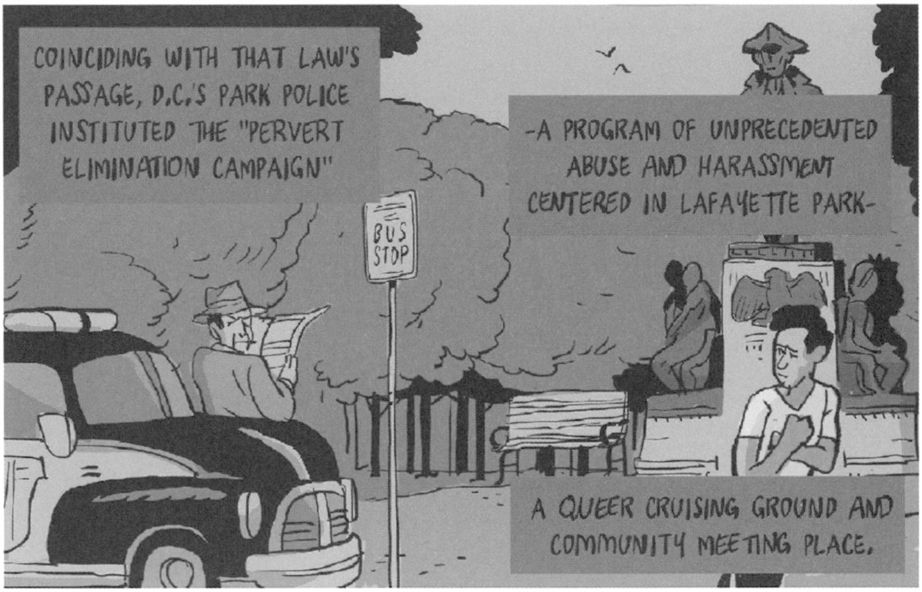
COINCIDING WITH THAT LAW'S PASSAGE, D.C.'S PARK POLICE INSTITUTED THE "PERVERT ELIMINATION CAMPAIGN"
-A PROGRAM OF UNPRECEDENTED ABUSE AND HARASSMENT CENTERED IN LAFAYETTE PARK-
A QUEER CRUISING GROUND AND COMMUNITY MEETING PLACE.
BUS STOP

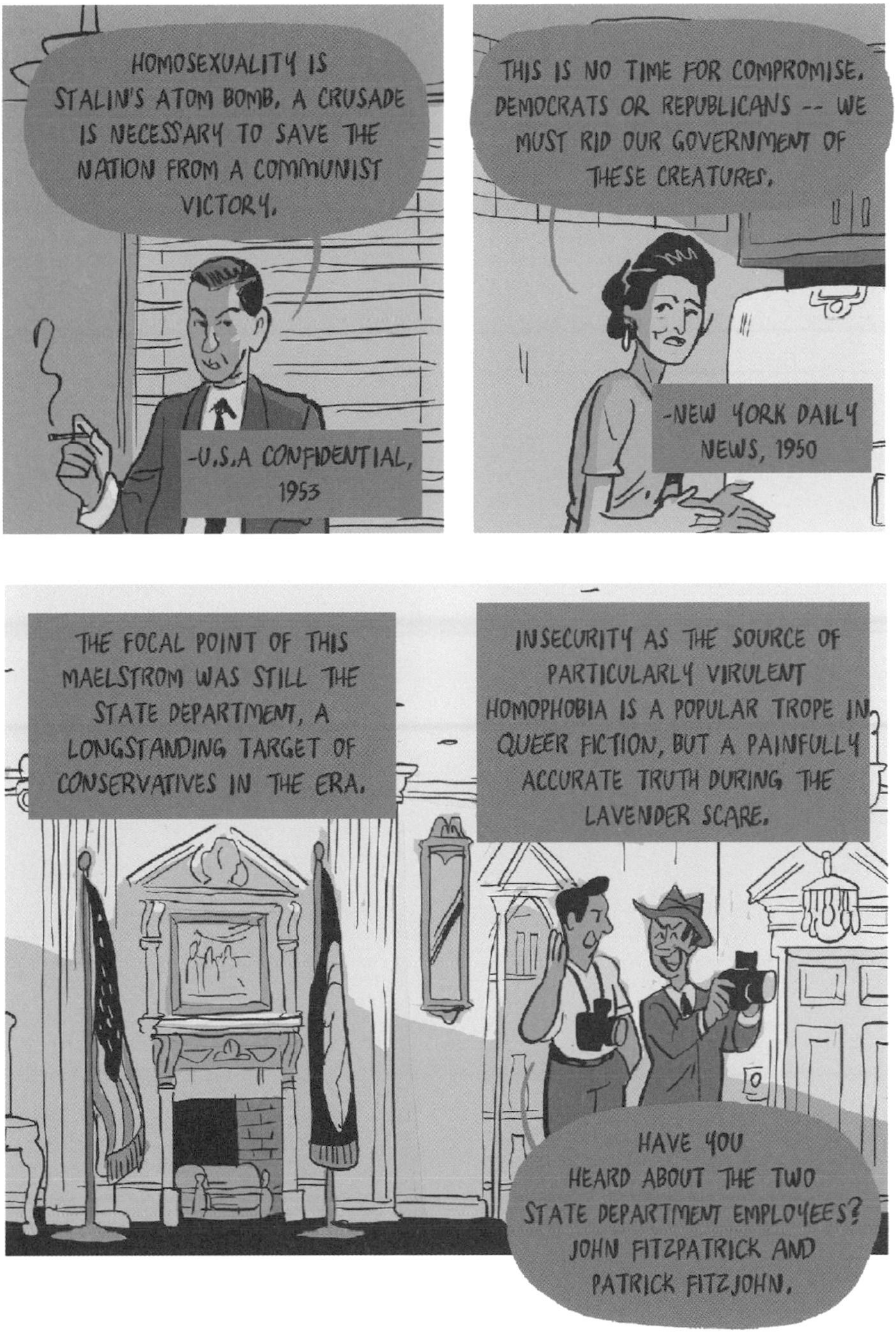
HOMOSEXUALITY IS STALIN'S ATOM BOMB. A CRUSADE IS NECESSARY TO SAVE THE NATION FROM A COMMUNIST VICTORY.
-U.S.A CONFIDENTIAL, 1953
THIS IS NO TIME FOR COMPROMISE. DEMOCRATS OR REPUBLICANS -- WE MUST RID OUR GOVERNMENT OF THESE CREATURES.
-NEW YORK DAILY NEWS, 1950
THE FOCAL POINT OF THIS MAELSTROM WAS STILL THE STATE DEPARTMENT, A LONGSTANDING TARGET OF CONSERVATIVES IN THE ERA.
INSECURITY AS THE SOURCE OF PARTICULARLY VIRULENT HOMOPHOBIA IS A POPULAR TROPE IN QUEER FICTION, BUT A PAINFULLY ACCURATE TRUTH DURING THE LAVENDER SCARE.
HAVE YOU HEARD ABOUT THE TWO STATE DEPARTMENT EMPLOYEES? JOHN FITZPATRICK AND PATRICK FITZJOHN.

AS ANTI-COMMUNIST HYSTERIA POISONED THE NATION, NON-CONFORMISTS OF ALL KINDS WERE ERRONEOUSLY SUBSUMED INTO AN INCREASINGLY RABID RHETORIC.

SHARP DIVISIONS EMERGED BETWEEN THOSE WITH THE FREEDOM OR WHEREWITHAL TO OPENLY EXPRESS A QUEER IDENTITY—

—AND THOSE FOR WHOM RESPECTABILITY WAS TOO SYNONYMOUS WITH THEIR LIVELIHOOD.

THE STATE DEPARTMENT'S RITUALISTIC FIRING OF HUNDREDS OF SUPPOSED HOMOSEXUALS A YEAR BECAME STANDARD PRACTICE AMONG ALL GOVERNMENT DEPARTMENTS.

THE TIGHT KNIT, EASY GOING QUEER COMMUNITY SHATTERED AS STATE SPONSORED PARANOIA SET IN.

EVEN A CASUAL CONVERSATION WITH A "KNOWN HOMOSEXUAL" WAS JUSTIFICATION FOR TERMINATION AND FEDERAL BLACKLISTING.

-OFTEN ON THE BASIS OF NOTHING MORE THAN HAVING A "MANNISH VOICE" IF YOU WERE A WOMAN OR "FEMININE POSTURE" IF A MAN.

ANXIETY OVER ITS REPUTATION INSPIRED A VEHEMENT ANTI-GAY CAMPAIGN WITHIN THE STATE DEPARTMENT.

EMPLOYEES THROUGHOUT THE '50S AND EARLY '60S WERE CONSISTENTLY FORCED TO ENDURE LONG AND HUMILIATING INTERROGATIONS CONCERNING THEIR SEXUAL BEHAVIOR—

IF A HOMOSEXUAL MUST WEAR THE MASK, HE CANNOT ASSOCIATE WITH THOSE WHO HAVE DISCARDED IT.

DONALD WEBSTER CORY, AUTHOR OF *THE HOMOSEXUAL IN AMERICA: A SUBJECTIVE APPROACH* (1951).

YOU LIVED NOT KNOWING WHAT WOULD HAPPEN NEXT. YOU WOULD BE SOCIALIZING WITH SOMEBODY, AND THEN THEY DISAPPEARED...

MADELEINE TRESS, FORCED TO DISAPPEAR HERSELF IN 1958

EVEN AMONG YOUR GAY FRIENDS, YOU NEVER KNEW WHO MIGHT BE PRESSURED TO INFORM ON YOU.

I CAN'T DESCRIBE THAT KIND OF FEAR.

FOR SOME, THE PRESSURES OF CONSTANT SURVEILLANCE AND HARASSMENT BECAME TOO MUCH.

EVENTUALLY, THE PRACTICE OF TARGETING OF GAYS AND LESBIANS AS UNDESIRABLE EMPLOYEES WAS PICKED UP BY THE PRIVATE SECTOR AS WELL. HOMOSEXUAL ADVOCACY GROUPS BEGAN TO FORM IN OPPOSITION.

ONE OF THE MOST FAMOUS OF THESE EARLY GROUPS, THE MATTACHINE SOCIETY, EXPLICITLY CITED THE GOVERNMENT PURGES OF THE LAVENDER SCARE AS THE PRIMARY MOTIVATION BEHIND THEIR FORMATION.

IN 1961, FRANK KAMENY FOUNDED THE

The Mattachine Society of Washington

For further information, contact:
Dr. Franklin E. Karmeny
5020 Cathedral Ave, N.W.

AN ORGANIZATION INDEPENDENT OF THE NATIONAL GROUP AND ONE COMMITTED TO INJECTING A NEW MILITANCY INTO THE MOVEMENT.

THEY WOULD BE ONE OF THE FIRST QUEER GROUPS TO EXPLICITLY FRAME THEIR ACTIVISM IN TERMS OF MINORITY IDENTITY AND CIVIL RIGHTS.

KAMENY HELD A PHD IN ASTRONOMY, WHICH, IN THE FIFTIES, MEANT THAT THE FEDERAL GOVERNMENT WAS ONE OF THE ONLY VIABLE EMPLOYERS IN HIS FIELD.

WHEN HE WAS FIRED DUE TO HOMOSEXUAL ACTIVITY, HE WAS WAS NOT ONLY LOSING A LIVING, BUT BEING BARRED FROM PURSUING HIS LIFELONG PASSION TO STUDY THE STARS.

IN THE
Supreme Court of the United States
October Term

—

No. 616

Franklin Howard Kameny, Petitioner

APPEALING TO JUDICIAL SYSTEM, KAMENY INITIALLY TRIED TO DISTANCE HIMSELF FROM HIS SEXUALITY, ASKING THAT HIS CASE BE GIVEN INDIVIDUAL CONSIDERATION.

FOR THE DISTRICT OF COLUMBIA CIRCUIT

AS THE YEARS PASSED HE REALIZED HIS MISTAKE: HIS SITUATION WAS NOT AN INDIVIDUAL ONE.

HE WAS PART OF A HUGE COMMUNITY OF PEOPLE BEING TREATED AS A SECOND CLASS CITIZENS BECAUSE OF THEIR SEXUALITY.

KAMENY AND THE MATTACHINE SOCIETY OF WASHINGTON BEGAN DEVELOPING AND DISTRIBUTING INFORMATIONAL PAMPHLETS—

POLICE

ADVISING QUEER PEOPLE OF THEIR RIGHTS AND HOW TO PROTECT THEMSELVES WHEN CONFRONTED WITH GOVERNMENT PERSECUTION.

If you are arrested...

"The Pocket Lawyer"

Mattachine

THE GROUP ALLIED WITH THE ACLU IN ORDER TO PROVIDE FORMAL LEGAL REPRESENTATION TO ANYONE AFFECTED BY THE GOVERNMENT"S HOMOPHOBIA.

THAT LED TO A STRING OF LEGAL VICTORIES THAT EFFECTIVELY PREVENTED THE GOVERNMENT FROM FIRING PEOPLE ON THE BASIS OF THEIR SEXUALITY ALONE. THE VERDICTS ATTAINED THROUGH THESE CASES BECAME KNOWN AS THE

Homosexual Bill of Rights

150

IN 1965, THEY WERE THE FIRST GAY GROUP TO PICKET THE WHITE HOUSE—

AN ENORMOUSLY CONTROVERSIAL DECISION FOR A COMMUNITY THAT, AT THE TIME, WAS OVERWHELMING COMMITTED TO SECRECY AND HETERONORMATIVE RESPECTABILITY POLITICS.

FOR SOME THOUGH, IT WAS AN ALMOST SPIRITUAL EXPERIENCE.

GAY IS GOOD

U.S. CLAIMS NO SECOND-CLASS CITIZENSHIP: WHAT ABOUT HOMOSEXUAL CITIZENS?

the America Employment Ba Competence, Ab Not Private Lif

I GAINED A LITTLE PIECE OF MY SOUL TODAY.

WITH THE HELP OF A SYMPATHETIC BLACK PRESS AND CAREFULLY CRAFTED LANGUAGE—

THE DEMONSTRATORS ESTABLISHED THEMSELVES WITHIN THE NATIONAL CONVERSATION IN THEIR OWN TERMS.

NOT ONLY AS A SEXUAL MINORITY GROUP—

BUT AS UNITED STATES CITIZENS, DESERVING OF THE SAME RIGHTS AND LIBERTIES THE CONSTITUTION GUARANTEED EVERY OTHER GROUP.

THOUGH STONEWALL IS COMMONLY SEEN AS THE BEGINNING OF THE GAY RIGHTS MOVEMENT, BY THE TIME THOSE GAY, LESBIAN, AND TRANS BAR PATRONS FOUGHT A ROUTINE POLICE RAID—

DAVID K. JOHNSON, QUEER HISTORIAN

—THE MOVEMENT HAD ALREADY WON ITS FIRST MAJOR LEGAL VICTORY AND HAD ESTABLISHED MUCH OF THE RHETORIC AND TACTICS IT WOULD DEPLOY OVER THE NEXT THIRTY YEARS.

GAY LIBERATION FRONT

IN 26 U.S. STATES, IT IS STILL LEGAL TO LOSE YOUR JOB FOR LIVING HONESTLY AS A QUEER PERSON.

FOR THE QUEER COMMUNITIES IN THOSE STATES, THE LAVENDER SCARE NEVER ENDED.

BUT IT CAN, IF THOSE OF US BENEFITTING FROM JUSTICE RECOGNIZE, LIKE KAMENY DID-
THAT AN ASSAULT ON ANY OF US IS AN ASSAULT ON ALL OF US.
GAY IS GOOD
TRANS LIVES MATTER
NB

MADY G

Boobs Aren't Binary

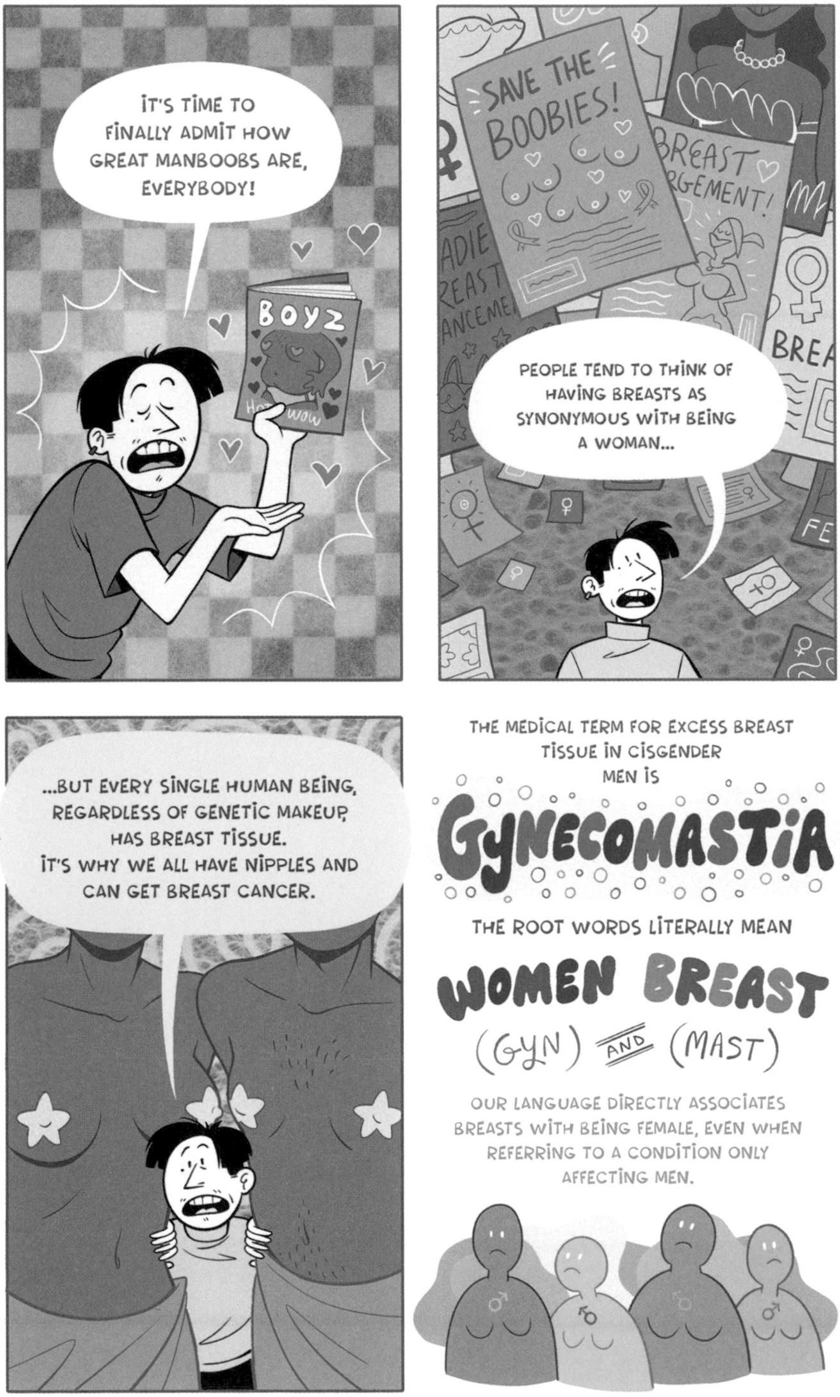
IT'S TIME TO FINALLY ADMIT HOW GREAT MANBOOBS ARE, EVERYBODY!
BOYZ
SAVE THE BOOBIES!
PEOPLE TEND TO THINK OF HAVING BREASTS AS SYNONYMOUS WITH BEING A WOMAN...
...BUT EVERY SINGLE HUMAN BEING, REGARDLESS OF GENETIC MAKEUP, HAS BREAST TISSUE. IT'S WHY WE ALL HAVE NIPPLES AND CAN GET BREAST CANCER.
THE MEDICAL TERM FOR EXCESS BREAST TISSUE IN CISGENDER MEN IS
GYNECOMASTIA
THE ROOT WORDS LITERALLY MEAN
WOMEN BREAST
(GYN) AND (MAST)
OUR LANGUAGE DIRECTLY ASSOCIATES BREASTS WITH BEING FEMALE, EVEN WHEN REFERRING TO A CONDITION ONLY AFFECTING MEN.

THE FEMINIZATION OF BREASTS CAN BE A GREAT SOCIETAL WEIGHT, ESPECIALLY AMONG TRANS MEN.

MANY TRANS GUYS AND NON-BINARY PEOPLE OPT FOR MASTECTOMIES TO RELIEVE THE RESULTING DYSPHORIA

THERE ARE ALSO MANY MASCULINE TRANS PEOPLE WHO DON'T MIND HAVING BREASTS AND WOULD RATHER NOT BIND - BUT STILL FEEL PRESSURED TO DO SO.

FOR EXAMPLE, "FREEBALLING" OFTEN RESULTS IN ME BEING MISGENDERED, EVEN WITH THE MOST BUTCH ATTIRE.

HAVE A GOOD DAY, MA'AM!

WROW, THANKS FOR THE REMINDER YOU WERE LOOKING AT MY TITS.

FEMININE BREASTS ARE ALSO OFTEN VIEWED AS IMPLICITLY SEXUAL - WHICH IS A PROBLEM WITHIN ITSELF.

MASCULINE BREASTS, ON THE OTHER HAND ARE OFTEN VIEWED AS UNSIGHTLY OR COMEDIC.

BREASTS ARE SOFT, SENSUAL BODY PARTS - NO MATTER TO WHOM THEY ARE ATTACHED.

THEY ALSO AREN'T SOMETHING MADE TO BE GAWKED AT OR ASHAMED OF.

WE ALL HAVE BREASTS IN SOME CAPACITY!

SOME JUST HAVE MORE FATTY TISSUE THAN OTHERS,

IT'S NOT THAT BIG A DEAL!

*NOT TO MINIMIZE ANY DYSPHORIA/AFFIRMATION THEY MAY CAUSE FOR SOME.

ALSO, IF CIS MEN WITH GYNECOMASTIA AND TRANS MEN WITHOUT TOP SURGERY SHOWED MORE SOLIDARITY WITH ONE ANOTHER, MAYBE THE NORMALIZATION OF MALE BREASTS WON'T BE FAR AWAY.

BOOBIE BROTHERS

LET'S SAY IT TOGETHER...

BOOBS ARE BEAUTIFUL

How Do You Adopt an Embryo?

AROUND THE TIME I WENT TO ART SCHOOL
AND STOPPED READING THE BIBLE EVERY
MORNING, I DETERMINED THAT
EMBRYOS AREN'T REALLY PEOPLE.

2002

2010

ALREADY A
PLANNED
PARENTHOOD
SUPPORTER.

2017

#SHOUT
YOUR
ABORTION

IT WAS THE COST OF ADMISSION INTO FEMINISM.

AND WHAT COST, REALLY?
I'M IN FULL SUPPORT OF A UTERUS HAVER'S
RIGHT TO CHOOSE.

BUT NOW I WAS ABOUT TO MEET A COUPLE OF
STRANGERS WHO WERE CONSIDERING
ME AND MY PARTNER
AS RECIPIENTS FOR THEIR EMBRYOS.

WE HAD MET ONLINE AND COURTED EACH OTHER OVER A FRENZY OF EAGER EMAILS.

EMBRYO DONATION IS ALSO WIDELY CALLED 'EMBRYO ADOPTION'.

WE LIKED THAT IT'S A METHOD IN-BETWEEN
ADOPTION AND BIOLOGICAL OPTIONS FOR
HAVING A BABY.

YOU RECEIVE EMBRYOS LEFTOVER FROM SOMEONE
ELSE'S IN-VITRO FERTILIZATION (IVF) PROCESS.

YOU DON'T HAVE A GENETIC CONNECTION TO YOUR
CHILD, BUT YOU GIVE BIRTH TO THEM.

IT COSTS SIGNIFICANTLY LESS THAN FULL IVF,
AND WAY LESS THAN MANY TYPES OF ADOPTION.

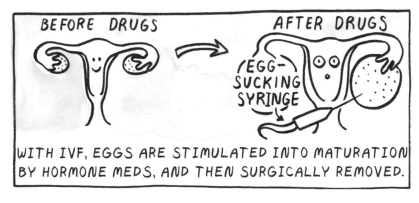

THE GOAL IS FOR ONE OR TWO EMBRYOS TO BE TRANSFERRED TO A UTERUS. SOMETIMES NONE SURVIVE. OTHER TIMES TEN OR MORE THRIVE.

EMBRYOS THAT AREN'T TRANSFERRED ARE FROZEN.

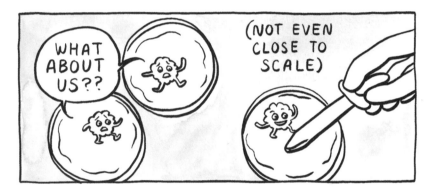

IT IS NOT UNUSUAL FOR THERE TO BE REMAINING FROZEN EMBRYOS AFTER A FAMILY IS COMPLETE.

AS THE PROCESS OF CRYOGENIC FREEZING HAS IMPROVED OVER THE PAST TWO DECADES, THE QUESTION OF WHAT TO DO WITH LEFTOVER EMBRYOS HAS BECOME MORE PRESSING.

IVF PATIENTS HAVE THREE MAIN OPTIONS:

DISCARD THEM

DONATE THEM for SCIENTIFIC RESEARCH

DONATE THEM to OTHERS WHO ARE TRYING to BECOME PARENTS

WHEN PEOPLE DECIDE TO DONATE THEIR EMBRYOS, THEY HAVE MORE CHOICES TO MAKE:

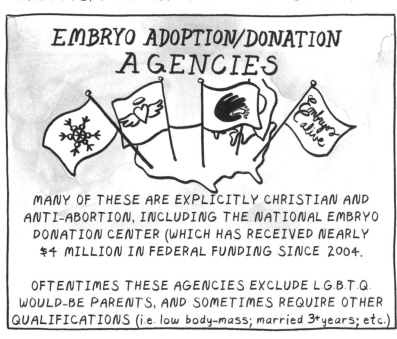

EMBRYO ADOPTION/DONATION AGENCIES

MANY OF THESE ARE EXPLICITLY CHRISTIAN AND ANTI-ABORTION, INCLUDING THE NATIONAL EMBRYO DONATION CENTER (WHICH HAS RECEIVED NEARLY $4 MILLION IN FEDERAL FUNDING SINCE 2004.

OFTENTIMES THESE AGENCIES EXCLUDE L.G.B.T.Q. WOULD-BE PARENTS, AND SOMETIMES REQUIRE OTHER QUALIFICATIONS (i.e. low body-mass; married 3+years; etc.)

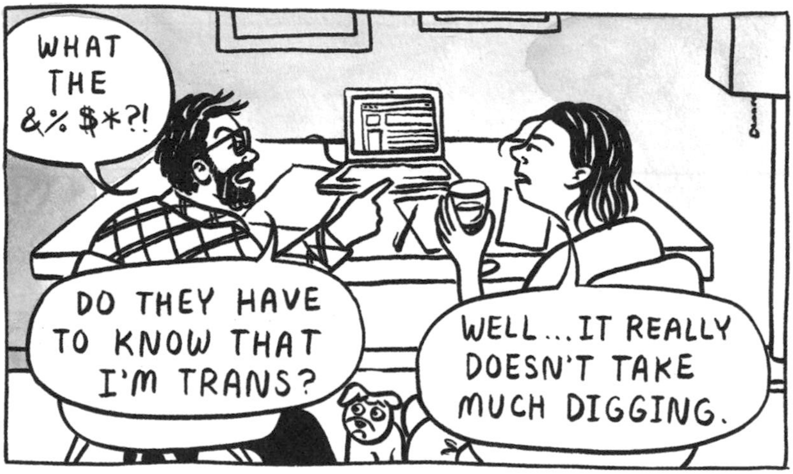
WHAT THE &%$*?!
DO THEY HAVE TO KNOW THAT I'M TRANS?
WELL... IT REALLY DOESN'T TAKE MUCH DIGGING.

162

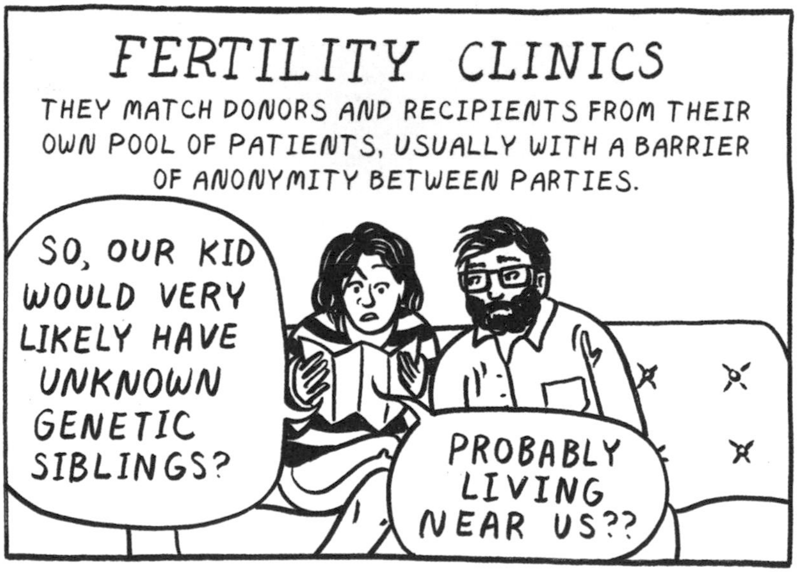
FERTILITY CLINICS
THEY MATCH DONORS AND RECIPIENTS FROM THEIR OWN POOL OF PATIENTS, USUALLY WITH A BARRIER OF ANONYMITY BETWEEN PARTIES.
SO, OUR KID WOULD VERY LIKELY HAVE UNKNOWN GENETIC SIBLINGS?
PROBABLY LIVING NEAR US??

WE HIT IT OFF, CAUTIOUSLY, WITH JEN AND BRIAN.
(Names have definitely been changed.)

WE PROBABLY WOULDN'T BE FRIENDS—
BUT COULD WE BE FAMILY?

WE TALKED ABOUT HOW THEY MET IN ASIA.

MY FRIEND'S MOM WOULD MAKE THIS NOODLE DISH...

PANCIT?

YEAH!

WE TALKED ABOUT THEIR DAUGHTER & ABOUT THEIR HEALTH.

THAT PART WAS LOADED WITH SIGNIFICANCE. WOULD OUR FUTURE KID HAVE TYPE 1 DIABETES, LIKE BRIAN?

DO WE CARE?

THE NEXT DAY

JEN, WHY DO YOU WANT TO DONATE?

IT'S NOT A RELIGIOUS THING.

I JUST CAN'T DESTROY THEM — WE WORKED SO HARD TO MAKE THEM.

IT CAN BE HARD TO FIND DONOR EMBRYOS THAT
AREN'T WHITE, BECAUSE THE MAJORITY OF IVF
PATIENTS ARE WHITE. (Much more could be said
about the history of IVF and eugenics.)

EMBRYO DONATION/ADOPTION ACCOUNTS FOR
A SMALL, BUT GROWING, NUMBER OF BIRTHS
IN THE U.S. AND ABROAD.

BUT IN A NUMBER OF COUNTRIES WITH A
THRIVING IVF INDUSTRY/PRACTICE,
LIKE GREECE AND THE CZECH REPUBLIC, THERE
ARE STRINGENT REQUIREMENTS FOR
ANYONE DONATING GENETIC MATERIAL.

THESE STANDARDS (higher than in the U.S.)
PREVENT AVERAGE COUPLES FROM DONATING
EMBRYOS. THUS, NO EMBRYO DONATION.

WE WERE JUST TRYING TO FIGURE OUT
HOW TO BECOME PARENTS.

A WEEK AFTER MEET-ING JEN & BRIAN, WE AGREED TO GO FOR IT.

WE'RE IN!

HITTING 'SEND' FELT MONUMENTAL.

A DAY LATER, THEY RESPONDED THAT THEY NEED TO BACK OUT—NO REASONS WERE GIVEN.

I GUESS THIS MEANS WE CREATE OUR OWN?

YEAH. I DON'T WANT TO WAIT A YEAR FOR ANOTHER CHANCE.

WE'VE STARTED THE PROCESS OF IVF WITH MY EGGS AND FILIPINO DONOR SPERM.

SOME PARTS HAVE BEEN EASIER THAN I EXPECTED.

I CAN SEE HOW YOU GOT USED TO INJECTING T*.

* TESTOSTERONE

SOME PARTS HAVE BEEN HARDER THAN I EXPECTED.

WHY DON'T WE HAVE A COUPLES' THERAPIST??!

UHH

WE'RE IN THE BIZARRE POSITION WHERE WE MIGHT HAVE TO DECIDE WHAT TO DO WITH LEFTOVER EMBRYOS OURSELVES (knock on wood).

THEY FEEL MORE LIKE PEOPLE
THAN I EVER EXPECTED.

JD BRAGER

LiveJournal Made Me Gay

WAS YOUR ADOLESCENT EXPERIENCE AS *CONFUSING* AS MINE WAS? I DIDN'T RECOGNIZE MYSELF IN ANYTHING I ENCOUNTERED. MOST OF THE IDEAS I HAD ABOUT QUEER AND TRANS PEOPLE CAME FROM SURREPTITIOUSLY WATCHING TV IN MY PARENTS' BASEMENT.

I KEPT MY FINGER ON THE POWER BUTTON JUST IN CASE.

MY FAMILY COMPUTER SAT IN THE MIDDLE OF THE LIVING ROOM LIKE A SHINING BEACON

IT WAS THE EARLY 2000s AND AT THE OTHER END OF THAT DIAL-UP DRONE LAY A WORLD OF POSSIBILITY.

169

THE FREE BLOGGING SITE LIVEJOURNAL WAS STARTED IN 1999— BY THE TIME I SET UP MY ACCOUNT IN THE MID '00s, AFTER A BRIEF STINT ON THE MORE GOTH "DEADJOURNAL", THERE WERE OVER TWO MILLION USERS, ORGANIZING THEMSELVES BY IDENTITY, AFFINITY, AND INTEREST.

I'M GONNA MAKE IT THROUGH THIS YEAR IF IT KILLS ME

I HAD AN EMBARASSING USERNAME INSPIRED BY THE NOVELS OF FRANCESCA LIA BLOCK. I SPENT TONS OF TIME ON LIVEJOURNAL WRITING ACHING, THINLY VEILED LOVE LETTERS AND VERY BAD FICTION, AND TRANSCRIBING DRAMATIC SONG LYRICS.

weekend in western illinois, the mountain goats

I DON'T THINK IDENTITY IS EVER SETTLED, BUT THESE DAYS, AS A *FULLY FORMED ADULT TRANSSEXUAL*™, I AM SURPRISED BY HOW OFTEN ONE LIVEJOURNAL COMMUNITY COMES UP IN CONVERSATION. IT WAS CALLED "BIRLS" - A PORTMANTEAU OF "GIRLS" AND "BOYS" THAT FEELS VERY ... DATED.

I DON'T REMEMBER HOW I FOUND BIRLS, BUT I REMEMBER I WANTED <u>IN</u>.

I FELT LIKE I COULDN'T POST UNTIL I CUT ALL MY HAIR OFF... OR AT LEAST UNTIL I GOT WHITE DREADS (UGH).

LIVEJOURNAL WASN'T JUST A BLOG PLATFORM— IT WAS EARLY SOCIAL MEDIA.

CERTAIN USERS WITH CERTAIN LOOKS GOT HIGHER ENGAGEMENT, WHICH SHAPED THE POSTING BEHAVIORS OF THE COMMUNITY.

WE WERE, EVEN IF WE DIDN'T REALIZE IT, CONSTANTLY NEGOTIATING THE BORDERS OF BIRLHOOD AS AN IDENTITY, AS A COMMUNITY OF BELONGING...

170

... AND AS A COMMUNITY OF DESIRE.

"Erotic recognition is an on ongoing dynamic of community involvement"

"Desire pervades birl talk... Commenting on the sexual allure of birls becomes a daily ritual of birl members reinforcing self confidence and collective bonding"

"Their mutual belonging rests on a mutual appreciation of their appeal as birls"

↑ page 190

THERE WAS EVEN A WHOLE SPIN-OFF COMMUNITY FOR NAKED PICS FOR BIRLS BY BIRLS

THE POLITICS OF DESIRE AND VISIBILITY WERE SHAPED BY THE SAME FORCES THAT THEY ARE IN THE REST OF THE WORLD.

NO ONE SWIPES FOR FATS OR FEMS

2019

EVERYONE IS SO SKINNY & WHITE...

2009

scroll
scroll

"TRANSGRESSIVE" DESIRE ON BIRLS OFTEN BOILED DOWN TO:

THINWHITEMASC 4 THINWHITEMASC

BIRLS WAS DEEPLY FLAWED, BUT FOUNDATIONAL TO MY UNDERSTANDING OF WHAT I WAS SUPPOSED TO BE IN ORDER TO BE QUEER AND TRANS.

IT GAVE ME A TEMPLATE THAT, EVEN IF I REJECTED IT LATER, WAS A PLACE TO BEGIN.

ALSO—A FRIEND FROM BIRLS TOOK ME TO MY FIRST GAY BAR AND GAVE ME MY FIRST BINDER.

It relieved a lot of pressure. Just a room to talk about your weird gender feelings in, without it being immediately pathologized or categorized. To me, that was a relief.

I remember counting down to the day I turned 18 so I could post nudes in birls2!

I think I met my first girlfriend in birls! I helped her workshop a poem for her girlfriend. Although she was a Libra that kept saying we weren't girlfriends, we were in love.

I remember feeling so young and overwhelmed by all these people... who seemed much more advanced in their identities than I felt.

172

WE MILLENIALS WERE SHAPED BY GROWING UP AT THE SAME TIME THAT THE WEB WAS COMING OF AGE.

HOW FOUNDATIONAL WAS THAT MACHINE FOR OUR GENERATION?

WE WERE FORGED IN THE STREAM OF EARLY CHAT ROOMS & MESSAGE BOARDS.

AS LIVEJOURNAL FIZZLED OUT/ GOT SOLD TO A SUPER-REPRESSIVE RUSSIAN COMPANY— BIRLS STAYED IN TOUCH OVER AIM OR BECAME IRL FRIENDS, FOLLOWED OR REDISCOVERED EACH OTHER ON TUMBLR, THEN INSTAGRAM.

I'M A TEACHER NOW!

MOST OF US FORMER BIRLS ARE *AT LEAST* IN OUR THIRTIES NOW... AND THE KIDS THESE DAYS HAVE THEIR OWN THINGS GOING ON.

I DELETED & PURGED MY LIVEJOURNAL WHEN I ENTERED THE "PROFESSIONAL" WORLD

WELP... IT MAY NOT GET BETTER, BUT IT GETS GAYER!

ARE YOU SURE?

ARE YOU SURE?

DELETE

NOW I DEEPLY REGRET THE LOSS OF THAT ARCHIVE OF TEEN DISCOMFORT!
xo JB

Sometimes I Call Myself Queer.
Sometimes I Feel Like a Liar.

173

WHEN I WAS 18...

...I GOT BLACK-OUT DRUNK WITH FRIENDS AFTER WE TRIED TO FIND A STRIP CLUB AND GOT 'LOST'.

I WAS GOING TO GIVE THEM THE ADDRESS OF A GAY NIGHTCLUB BUT GOT COLD FEET.

BARS MAKE ME NERVOUS.

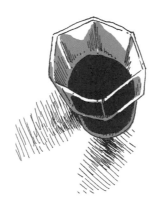

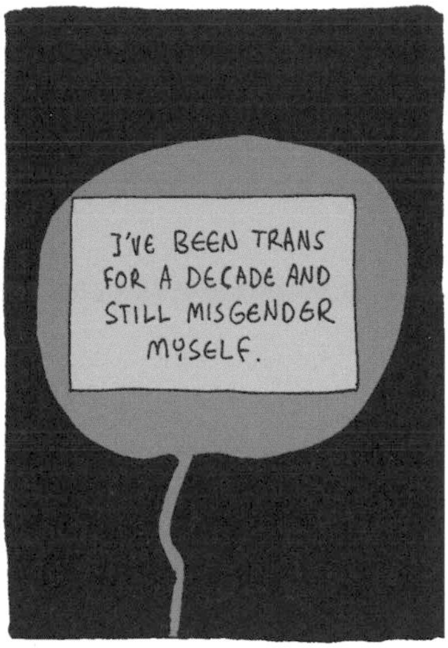
I'VE BEEN TRANS FOR A DECADE AND STILL MISGENDER MYSELF.

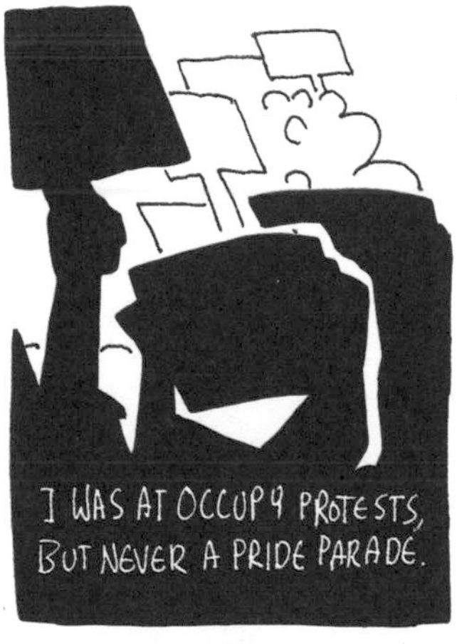
I WAS AT OCCUPY PROTESTS, BUT NEVER A PRIDE PARADE.

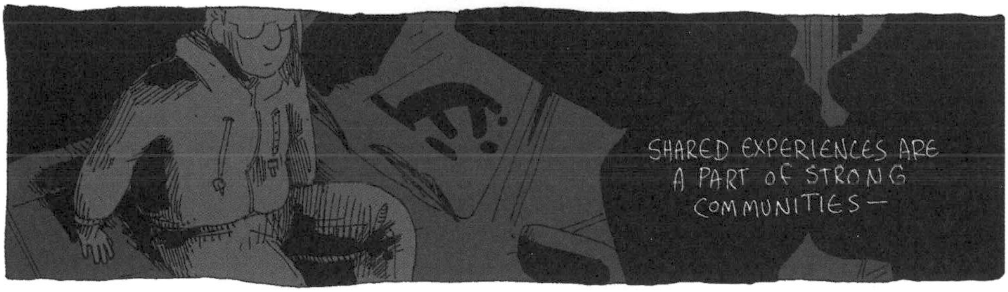
SHARED EXPERIENCES ARE A PART OF STRONG COMMUNITIES—

—AND THE QUEER
COMMUNITY IS
SUCH A PART OF
PEOPLES' IDENTITIES
THAT IT MAKES ME—

—FEEL LIKE
A LIAR.

IT FEELS THAT MUCH
MORE DIFFICULT TO
PARTICIPATE IN
THESE SPACES WITHOUT
THOSE EXPERIENCES.

AND IF I'M NOT
PARTICIPATING,
WHY CALL MYSELF
QUEER **AT ALL**?

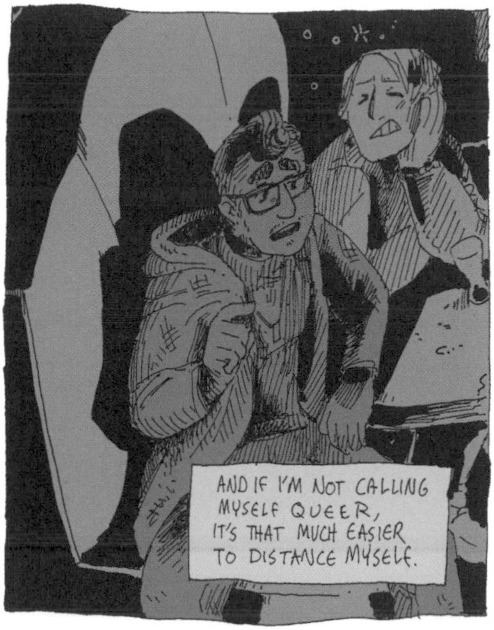
AND IF I'M NOT CALLING MYSELF QUEER, IT'S THAT MUCH EASIER TO DISTANCE MYSELF.

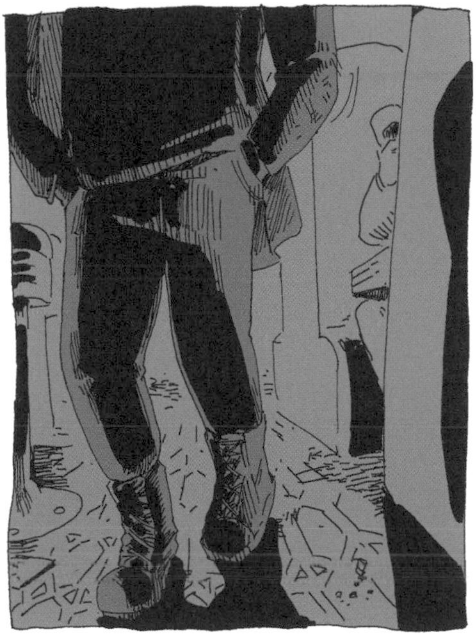

DESPITE BEING BOTH GAY AND TRANS —

I DON'T FEEL LIKE I'VE EARNED THESE SPACES.

I'VE ALWAYS HAD TO CAREFULLY BUILD THE SPACES WE **CAN** INHABIT BY HAND.

WHEN LABELING YOURSELF,
EVEN IN A SELF-AFFIRMING WAY,
OTHERS STILL PROJECT THEIR
IDEAS OF WHO YOU COULD
OR SHOULD BE.

EVEN WITH SOMETHING
AS BROAD AS 'QUEER',
IT'S NOT HARD TO FEEL
LIKE YOU AREN'T WHO
YOU ARE EXPECTED
TO BE.

I'M NOT IN A ROMANTIC OR SEXUAL RELATIONSHIP WITH ANY MALE-IDENTIFIED PERSON —

— I'M POLY, BUT I'M MARRIED, EVEN THAT ALONE IS ENOUGH TO CONFUSE AND ALIENATE OTHER QUEER PEOPLE.

"I USED TO WORK AT A 'QUEER PUNK ROCK ICE CREAM SHOP,' BUT GOT TOLD TO MY FACE BY A COWORKER THAT 'PEOPLE WHO USE THEY PRONOUNS PISS ME OFF' - I USE THEY PRONOUNS. THEY KNEW THIS — MAYBE THEY FORGOT.

LATER I GOT FIRED FOR 'YELLING AT A CUSTOMER WHO MISGENDERED ME.' I'VE NEVER YELLED AT ANYONE WHILE ON THE CLOCK IN MY ENTIRE LIFE, ESPECIALLY NOT ABOUT GENDER."
—ANONYMOUS

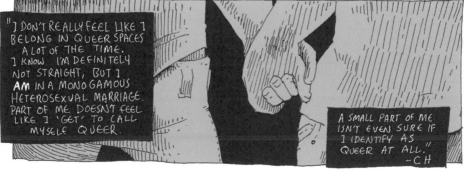

"I DON'T REALLY FEEL LIKE I BELONG IN QUEER SPACES A LOT OF THE TIME. I KNOW I'M DEFINITELY NOT STRAIGHT, BUT I **AM** IN A MONOGAMOUS HETEROSEXUAL MARRIAGE. PART OF ME DOESN'T FEEL LIKE I 'GET' TO CALL MYSELF QUEER.

A SMALL PART OF ME ISN'T EVEN SURE IF I IDENTIFY AS QUEER AT ALL."
—CH

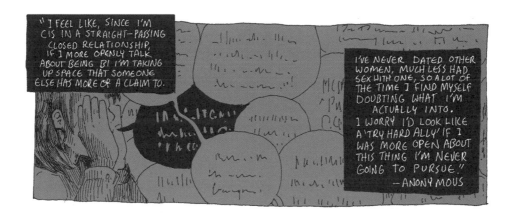

"I FEEL LIKE, SINCE I'M CIS IN A STRAIGHT–PASSING CLOSED RELATIONSHIP, IF I MORE OPENLY TALK ABOUT BEING BI I'M TAKING UP SPACE THAT SOMEONE ELSE HAS MORE OF A CLAIM TO.

I'VE NEVER DATED OTHER WOMEN, MUCH LESS HAD SEX WITH ONE, SO A LOT OF THE TIME I FIND MYSELF DOUBTING WHAT I'M ACTUALLY INTO.
I WORRY I'D LOOK LIKE A 'TRY HARD ALLY' IF I WAS MORE OPEN ABOUT THIS THING I'M NEVER GOING TO PURSUE."
—ANONYMOUS

OUR COLLECTIVE ANXIETIES AND DISASSOCIATION WITH QUEER SPACES—

IRIS
3:04

–IS THIS DUE TO OUR DISASSOCIATION WITH THE COMMUNITY AT LARGE, OR A CONFLICT WITH THE WORD 'QUEER' ITSELF?

CAN WE FEEL ALIENATED FROM WHO OTHERS THINK WE SHOULD BE, BUT TAKE COMFORT IN THAT WE'RE BECOMING WHO WE WANT TO BE?

THERE IS A CERTAIN COMFORT IN CHANGE -
BUS STOP
71
4432
-WHEN YOU KNOW THAT OTHERS ARE CHANGING WITH YOU.

A Lifetime of Coming Out

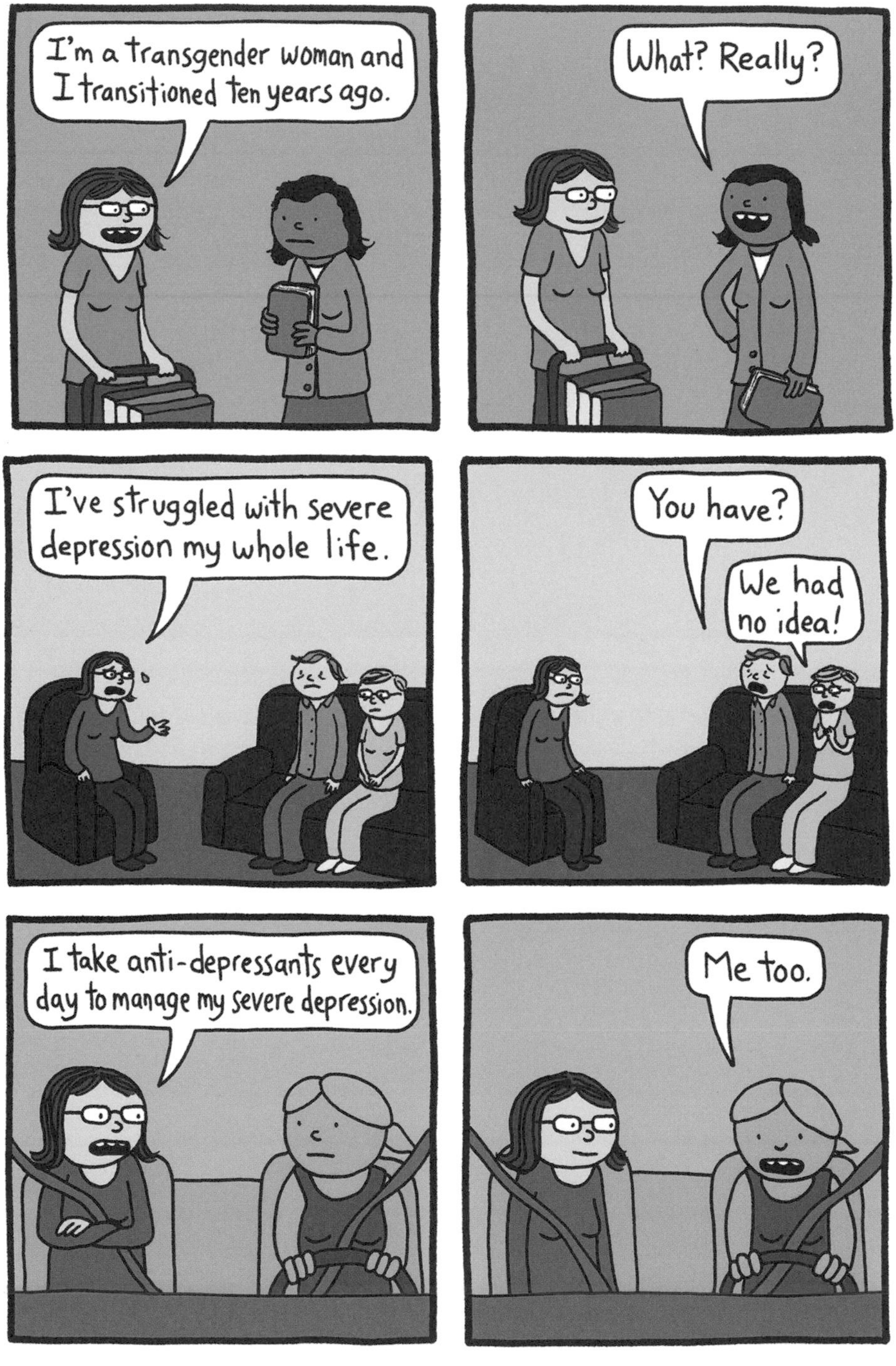
I'm a transgender woman and I transitioned ten years ago.
What? Really?
I've struggled with severe depression my whole life.
You have?
We had no idea!
I take anti-depressants every day to manage my severe depression.
Me too.

I spent most of my 20s drunk and on drugs to avoid dealing with my sexuality, gender-identity, and depression.
That must have been hard.
I've never seen The Godfather, Fight Club, Titanic, or about 100 other "classic" films.
WHAT? ARE YOU KIDDING ME?!
joey alison sayers

I Am More Than My Chromosomes

186

IT'S NOT THAT I THINK THERE'S SOMETHING WRONG WITH BEING A WOMAN...

... IT'S JUST SOMETHING I DON'T IDENTIFY WITH.

I HAVE NEVER FELT THAT MY BODY BELONGS TO ME.

HMM, THIS HAS MY NAME ON IT...

ELÍSABET RÚN

...BUT I'M NOT SURE THAT IT FITS.

I DON'T HAVE AN EXPLANATION,

BUT EVERY FEMININE FEATURE ON MY BODY CAUSES ME SHAME.

EVEN MY VOICE.

STILL, THOSE FEATURES ARE ALWAYS THE FIRST THING PEOPLE SEE.

Good morning ...

THEY IMMEDIATELY WANT TO CATEGORIZE ME BY SOMETHING I DON'T RELATE TO AT ALL.

... miss!

BUT THIS IS THE WAY IT IS FROM (AND EVEN BEFORE) THE MOMENT WE'RE BORN.

And do you want to know the sex?

KNOWING THE SEX ISN'T ABOUT KNOWING THE BABY'S GENITALIA.

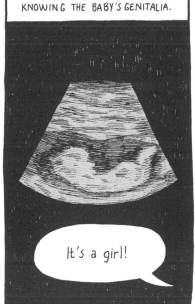

It's a girl!

IT'S ABOUT HOPES AND EXPECTATIONS WHICH START FORMING AS SOON AS WE CAN TALK ABOUT <u>IT</u> AS <u>HIM</u> OR <u>HER</u>.

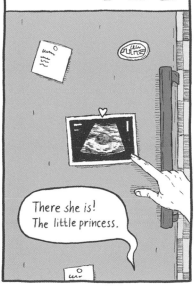

There she is! The little princess.

IT'S ABOUT IDEAS WHICH ARE SO DEEP-ROOTED THAT THEY SOMETIMES FEEL INNATE.

And it's a little princess!

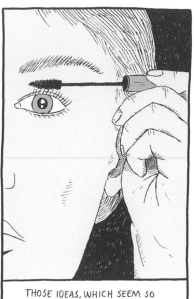

THOSE IDEAS, WHICH SEEM SO INHERENT, HAUNT US THROUGH OUR ENTIRE LIVES.

THEY SEEM SO INSTINCTIVE THAT MOST OF US DON'T NOTICE HOW TRAPPED WE ARE.

IT ISN'T UNTIL YOU TRY TO BREAK OUT OF THESE IDEAS THAT THEIR FIRM GRASP BECOMES VISIBLE

KNOCK KNOCK

AND YOU REALIZE HOW MUCH OF OUR EXISTENCE IS DETERMINED BY CHROMOSOMES.

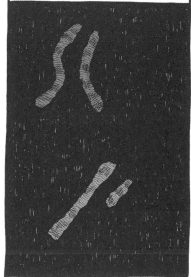

THERE ARE CERTAINLY INSTANCES WHERE GENDER DIVISION HAS A PURPOSE,

BUT WHY DOES YOUR TYPE OF BODY MATTER WHEN YOU'RE BUYING A PLANE TICKET?

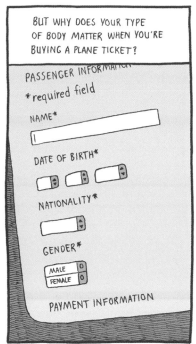

THERE ARE SO MANY EXAMPLES OF UNNECESSARY GENDER DIVISION.

WHAT DO PEOPLE REALLY WANT TO KNOW WHEN THEY ASK ABOUT GENDER?

You see, I've noticed that women are more often blahblahblah...
Of course! Because they were raised that way.
While men are always blahblahblah...
Exactly, because they grew up with those ideas.
THIS DIVISION INTO MEN AND WOMEN IS POINTLESS, BECAUSE IT FOCUSES ON WHAT MAKES US DIFFERENT,
WHEN IN FACT WE HAVE MUCH MORE IN COMMON.

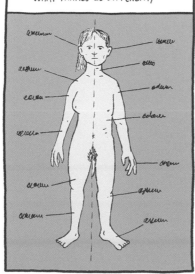

I KNOW THAT PEOPLE ARE JUST BEING POLITE,

Good morning, miss. How can I help you?

BUT I FIND IT SUCH A DISRESPECTFUL OVERSIMPLIFICATION TO CATEGORIZE A WHOLE PERSON

BASED ON SOMETHING AS INSIGNIFICANT AS THEIR CHROMOSOMES.

193

INDEED, YOU PAY MORE ATTENTION TO THE CATEGORIES WHEN YOU FIT INTO NEITHER.

TOILETS

AND IT HURTS MORE WHEN EVERYTHING REMINDING YOU OF GENDER BRINGS YOU SHAME.

Let the woman pass, buddy.

BUT WE ARE ALL STUCK
IN THIS SORTING MACHINE,

AND IT IS US WHO ARE
KEEPING IT GOING.

IT SEEMS ALMOST IMPOSSIBLE
TO CHANGE A FORMULA SO INGRAINED
THAT IT IS EVEN PART OF GRAMMAR
IN MOST LANGUAGES.

I'm so tired of this!

*IN MY NATIVE ICELANDIC,
THIS SENTENCE IS DEPENDING
ON THE SPEAKER'S GENDER.

IT IS CARVED INTO THE WORDS
WE USE ABOUT OURSELVES.

BUT IT WASN'T ANYONE OTHER THAN
US WHO INVENTED THIS FORMULA.

I THINK IT'S ABOUT TIME TO REVIEW THIS FORMULA,

Excuse me!

AND RESPECT THAT WE ARE SO MUCH MORE

Do you see any better with this? I'm right here!

THAN JUST TWO KINDS OF CHROMOSOMES.

IMAGINE BEING ABLE TO GO OUTSIDE

AND SIMPLY BE A PERSON.

Good morning!

Jussie Smollett Doesn't Negate the Reality of Hate Crimes

The Jussie Smollett incident has been quite the emotional rollercoaster for both the black and LGBTQ community, from initial claims of a racist assault to Smollett being charged with staging the attack on himself.

196

It's hard to wrap my head around what could drive someone to do something so ridiculous, so selfish, and most importantly, so damaging to already vulnerable communities...

Black and queer people are already accused of exaggerating, being paranoid, and sometimes outright lying about hateful encounters.

I can only think of the times where hateful lies have gotten people killed. Emmett Till was a 14-year-old boy when he was tortured and eventually shot to death for allegedly making advances on a 21-year-old white woman in the segregated south of 1955, an important catalyst for the beginnings of the Civil Rights Movement.

It wasn't until six decades later, in 2017, that the woman in question admitted to totally lying about the boy grabbing and menacing her.

That part is not true.

- Told to historian Timothy B. Tyson

And of course, simply existing as you are
can get you killed or imprisoned in many countries.

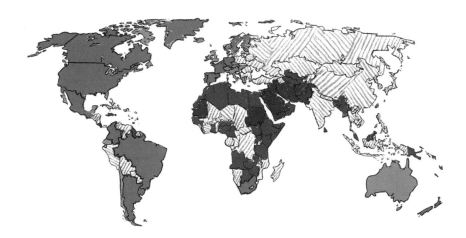

SAME SEX RELATION LAWS WORLDWIDE

Source: International Lesbian, Gay, Bisexual,
Trans and Intersex Association, May 2017

◼ MARRIAGE   ◼ DEATH PENALTY

◻ PARTNERSHIP   ◼ IMPRISONMENT

▨ DECRIMINALIZED OR ILLEGAL WITH NO
         PENALISING LAW

I've had all kinds of unfortunate encounters in my life, but still I consider myself lucky. When I was but a young, odd middle schooler living in Southern California, my friend circle was pretty gay. I'd never felt more at home.

As if puberty wasn't enough to deal with, some of us were also considering coming out to family. But one day, we got terrible news. A kid from a school a little further up the coast had been shot in the back of the head in the middle of English class by a fellow student.

Lawrence King was a 15-year-old boy who liked to wear heeled boots, jewelry, and asked his teacher to call him Leticia. He was openly proud of liking boys, and had publicly asked a classmate to be his valentine.

That classmate came to school next day with the gun that ended his life.

Everyone seemed to be saying that Lawrence wouldn't have been killed if he wasn't so obvious about it. We wondered if our peers were capable of doing the same.

I clearly remember advising my friends to put a hold on coming out. It didn't feel right to hide. But it didn't feel safe to do anything else.

What Jussie Smollett is said to have done is not a
reflection of our truth, or even a trend in our country.
But it seems that those who wish to deny the truth
of hate in America will find any way to do so.

HATE CRIMES IN MAJOR US CITIES

Source: Center for the Study of Hate and Extremism
CSU San Bernardino, May 2018

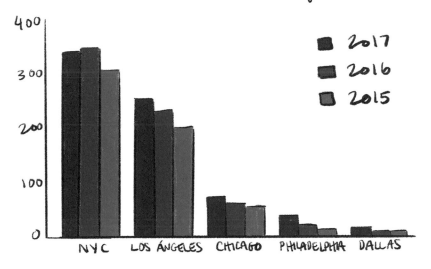

The truth is, there is nothing to gain from being a victim.
We are not victims. We do not want sympathy.
We want acknowledgment.

We don't want to just survive,
we want to live in peace, as we are.

It's All for the Breast

I'M OFTEN REMINDED OF HOW FEMININE I LOOK AND DRESS. IT'S STRANGE TO THINK HOW MUCH I'VE CHANGED.

HEY LEX, I DON'T THINK I'VE EVER SEEN YOU IN PANTS. DO YOU EVEN OWN ANY?

SOMETIMES I WEAR LEGGINGS AS PANTS...

LEGGINGS ARE NOT PANTS.

MY TEEN SELF WOULD HATE HOW WE TURNED OUT.

TEN YEARS AGO

HEY LEX, I DON'T THINK I'VE EVER SEEN YOU IN A SKIRT, DO YOU EVER WEAR THEM?

205

NEVER!!

I'VE ALWAYS BEEN SOMEONE WHO'S GONE AGAINST THE GRAIN.

I HATE BACKSTREET BOYS. I ONLY LIKE BATS.

AS FAR AS I WAS CONCERNED, NO ONE COULD TELL ME WHAT TO DO, OR WHO TO BE.

WHAT THE...? HANG ON A MINUTE.

BUT THEN MY BODY SUDDENLY DECLARED THAT I WAS A WOMAN, WITHOUT CONSULTING ME.

HEY! SLOW DOWN!

I WASN'T READY TO DECIDE EITHER WAY, SO I PUT MY FOOT ON THE BRAKES AND STARTED HEADING IN THE OTHER DIRECTION.

I'M A DUDE NOW. AND I STILL HATE THE BACKSTREET BOYS.

THAT ONE SONG IS GOOD, THOUGH.

THEY SAY, "CLOTHES MAKETH THE MAN," AND THIS IS EVEN TRUER WHEN YOUR CUP RUNNETH OVER.

OH COME ON, I WAS JUST FITTED.

AROUND 14, I STARTED WEARING A LOT OF LAYERS AND DARK COLOURS, TO HIDE WHAT I DIDN'T WANT PEOPLE TO SEE.

IT CAME AT A PRICE.

AUSTRALIAN SUN

PERMANENTLY SWEATY MESS

WORTH IT.

I FOUND THAT IF I GAVE PEOPLE THE OVERALL IDEA OF "DUDE" THEN THAT'S WHAT THEY SAW.

PEOPLE SEE WHAT THEY EXPECT TO SEE.

EVERY TIME SOMEONE READ ME AS MALE

I FELT IN CONTROL

DUDE

MISTER

SIR

BRO!

THAT GUY OVER THERE

MATE

I WAS IN CHARGE OF HOW PEOPLE SAW ME AND INTERACTED WITH ME.

BABY FACED BOY

WOMAN

AS LONG AS MY PARENTS WEREN'T AROUND.

EXCUSE ME, SIR?

ACTUALLY, COULD YOU JUST IGNORE THE ELEPHANT IN THE ROOM AND CALL ME MA'AM?

EVEN WHEN STUCK IN MY SCHOOL UNIFORM, I MANAGED TO MAINTAIN A CERTAIN LEVEL OF MASCULINITY.

OI! IS THAT A DUDE IN A DRESS?

HAH! YEAH, PRETTY MUCH.

MY PARENTS KNEW I WAS ONE OF THE WIERD KIDS AND TRIED TO PROTECT ME, BUT THERE WAS NO NEED.

UGH. WHY CAN'T I WEAR A SUIT TO THE DANCE??

I'M JUST... I'M WORRIED THE OTHER KIDS WILL CALL YOU A LESBIAN.

HAVE YOU SEEN ME?

THEY ALREADY DO!!

NO ONE GAVE ME A HARD TIME FOR BEING A LESBIAN, BUT I WAS THREATENED SEVERAL TIMES FOR "BEING A FAG".

IT NEVER CAME TO BLOWS BECAUSE THEY'D REALISE I HAD BOOBS AND WOULD LEAVE ME SHAKEN BUT UNHARMED.

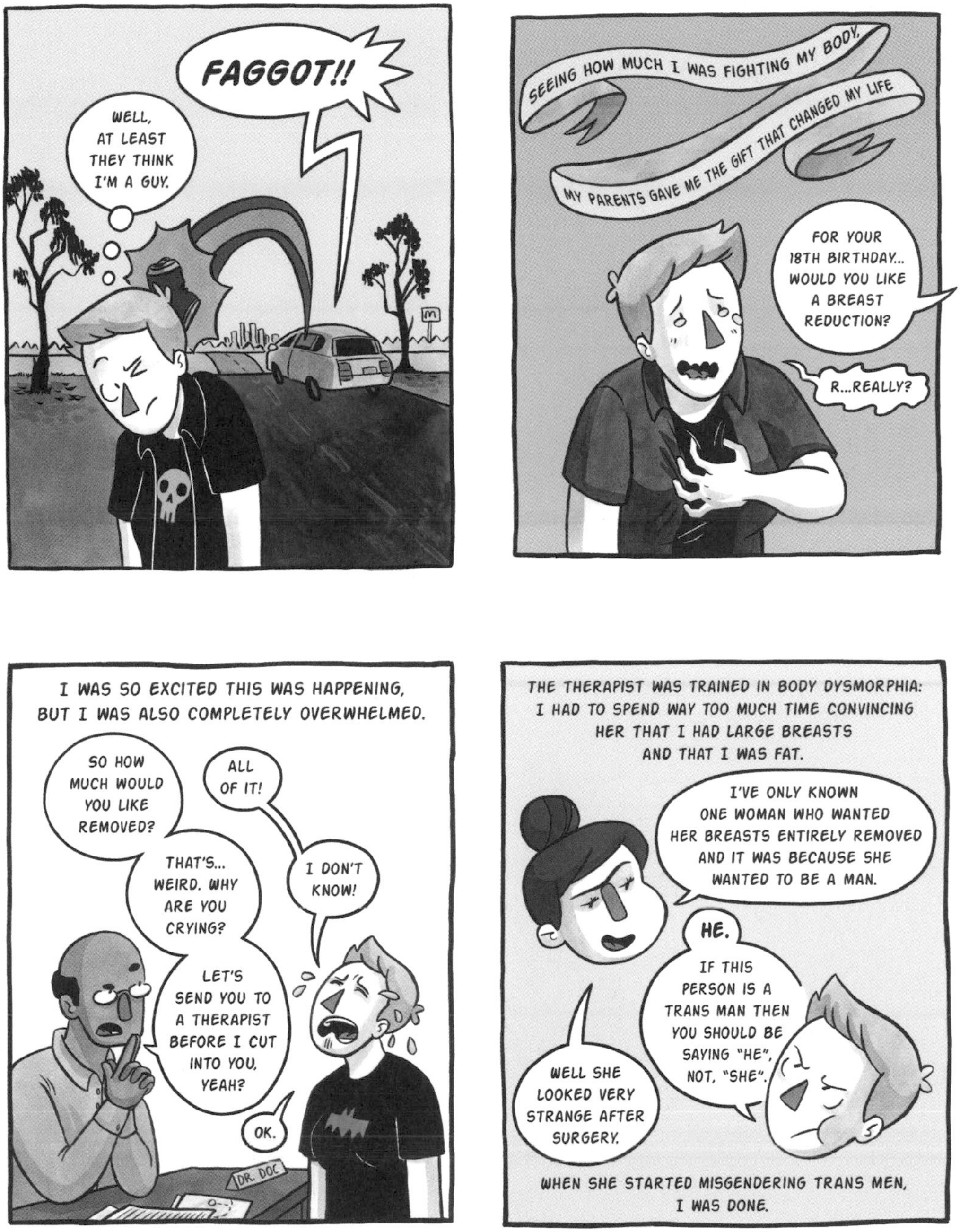
FAGGOT!!
WELL, AT LEAST THEY THINK I'M A GUY.
SEEING HOW MUCH I WAS FIGHTING MY BODY,
MY PARENTS GAVE ME THE GIFT THAT CHANGED MY LIFE
FOR YOUR 18TH BIRTHDAY... WOULD YOU LIKE A BREAST REDUCTION?
R...REALLY?
I WAS SO EXCITED THIS WAS HAPPENING, BUT I WAS ALSO COMPLETELY OVERWHELMED.
SO HOW MUCH WOULD YOU LIKE REMOVED?
ALL OF IT!
THAT'S... WEIRD. WHY ARE YOU CRYING?
I DON'T KNOW!
LET'S SEND YOU TO A THERAPIST BEFORE I CUT INTO YOU, YEAH?
OK.
DR. DOC
THE THERAPIST WAS TRAINED IN BODY DYSMORPHIA: I HAD TO SPEND WAY TOO MUCH TIME CONVINCING HER THAT I HAD LARGE BREASTS AND THAT I WAS FAT.
I'VE ONLY KNOWN ONE WOMAN WHO WANTED HER BREASTS ENTIRELY REMOVED AND IT WAS BECAUSE SHE WANTED TO BE A MAN.
HE.
IF THIS PERSON IS A TRANS MAN THEN YOU SHOULD BE SAYING "HE", NOT, "SHE".
WELL SHE LOOKED VERY STRANGE AFTER SURGERY.
WHEN SHE STARTED MISGENDERING TRANS MEN, I WAS DONE.

IF YOU WON'T TAKE IT ALL, JUST TAKE AS MUCH AS POSSIBLE.

OH YEAH, AND TRIM DOWN THE NIPS TO MATCH.

DR. DOC

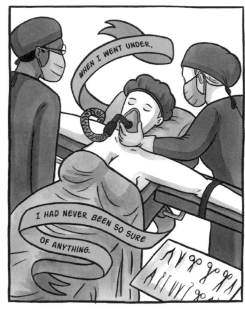

WHEN I WENT UNDER,

I HAD NEVER BEEN SO SURE

OF ANYTHING.

210

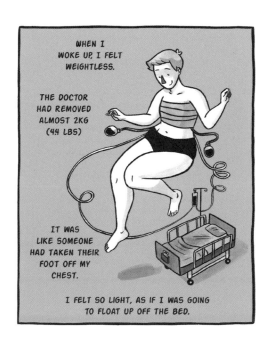

WHEN I WOKE UP, I FELT WEIGHTLESS.

THE DOCTOR HAD REMOVED ALMOST 2KG (44 LBS)

IT WAS LIKE SOMEONE HAD TAKEN THEIR FOOT OFF MY CHEST.

I FELT SO LIGHT, AS IF I WAS GOING TO FLOAT UP OFF THE BED.

WITHOUT SUCH AN OBVIOUS MARKER OF WOMANHOOD, I STARTED TO BECOME MORE COMFORTABLE WITH BEING FEMALE.

I DIDN'T HAVE TO WORRY ABOUT
DEFENDING MY MASCULINITY.

I COULD JUST

BE MYSELF

211

AND APPARENTLY, I'M A WOMAN.

SRSLY?
ALL THAT JUST
TO FIND OUT I'M
CIS-GENDERED?
SHEESH.

I GUESS I'D JUST BEEN CARRYING
TOO MUCH BAGGAGE.

Witch Camp

I'm a queer, nonbinary person, and always have been.

I didn't always know it, though.

Growing up in a community where words like "queer" and "nonbinary" are never talked about, can make it seem like queer, nonbinary people simply don't exist.

Except for that persistent, nagging feeling that something's "wrong" with you.

(which other kids often suspected, too.)

I don't think that is a girl!!!

But every now and then, I'd meet a kid who seemed somehow *familiar*.

Her name was Annie, and she smelled like the forest.

The other girls called her ugly.

But I liked how she looked.

One night, after lights-out, Annie convinced our cabin to play a game:

LIGHT AS A FEATHER, STIFF AS A BOARD

I remember her hands on my arm.

And mine on hers.

But Annie took the game too far.

I SEE HER SHE'S COM-ING

SHE'S COMING TO GET US

Someone must've run for the counselors' cabin, because a moment later—

WHAT IS GOING ON HERE?!

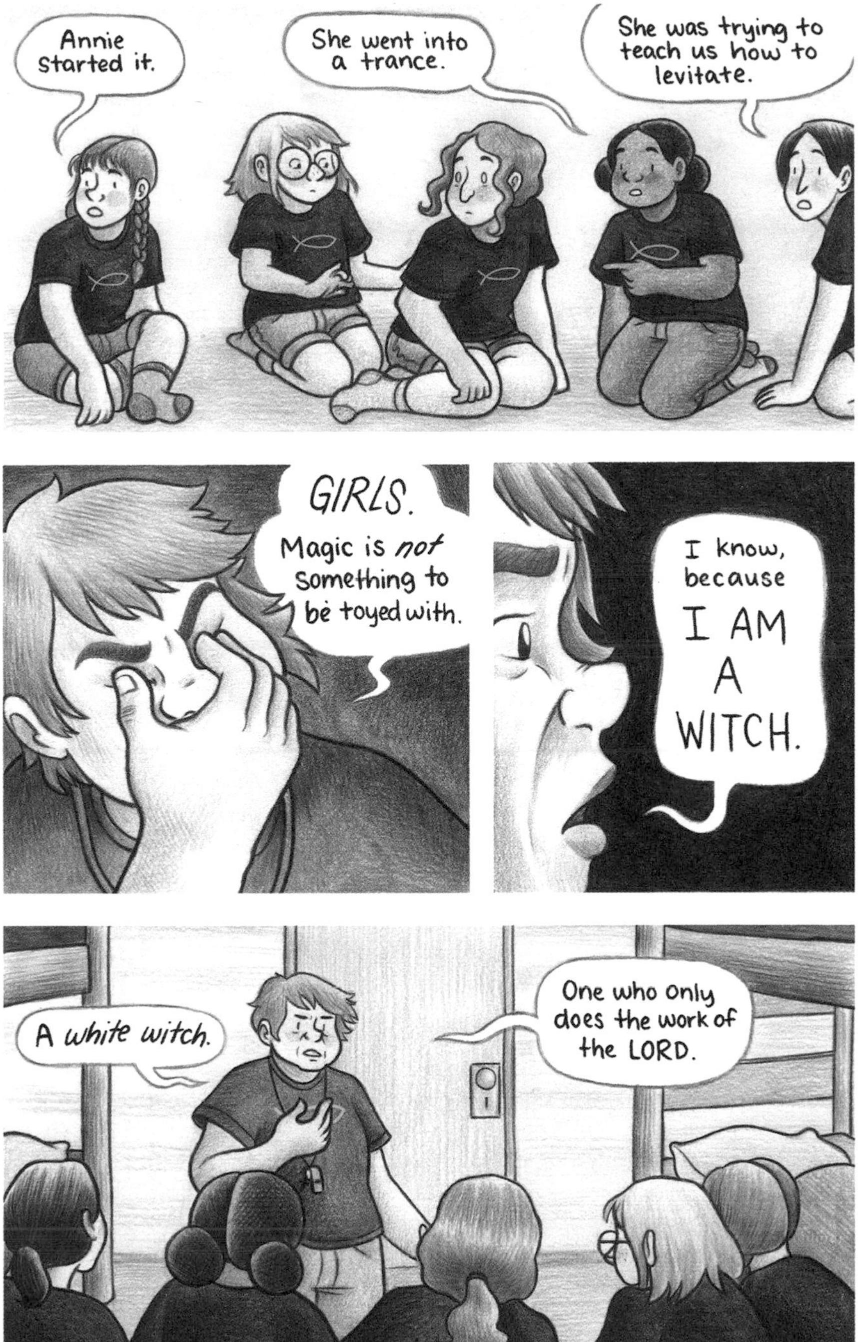
Annie started it.
She went into a trance.
She was trying to teach us how to levitate.
GIRLS.
Magic is *not* something to be toyed with.
I know, because I AM A WITCH.
A *white witch.*
One who only does the work of the LORD.

Was that it, then?

The thing that made me "different"–

Somehow, I was a witch?

I supposed a real witch would know how to recognize others.

The next morning, Annie was gone.

The counselors said they found her hiding in the woods later and called her parents.

But we never saw her again.

The person who drove me home that day was the white witch.

Scared as I was, I had to ask.

How could you tell I'm a...

...witch?

Everyone has a little light inside— one that never goes out, even after we die.

But some people's shine a little brighter than others'.

If you have it yourself, you can learn to see it in others.

God gave us that light, so it's our responsibility to use it to be a guide for others.

JULIA BERNHARD

Take a Hint

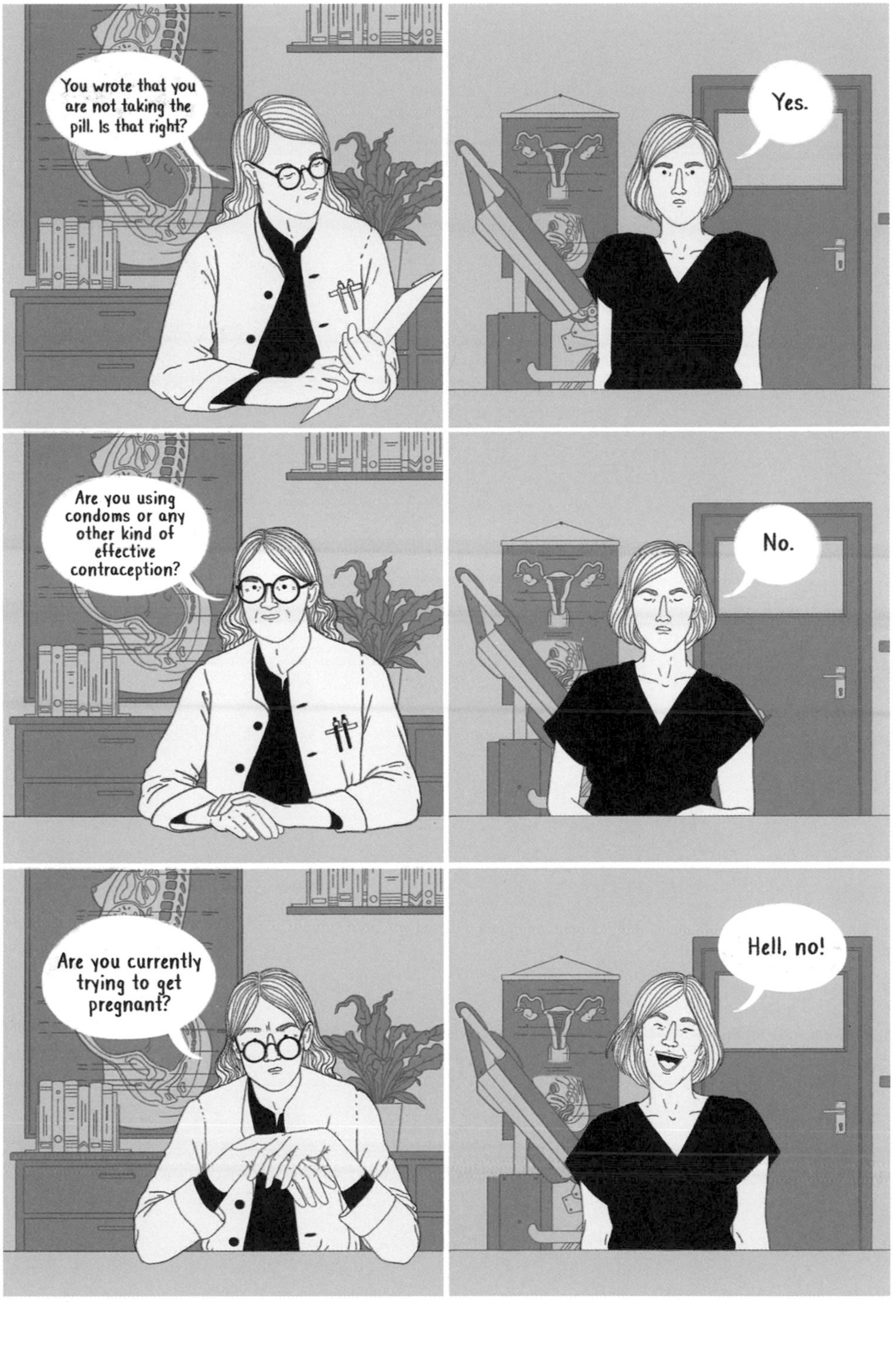
You wrote that you are not taking the pill. Is that right?
Yes.
Are you using condoms or any other kind of effective contraception?
No.
Are you currently trying to get pregnant?
Hell, no!

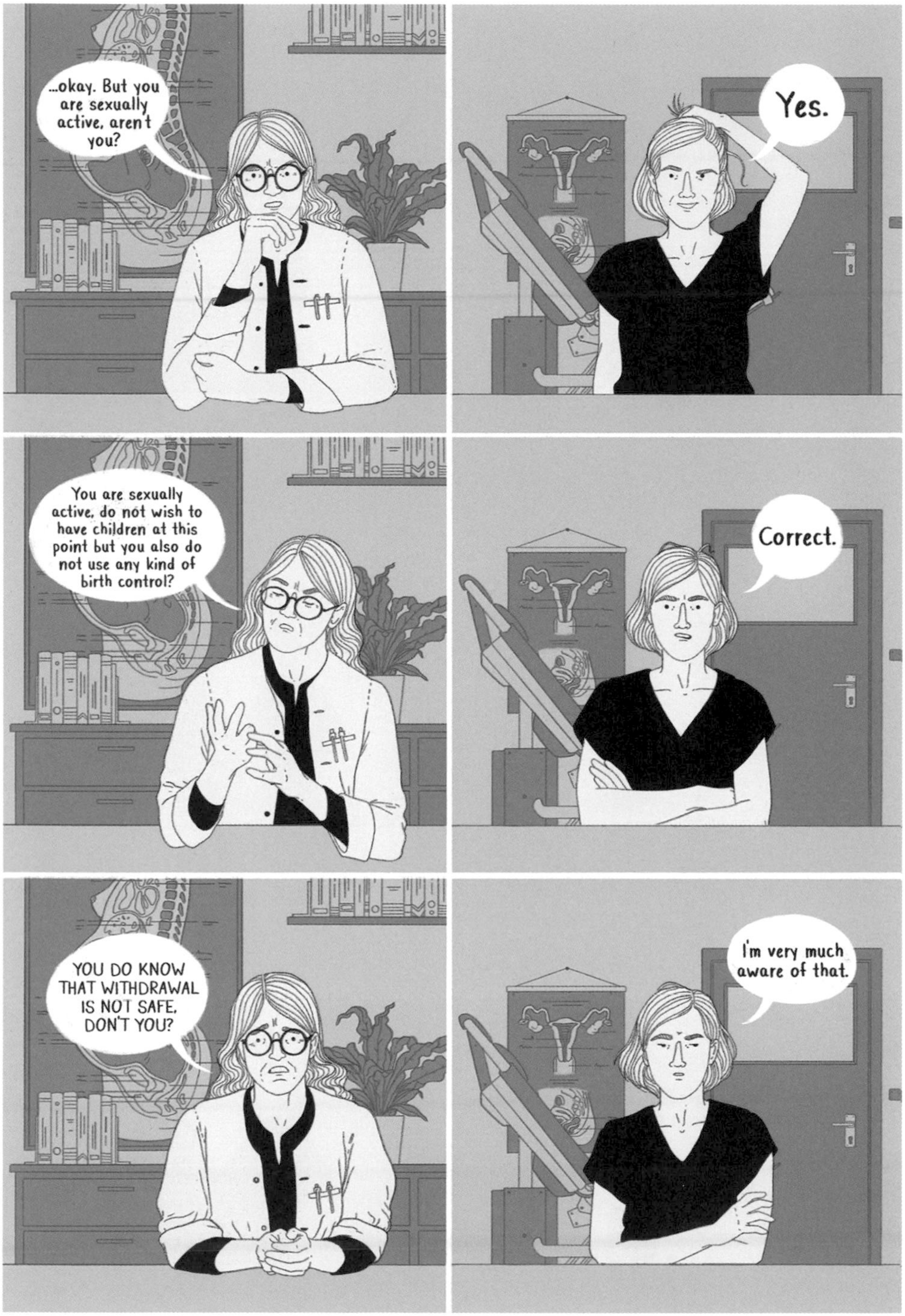

...okay. But you are sexually active, aren't you?
Yes.
You are sexually active, do not wish to have children at this point but you also do not use any kind of birth control?
Correct.
YOU DO KNOW THAT WITHDRAWAL IS NOT SAFE, DON'T YOU?
I'm very much aware of that.

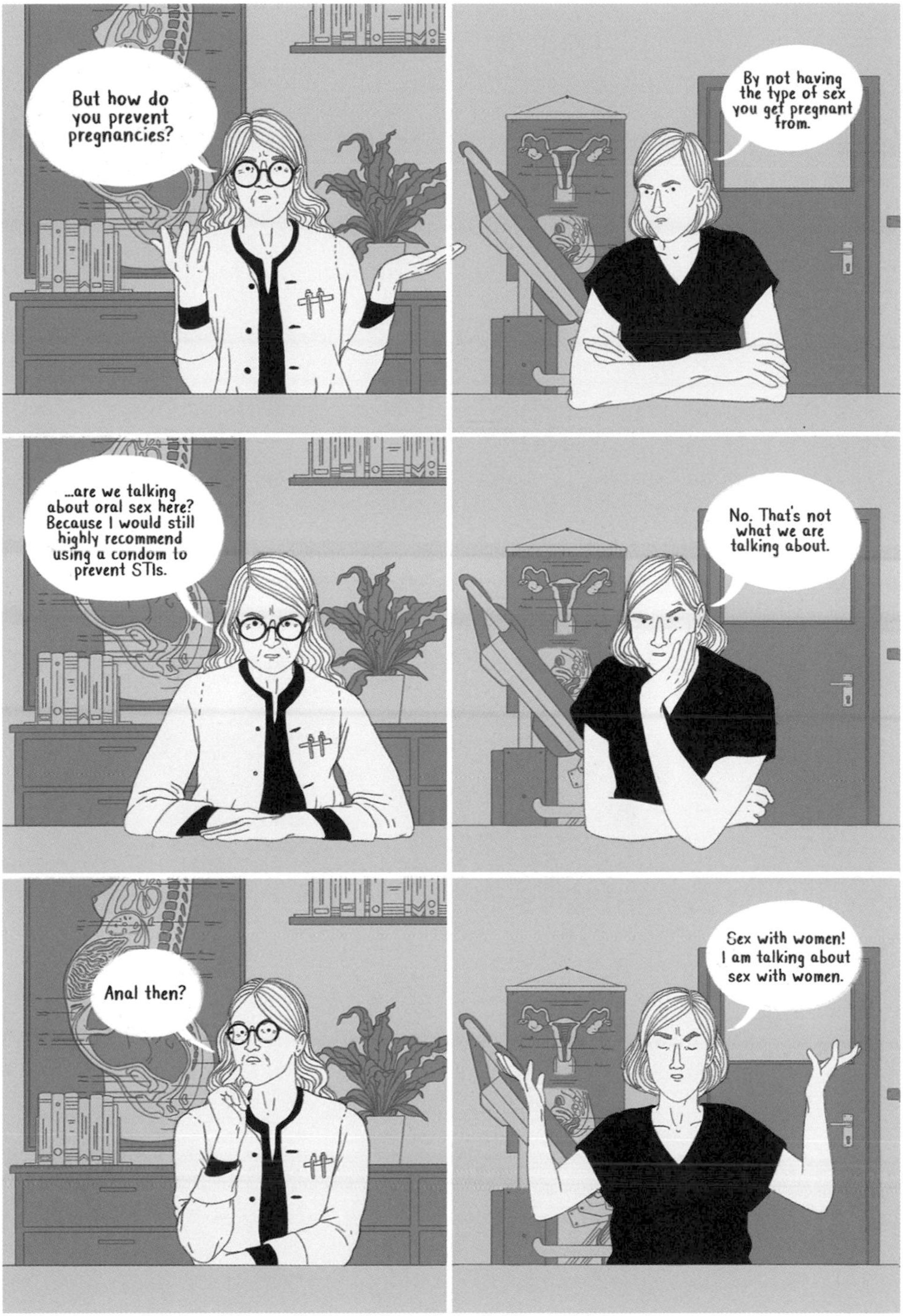
But how do you prevent pregnancies?
By not having the type of sex you get pregnant from.
...are we talking about oral sex here? Because I would still highly recommend using a condom to prevent STIs.
No. That's not what we are talking about.
Anal then?
Sex with women! I am talking about sex with women.

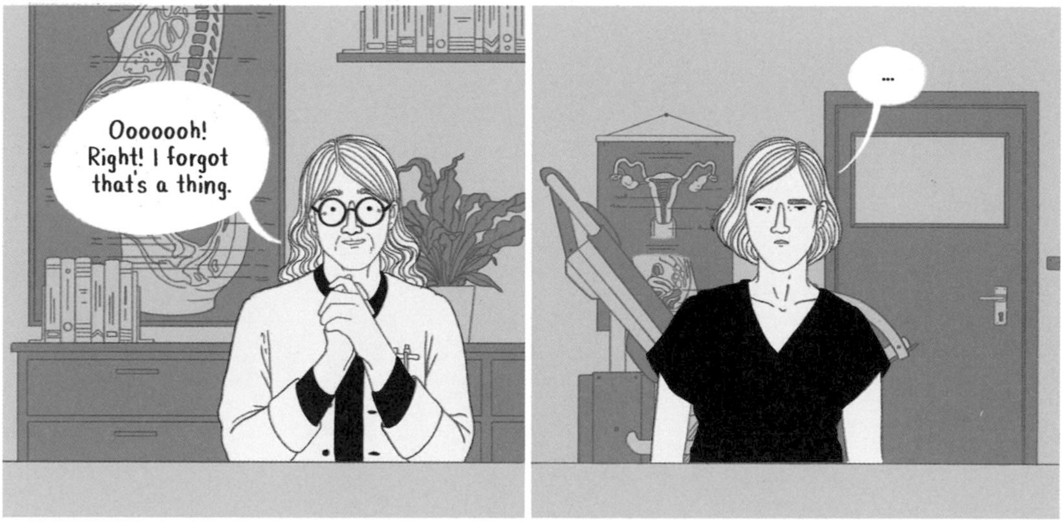
Ooooooh! Right! I forgot that's a thing.
...

The American Revolution's Greatest Leader Was Openly Gay

Maybe the most important military leader in the American Revolution was

FRIEDRICH WILHELM AUGUST HEINRICH FERDINAND STEUBEN,

IMMIGRANT, HOMOSEXUAL and ALL-AROUND BADASS!

"Baron von Steuben" hailed from Prussia, where he:

was injured in battle...

became a prisoner of the Russians...

223

got injured in battle AGAIN,

and became a famous captain in the Seven Years' War.

However, Steuben lived openly as a homosexual before the term even existed...

and it got him in a lot of trouble.

When the Seven Years War ended, Steuben was expelled from Germany on charges of Sodomy.

GEHEN!

He fled to France, but nobody wanted him there, either.

NON.

In 1777, Benjamin Franklin was in Europe on behalf of General George Washington. He was looking for military experts he could recruit to the Continental Army.

America was in no position to win a war against Britain. They desperately needed experienced soldiers.

Franklin knew about Von Steuben's past, but still decided to write a letter of recommendation to George Washington.

Rather than focus on the scandal, the letter emphasized "his distinguished character and known abilities."

It's unclear exactly what Washington knew about Von Steuben, but in short time the new recruit proved his worth as a military commander.

In a matter of months and without speaking English, Steuben was promoted to the rank of Inspector General.

Thank God...

He trained soldiers how to survive in a war. Not just how to fight, but how to set up camp...

maintain supply lines...

and avoid disease.

LATRINE
MESS TENT

Steuben's exacting standards saved countless lives and became the mold for the American Military.

REGULATIONS
FOR THE
Order and Difcipline
OF THE
TROOPS
OF THE
UNITED STATES
PART I

The "Blue Book" training manual he created was taught to American soldiers for nearly a century.

Rumors about Von Steuben's "tastes" were common knowledge and reported in the American Press.

One story claimed that Von Steuben loved to host cocktail nights for his favorite cadets...

no clothing allowed.

General Steuben remained a vital and successful part of the Continental Army for the remainder of the war.

President George Washington rewarded his prized General with an estate in Valley Forge, the site of perhaps his greatest military victory.

The two men regarded one another highly, and exchanged letters for the rest of their lives.

Steuben spent his final years with two younger men he had served with in the war.

Captain Benjamin Walker

and

Brigadier General William North. (Later a US Senator)

He adopted both as his "sons," but speculation about their relationships remain.

Today, German-Americans celebrate "Von Steuben Day" every September.

·MILITARY·INSTRUCTION·

Von Steuben Memorial
· Washington DC ·

At parades and parties nationwide, they honor Steuben's contributions to the American Revolution (but mostly gloss over the gay stuff).

Our understanding of sexuality and love are different than in the 18th century.

To complicate things, evidence of homosexuality is often hidden from the pages of history.

Queer people have always played an important role in a world events, we often just don't know about it.

In his lifetime, Baron Von Steuben lived fearlessly and died a hero to a new nation.

Whom he chose to love was of secondary importance to our Founding Fathers.

What mattered were his skills, expertise, and integrity.

We need to recognize the contributions of LGBTQ servicemen and women when honoring our troops.

Especially those who even today are afraid to serve their country openly.

What's It Like to Raise Kids in Malaysia When You're LGBT?

THE RULING PARTY AGGRESSIVELY PUSHES THE "BRAND IMAGE" THAT THIS SOUTHEAST ASIAN NATION IS A "COUNTRY THAT ALLOWS FREEDOM OF BELIEF, AND HONORS AND RESPECTS ALL RELIGIONS."

DESPITE THAT, THE OLD CLICHÉ ABOUT QUEERS PREYING ON KIDS IS ENDEMIC—

+ FIRLY AFWIKA, API FELLOW

THE PRIME MINISTER, NAJIB RAZAK, FAMOUSLY COMPARED LGBT RIGHTS GROUPS TO ISIS, STATING:

THEY WERE "TARGETING THE YOUNGER GENERATION TO SPREAD THEIR IDEOLOGIES."

IN THE FACE OF A DEPRECIATING CURRENCY AND WIDESPREAD ACCUSATIONS OF CORRUPTION, NAJIB COULD CERTAINLY USE A CONVENIENT SCAPEGOAT FOR THE NATION'S WOES.

"NOWADAYS IN MALAYSIA YOU READ SO MANY THINGS IN NEWSPAPER ARTICLES OR WRITE-UPS ABOUT LGBT's ... BECAUSE THEY ARE GOING INTO SCHOOLS AND INFLUENCING CHILDREN."

RAHMAN ADAM IS THE DIRECTOR OF A GOVERNMENT-BACKED MUSICAL, ASMARA SONGSANG (ABNORMAL DESIRES).

THE MUSICAL, A SCREWBALL COMEDY ABOUT A GROUP OF GENDER-BENDING DELINQUENTS, AIMS TO "ALERT YOUNGSTERS TO THE BAD THINGS ABOUT LGBT."

PROPAGANDA LIKE THAT CAN MAKE COMING OUT AS LGBT-EVEN TO YOUR OWN KIDS-A RISKY PROSPECT.

AT FIRST WE DIDN'T TELL TONY, OUR SON, THAT I WAS A TRANS MAN. WE DIDN'T START WITH THAT BECAUSE I DIDN'T KNOW HOW HE'D REACT, AND I DIDN'T WANT HIS BIOLOGICAL DAD TO FIND OUT.

ALEX, 29, FREELANCER

IT WOULD'VE MADE THINGS COMPLICATED IN TERMS OF CUSTODY.. BUT THEN TONY WOULD ASK QUESTIONS LIKE "CAN TWO BOYS GET MARRIED?" WE WERE LIKE, "YEAH OF COURSE!"

SNAP

TONY WAS NEVER TAUGHT IT WAS WRONG.

ASHA, 36, FAMILY LAWYER

EVEN THOUGH HIS BIOLOGICAL DAD IS FROM A VERY CONSERVATIVE, VERY TRADITIONAL, VERY...

VERY INDIAN? HA HA

VERY OLD-SCHOOL INDIAN. WHEN ASHA FIRST GOT MARRIED TO HIM, SHE COULDN'T SIT ON THE SOFA WITH HIM, ASHA HAD TO SIT AT HIS FEET.

TONY KNOWS THAT IF HE WEARS NAIL POLISH WHEN HE'S AT HIS MUM'S, HE NEEDS TO REMOVE IT BEFORE HE GOES HOME, WHICH I SAW HAPPENING SINCE HE WAS FOUR OR FIVE.

I LIKE THE RED FINGER COLOR!

TONY, 7, ASHA & ALEX'S SON

TONY'S SO OBSESSED WITH DRAWING ALEX THESE DAYS.

LOOK AT THOSE ARMS, I'M A BEEFCAKE!

Daddy

IF WE WENT TO COURT TO SEEK FULL CUSTODY, I COULDN'T TAKE ALEX. WE'RE NOT MARRIED, SO HE DOESN'T EXIST.

IF I TALKED ABOUT HIM IN COURT, I'D HAVE TO DISCLOSE THAT HE'S TRANS. THEY'D TAKE ONE LOOK AT HIS IDENTITY CARD, AND DECIDE I'M IN A SAME-SEX RELATIONSHIP.

NAVIGATING THE LEGAL SYSTEM IS TRICKY WHEN YOU'RE A DEMONIZED MINORITY. IN RAHMAN'S MUSICAL, THE LGBT CHARACTERS GET HIGH, PARTY AND BEDEVIL MUSLIM WORSHIPPERS AT A LOCAL MOSQUE.

THE SUPPOSED ANTAGONISM BETWEEN QUEERNESS AND MALAYSIA'S 19.5 MILLION SUNNI'S IS A GODSEND TO VINDICTIVE PARENTS SEEKING CUSTODY.

WHEN TAL, MY EX HUSBAND, HAD ONE OF HIS WEEKENDS WITH LIZ, HE TOOK HER TO A SHARIA LAWYER, WHO ASKED IF HER MOM IS 'NORMAL'!

SHAFINA, 36, WORKS AT AMNESTY

BECAUSE SHE DOESN'T HAVE ANY OF THE SOCIETAL HANGUPS ABOUT SEXUALITY, LIZ WAS LIKE 'YEAH, MY MOM'S A LESBIAN, SHE HAS A GIRLFRIEND."

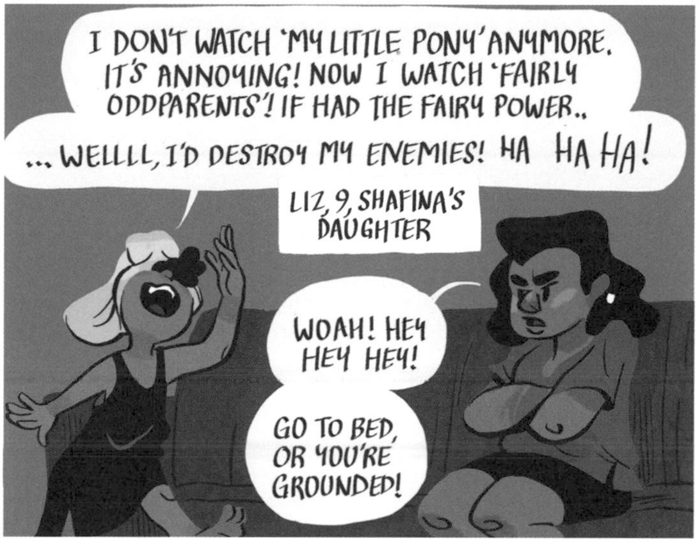
I DON'T WATCH 'MY LITTLE PONY' ANYMORE. IT'S ANNOYING! NOW I WATCH 'FAIRLY ODDPARENTS'! IF HAD THE FAIRY POWER..
... WELLLL, I'D DESTROY MY ENEMIES! HA HA HA!
LIZ, 9, SHAFINA'S DAUGHTER
WOAH! HEY HEY HEY!
GO TO BED, OR YOU'RE GROUNDED!

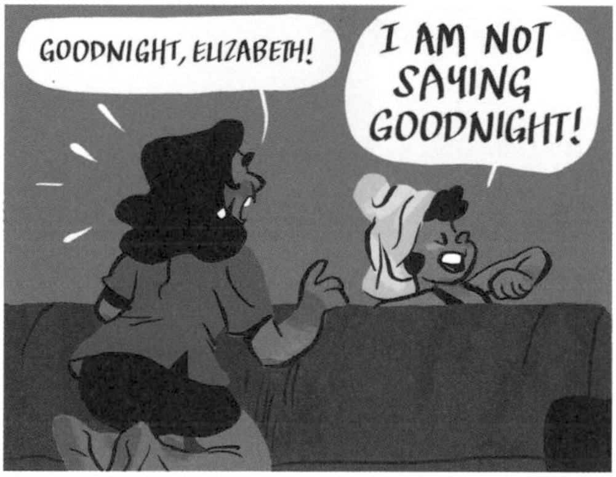
GOODNIGHT, ELIZABETH!
I AM NOT SAYING GOODNIGHT!

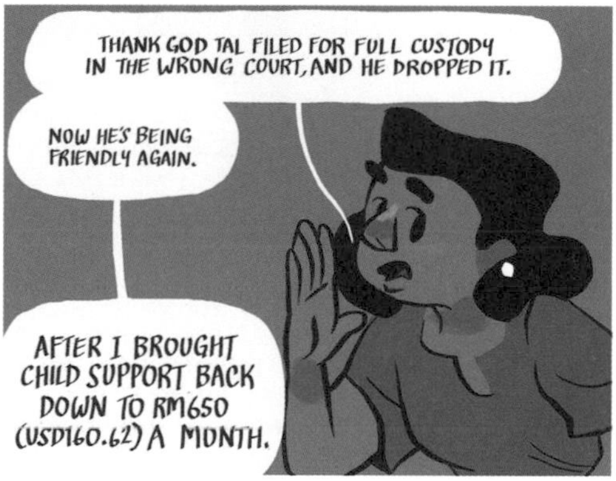
THANK GOD TAL FILED FOR FULL CUSTODY IN THE WRONG COURT, AND HE DROPPED IT.
NOW HE'S BEING FRIENDLY AGAIN.
AFTER I BROUGHT CHILD SUPPORT BACK DOWN TO RM650 (USD160.62) A MONTH.

THAT'S A LOT OF STUPID DRAMA, FOR WHAT? BECAUSE HE COULDN'T GET HIS SHIT TOGETHER AND TALK!

BUT THAT'S ALL YOU HAVE TO DO TO GET CUSTODY. PROVE I'M A 'BAD' MUSLIM.

PROPAGANDA SUGGESTING LGBT FOLKS ARE ISLAMIC 'DEVIANTS' IS RAMPANT. KINDLY MUSLIM PREACHERS IN THE MUSICAL TRY TO CONVINCE THE REBELLIOUS QUEERS TO CHANGE THEIR WICKED WAYS. THOSE WHO DON'T ARE SUDDENLY STRUCK DEAD BY LIGHTNING.

234

THIS ENDING IS IN LINE WITH THE 2010 FILM CENSORSHIP BOARD'S GUIDELINE DICTATING THAT ALL QUEER CHARACTERS SHOULD 'REPENT OR DIE' BY THE TIME THE CREDITS ROLL.

I'M MUSLIM, I'M QUEER AS HELL, AND I'M NOT GONNA LET THE HARDLINERS PUSH ME OUT OF MY OWN RELIGION. I DON'T WANT TO HIDE THIS STUFF FROM LIZ..

I TRY TO TALK ABOUT IN A WAY THAT REFLECTS A NORMAL RELATIONSHIP, WHERE PEOPLE RESPECT EACH OTHER AND HAVE HEALTHY BOUNDARIES.

ON THE OTHER HAND, I'M LIKE, WHAT IS SHE GONNA SAY TO HER FRIENDS?

IT WAS ALWAYS A LITTLE AWKWARD IN SITUATIONS WITH OTHER PARENTS, I FELT LIKE, THEY'D LOOK AT ME AND THINK, 'WHY THE FUCK IS SHE HERE?'

IT'S LIKE, OH, I'M SHAFINA'S "FRIEND," WHO'S ALWAYS AROUND, Y'KNOW?'

NAGA, 29, FREELANCE JOURNALIST (SHAFINA'S EX)

ME AND TAL USED TO BE FRIENDS WHEN SHAFINA AND ME FIRST GOT TOGETHER. WE'D HAVE DRINKS, GO DANCING, WHATEVER.

I EVEN TOLD HIM, LISTEN, IT'S NOT LIKE I'M TAKING YOUR PLACE, YOU'LL ALWAYS BE LIZ'S FATHER.

235

THEN HE STARTED THREATENING TO CALL JAIS OR JAKIM (THE RELIGIOUS POLICE) ON US, JUST BECAUSE OF HIS BRUISED MALE EGO.

AFTER A WHILE, I REALIZED THEY WERE ALL EMPTY THREATS, Y'KNOW? LIKE, IF YOU WANNA FUCKIN' DO SOMETHING, THEN DO SOMETHING. QUIT THREATENING US.

LACK OF SUPPORT FROM LAW ENFORCEMENT IS NOT UNCOMMON FOR LGBT PARENTS IN MALAYSIA. LGBT CHARACTERS IN RAHMAN'S MUSICAL SERVE AN UNSEEN 'BIG BOSS' WHO PAYS THEM TO DESTROY PUBLIC PROPERTY AND UNDERMINE PUBLIC MORALS—

WHEN YOUR LIFESTYLE IS CRIMINALIZED, IT CAN BE HARD TO GET THE POLICE ON YOUR SIDE.

I WAS KIDNAPPED BY FIVE MASKED MEN, WHO MAXED OUT ALL MY CARDS. I PRAYED FOR MY SAFETY AND FOR MY KIDS.

THERE WAS NO POLICE REPORT.

KATAN, 62, WORKS AT AN ENERGY COMPANY

WHEN I WAS RELEASED FOUR DAYS LATER, MY EXTENDED FAMILY ACCUSED MY BOYFRIEND OF BEING INVOLVED.

MY BOYFRIEND, [LAN] FELT SO BAD THAT HE LEFT ME.

I GUESS MY DAD'S FAMILY BLAMED DAD'S BOYFRIEND, LAN, FOR THE KIDNAPPING BECAUSE HE WAS AN EASY TARGET, AN OUTSIDER. UNCLE LAN WAS THE SWEETEST FUCKING PERSON IN THE WORLD.

KLARISSA, 32, FILM PRODUCER IN L.A. (KATAN'S DAUGHTER)

FOR AN ILLUSTRATION OF HOW NATIONALISM AND ISLAMIC CONSERVATISM ARE LINKED IN MALAYSIA, CONSIDER THIS— THE DIVINE RETRIBUTION SCENE IS FOLLOWED IMMEDIATELY BY ALL CAST MEMBERS (EVEN DEAD CHARACTERS) SINGING AN ANTHEM FOR NATIONAL UNITY.

THIS POTENT BLEND OF PATRIOTISM AND HOMOPHOBIA OFTEN LEADS TO A CULTURE OF INTENSE SECRECY.

236

BEING GAY WAS NEVER A PROBLEM FOR ME AT WORK.

I HAD TO BEHAVE MYSELF. I'M NOT A HARD-CORE GAY WHO CAN'T CONTROL HIMSELF, YOU KNOW? A FLIRT. MY KIDS WERE TOO YOUNG TO UNDERSTAND.

THE MORAL POLICING GOT WORSE AS WE GREW UP. MY BROTHER WAS BULLIED AT HIS METHODIST BOYS SCHOOL. EVEN MY TEACHERS WOULD SNEAK IN SOME REALLY, REALLY KEPOH (NOSY) QUESTIONS.

LIKE, "OHH, SO YOUR'S DAD'S BEST FRIEND LIVES WITH YOU?" MY PARENTS NEVER REALLY CAME TO TERMS WITH THEMSELVES. LYING WAS JUST A WAY OF LIFE.

THAT SORT OF STICKS WITH YOU, AS A KID.

CULTURAL INDOCTRINATION SPREAD TO MALAYSIAN CLASSROOMS TOO. WHEN THE 'ASMARA SONGSANG' MUSICAL WENT ON TOUR, FREE TICKETS WERE PROVIDED FOR STUDENTS.

THE EDUCATION MINISTRY RELEASED A SET OF GUIDELINES FOR PARENTS TO SPOT 'SYMPTOMS' OF GAYNESS IN STUDENTS. THESE INCLUDED "WEARING V-NECK T-SHIRTS" AND A "LACK OF INTEREST" IN THE OPPOSITE SEX.

238

THE LGBT CHARACTERS IN 'SONGSANG' ARE SPOILED, RICH AGITATORS, EDUCATED IN THE WEST.

NAJIB RAZAK, THE PRIME MINISTER SAID:

"LGBTs, PLURALISM, LIBERALISM-ALL THESE 'ISMS' ARE AGAINST ISLAM AND IT IS COMPULSORY FOR US TO FIGHT THESE."

THE MESSAGE HAMMERED HOME AGAIN AND AGAIN IS THAT QUEERNESS IS NOT WHOLESOME-AND THAT LGBT RIGHTS ARE ANTITHETICAL TO FAMILY, AND TO THE MALAYSIAN IDENTITY.

WE NEVER HAD TO HIDE ANYTHING FROM UNCLE LAN'S FAMILY. MY DAD'S SIDE IS FROM THE CITY, AND SUPPOSEDLY CITY FOLK ARE MORE OPEN MINDED, BUT UNCLE LAN'S FAMILY?

THEY WERE FROM THE KAMPUNG (VILLAGE), THEY'RE MALAY, THEY'RE MUSLIM, THEY'RE TRADITIONAL-

AND THEY ALWAYS WELCOMED US.

UNCLE LAN WAS HILARIOUS! WE'D ALWAYS PRETEND HE WAS A CHEF ON TV WHEN HE WAS IN THE KITCHEN. HE'D ALWAYS BE LIKE, 'OOOOOOH, BES KAN, TUAN TUAN DAN PUAN PUAN?" (ISN'T IT TASTY, LADIES & GENTS)

HA HA HA HA HA HA HA HA!

WHEN LAN HAD TO LEAVE, IT DEVASTATED ME. I HATED MYSELF. BUT MY CHILDREN WERE STILL WITH ME, AND I LOVED THEM.

LIFE HAD TO GO ON.

IN RAHMAN'S MUSICAL, THE LGBT CHARACTERS IGNORE THE RULES OF SOCIETY, ARROGANTLY CHOOSING THEIR OWN REALITY—

"DUNIA KITA DUNIA FANTASI!" (OURS IS A WORLD OF FANTASY!)

IN FACT, LGBT PARENTS IN MALAYSIA DO INHABIT A SEPARATE WORLD. ONE GOVERNED BY CONFUSING RULES, INVISIBLE TO MOST MALAYSIANS.

BUT THESE FAMILIES DIDN'T CHOOSE THAT WORLD—THEY ARE KEPT THERE BY AN INTOLERANT AND INDIFFERENT SYSTEM.

239

DISCLAIMER: TO PROTECT THE PRIVACY OF CERTAIN INDIVIDUALS, NAMES & IDENTIFYING DETAILS HAVE BEEN CHANGED.
CREDIT TO ALIA ALI'S REVIEW OF "ASMARA SONGSANG"-"OH, INVERTED WORLD" FOR SPECIFIC MUSICAL PLOT DETAILS AVAILABLE AT HTTP://BLOG.KAKISENI.COM/2013/03/OH-INVERTED-WORLD/

The Wonderfully Queer World of Moomin

DURING THE SUMMER IF 1914, IN A COTTAGE IN HELSINKI, FINLAND, AN UNSTOPPABLY QUEER CREATIVE FORCE WAS BORN.

BORN TO A SCULPTOR FATHER AND ILLUSTRATOR MOTHER, TOVE JANSSON WAS NO STRANGER TO THE ARTS. SHE WROTE AND ILLUSTRATED HER FIRST CHILDREN'S BOOK BY AGE 14, AS HER MOTHER DESIGNED POSTAGE STAMPS.

240

TOVE'S FIRST JOB WAS AT THE SWEDISH SATIRE MAGAZINE 'GARM'. SHE MADE A LIVING DRAWING ANTI-FASCIST ILLUSTRATIONS, WHICH SHE DID WELL INTO THE 1950S.

TOVE SPENT MUCH TIME IN SWEDEN'S STOCKHOLM ARCHIPELAGO. ISLANDS, FOR HER, WERE AN UNSHAKABLE SYMBOL OF STRENGTH AND FREEDOM. IT WAS THIS INSPIRATION THAT SPARKED THE FIRST NOVEL OF HER NOW INTERNATIONALLY RENOWNED SERIES: "THE MOOMINS".

TOVE CREATED THE MOOMINS DURING THE WINTER WAR BETWEEN FINLAND AND THE USSR IN 1939, AMIDST WWII. TOVE FELT THAT ALL COLOR HAD DIED, SO SHE DECIDED TO MAKE A BLACK AND WHITE BOOK WITH A HAPPY ENDING.

WHILE STUDYING IN PARIS, TOVE MET TUULIKKI PIETILÄ AND ASKED HER TO DANCE. TUULIKKI (OR TOOTI), REJECTED HER, AS HOMOSEXUALITY WAS STILL ILLEGAL IN FINLAND AT THE TIME.

A FEW CHARMING DRAWINGS OF FAT STRIPED CATS LATER, AND THE PAIR WERE VISITING EACH OTHER IN SECRET VIA ATTIC PASSAGEWAYS BACK IN HELSINKI.

THE MOOMIN BOOK SERIES BECAME POPULAR AROUND THE WORLD. THE NINE BOOKS SPAWNED A COMIC STRIP, NUMEROUS ANIMATED FILMS AND TV SERIES, A MUSIC ALBUM, AND EVEN A SMALL THEME PARK IN FINLAND.

LITTLE MOOMINTROLL AND HIS FRIENDS BECAME BELOVED ICONS TO CHILDREN AND ADULTS ALIKE. AND TOVE KEPT TELLING THEIR STORIES.

IN THE EARLY 1960S, TOVE AND TOOTI MOVED TO AN ISOLATED ISLAND IN THE GULF OF FINLAND, WHERE THEY LIVED TOGETHER FOR 30 SUMMERS. THE PAIR PAINTED, LISTENED TO FRENCH RECORDS, TRAVELED THE WORLD TOGETHER, AND WERE VERY MUCH IN LOVE.

TOVE'S VIBRANT QUEERNESS IS WELL-DOCUMENTED IN HER WORK. TUULIKKI APPEARS AS THE ANDROGYNOUS EXPLORER TOO-TICKY, AND TOVE'S EX-LOVER VIVICA BANDLER – A THEATRE DIRECTOR WITH WHOM TOVE HAD A WHIRLWIND AFFAIR – TAKES ON THE CHARACTER OF BOB.

'MOOMINLAND MIDWINTER' AND 'MOOMINVALLEY IN NOVEMBER' WERE TOVE'S LAST MOOMIN NOVELS – THE FIRST DEDICATED TO THE DEATH OF HER FATHER, THE SECOND MOURNING HER MOTHER. THE FINAL BOOK FEATURES A FORLORN AND EMPTY MOOMINHOUSE WITH NOBODY LEFT.

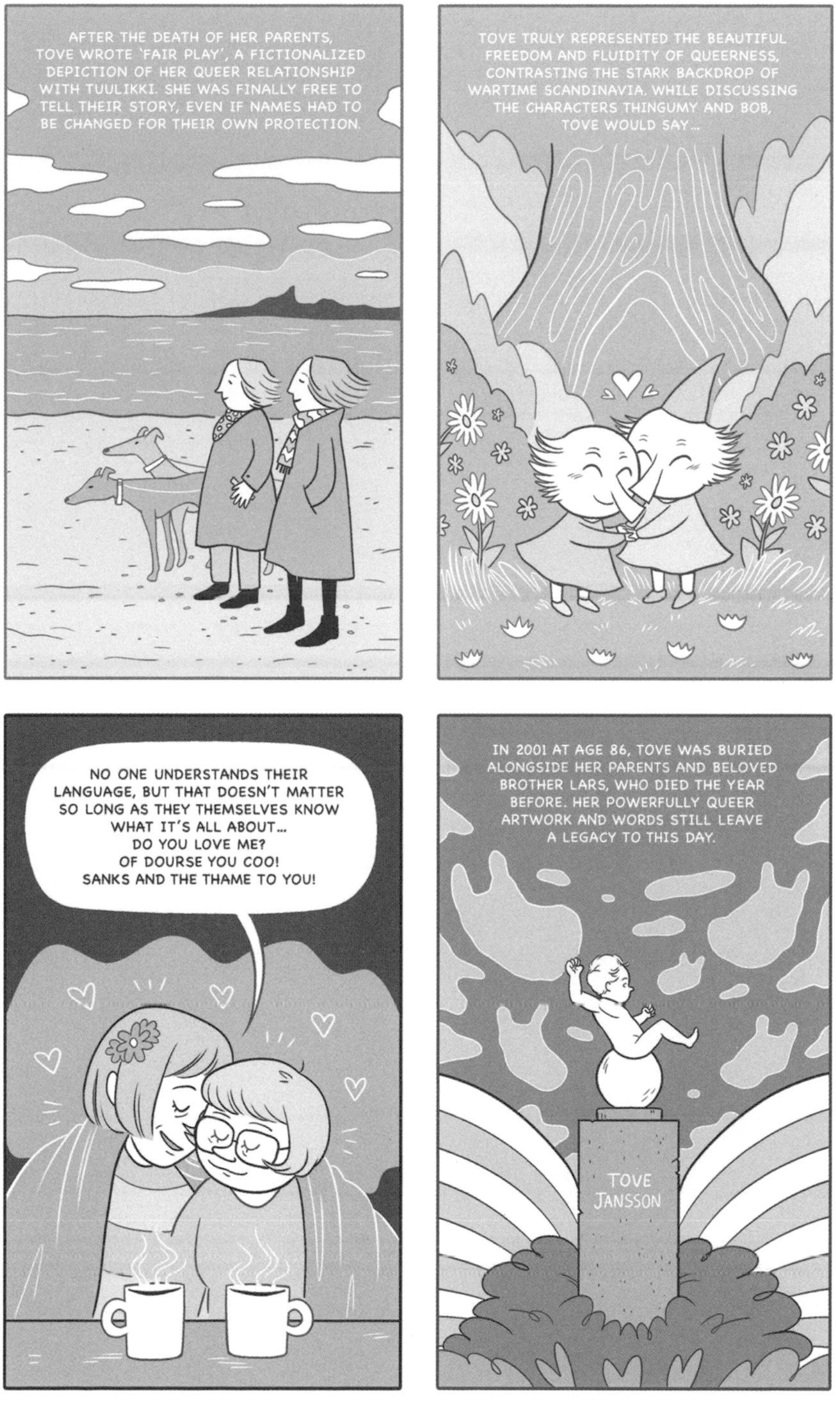
AFTER THE DEATH OF HER PARENTS, TOVE WROTE 'FAIR PLAY', A FICTIONALIZED DEPICTION OF HER QUEER RELATIONSHIP WITH TUULIKKI. SHE WAS FINALLY FREE TO TELL THEIR STORY, EVEN IF NAMES HAD TO BE CHANGED FOR THEIR OWN PROTECTION.
TOVE TRULY REPRESENTED THE BEAUTIFUL FREEDOM AND FLUIDITY OF QUEERNESS, CONTRASTING THE STARK BACKDROP OF WARTIME SCANDINAVIA. WHILE DISCUSSING THE CHARACTERS THINGUMY AND BOB, TOVE WOULD SAY...
NO ONE UNDERSTANDS THEIR LANGUAGE, BUT THAT DOESN'T MATTER SO LONG AS THEY THEMSELVES KNOW WHAT IT'S ALL ABOUT... DO YOU LOVE ME? OF DOURSE YOU COO! SANKS AND THE THAME TO YOU!
IN 2001 AT AGE 86, TOVE WAS BURIED ALONGSIDE HER PARENTS AND BELOVED BROTHER LARS, WHO DIED THE YEAR BEFORE. HER POWERFULLY QUEER ARTWORK AND WORDS STILL LEAVE A LEGACY TO THIS DAY.
TOVE JANSSON

JOEY ALISON SAYERS

Judge Not

I have some serious reservations about what your religion gets up to.
Now, now. It's not polite to criticize people's religions.
Anyway, Senator, please accept this five million dollar donation to support your bill outlawing trans people going pee.
Hey, that's not cool!
Shhh. Be polite.

The Important Pundit in: Silent Horror

Contributors

Dorian Alexander is a PhD student at the University of Washington where they study queer narrative and revolutionary fiction. They teach history at Seattle Central College and is one of the editors for *Drawing the Past: Comics and the Historical Imagination*, an upcoming book series exploring how comics shape our understandings of history.
🐦 **@mutantrights21**

Julia Bernhard is a German cartoonist and illustrator based in Mainz and Berlin. Her cartoons have been published by *The New Yorker*, *The Nib*, *The Lily* and many more. Her comic debut *Wie gut, dass wir darüber geredet haben* was published by the renowned German Avant-Verlag in 2019.
📷 **@juliabernhardcomics**

Archie Bongiovanni is a cartoonist and illustrator living in Minneapolis. They are the co-creator of *A Quick And Easy Guide To They/Them Pronouns* and their newest graphic novel, *Grease Bats*, was released by BOOM! Studios fall 2019. They've been featured on Autostraddle, Vice, Everyday Feminism, and *The Nib*.
🐦 **@babywrist**

JB Brager is a comics artist and teacher. They are a Sagittarius sun, Aquarius rising, Aries moon, and have a PhD in Gender Studies. They identify as a late bloomer.
📷 **@jbbrager**

246

Sage Coffey is a non-binary cartoonist in Chicago, IL who loves bugs and wrestling. Sage has done work for *The Nib* (obviously!), *The Washington Post*, and illustrated *I AM NOT A WOLF*, a choose-your-own-path novel from Unbound Press. (They/them).
🌐 **sagecoffey.com**

Rosa Colón Guerra is a comic artist and illustrator living in San Juan, Puerto Rico. Her work has been published in *The Nib*, *The Believer*, *The Lily*, and in the Eisner Winner *Puerto Rico Strong* by Lion Forge.
🐦 **@sodapopcomics**

Shelby Criswell is an illustrator and troublemaker in SATX. They've done some cool stuff for *The Nib*, *Oh Joy Sex Toy*, and one time designed a VIP pass for Nelly, somehow? They're working on a cool book at the moment with Matthew Erman.
🐦 **@shelby_criswell**

Max Dlabick is an illustrator and comicker that crawled out of the mudbanks of the Mississippi River. They draw webcomics like *André and Karl* and *Stick and Poke* and will continue to put comics on the web for years to come.
🐦 **@mdlabick**

Dylan Edwards is a queer & trans comic creator, best known for *Transposes* and *Valley of the Silk Sky*. He is the recipient of the Association of LGBTQ Journalists' 2016 Excellence in Transgender Coverage Award for *How I Told My Grandma I'm Transgender* and the Prism Comics 2017 Best Short Form Comic Award for *Nothing Wrong With Me*.
🌐 **studiondr.com**

Trinidad Escobar is the author of forthcoming graphic novel *Of Sea And Venom*, published by FSG. She lives with her son and partner in the Bay Area, California.
📷 **@escobarcomics**

Mady G is a cartoonist, illustrator, and author based in NY's Hudson Valley. Their educational graphic novel, *A Quick And Easy Guide to Queer And Trans Identities*, from Limerence/Oni Press, has received multiple awards in both the US and Canada
🐦 @madygcomics

Melanie Gillman is a cartoonist who specializes in LGBTQ books for kids and teens. They are the creator of the webcomic and graphic novel *As the Crow Flies*, published in 2017 by Iron Circus Comics, and winner of the 2018 Stonewall Honor Award. Their newest book, *Stage Dreams*, was published by Lerner/Graphic Universe in 2019.

Alex Graudins is a cartoonist based in RI. She illustrated *Science Comics: The Brain* and *History Comics: The Great Chicago Fire* and likes to make comics about living with anxiety.
📷 @toonyballoony

Levi Hastings is a queer illustrator and cartoonist based in Seattle. A frequent contributor to *The Nib*, he's currently working on a full-length graphic novel adaptation of Washington's Gay General with Josh Trujillo.
📷 @LeviHastingsArt

Binglin Hu is a Baltimore-based graphic designer by day and cartoonist/illustrator by night. They seek joy in creating sincere and colorful work about love, life, loss, and furries.
🌐 binglinhu.com

Robyn Jordan is a cartoonist and public-school art teacher based in Seattle. She regularly self publishes mini-comics. Her memoir and journalism stories have been featured in Vox, Huffington Post, *The Stranger*, *Seattle Weekly*, *The Nib*, and *Mutha Magazine*.
📷 @robynjordanvolcano

Shing Yin Khor is a Malaysian-American cartoonist and installation artist exploring immigrant identity and memory. They are the author of the road trip memoir *The American Dream? A Journey on Route 66*, from Lerner Publishing, and won an Ignatz Award in 2018 with their minicomic *Say It With Noodles*.
🐦 @sawdustbear

Maia Kobabe is a nonbinary, queer author and illustrator from the Bay Area. Eir first book, *Gender Queer: A Memoir*, was published by Lion Forge in May 2019. Maia's work can be found on instagram and patreon.com/maiakobabe.
📷 @redgoldsparks

Kazimir Lee is a Lambda Award-winning cartoonist and illustrator based in Brooklyn, New York. They are a queer parent, pornographer, and journalist, and have contributed to *Oh Joy Sex Toy* and *Slate*. They're sorry.
🌐 kazimirlee.com

Matt Lubchansky is a cartoonist and illustrator in Queens, NY. They are the associate editor of *The Nib*.
🐦 @Lubchansky

Mariah-Rose Marie is a comic artist, illustrator, educator, and poet based in Los Angeles, CA where she sometimes storyboards for TV.
📷 **@biophonies**

Ria Martinez is a cartoonist and illustrator based in New Jersey. You can find their comics work in *ELEMENTS: Earth A Comic Anthology by Creators of Color!*, *Rumble Royale*, and *Bad Mojo*. They also co-created and are the lead artist for the webcomic *Casual Hex*. Their latest work can be seen in the mobile game *FictIf* created by Nix Hydra.

Jason Michaels is a writer and renaissance man (has worked a lot of day jobs) based out of the Hudson Valley. A player of games and hater of fascists, he spends his time thinking about the former and yelling at the latter.
🐦 **@flotsamandjason**

Sarah Mirk is a visual journalist who writes and edits books, articles, and nonfiction comics. She is also a somewhat obsessive zine maker.
🐦 **@sarahmirk**

248

Sfé R. Monster is an award winning trans & queer Canadian comic maker; creator of *Beyond: The Queer Sci-Fi & Fantasy Comic Anthology*, and their comic *Eth's Skin.* They most recently adapted *Minecraft* into a graphic novel for Dark Horse Comics.
📷 **@sfemonster**

Hazel Newlevant is a cartoonist whose works include *No Ivy League*, *Sugar Town*, and *If This Be Sin*. They have edited and published the anthologies *Chainmail Bikini* and *Comics for Choice*.
🐦 **@HNewlevant**

Breena Nuñez is an Afro Central American cartoonist and educator born and raised in the Bay Area. They received an MFA in Comics from California College of the Arts and have contributed a story in *Drawing Power: Women's Stories of Sexual Violence, Harassment, and Survival*.

Nero O'Reilly is an indigenous Latinx erotic cartoonist living in Seattle, WA. His work has been published by Slipshine, Iron Circus Comics, Fortuna Media, and more.
🌐 **itsnero.com**

Elísabet Rún is an Icelandic comic artist and illustrator, whose work focuses mainly on politics, gender, and mental health.
📷 **elisabetrun**

Joey Alison Sayers is a cartoonist living in Oakland, CA. Her work has appeared in *Mad* magazine, the *Best American Comics* anthology, and she is the current writer of the daily comic strip *Alley Oop*.
🐦 **@joeyalison**

Taneka Stotts is an award-winning comics creator and television writer based in Los Angeles, CA. They have won the 2017 Ignatz and 2018 Eisner awards for best anthology. A co-founder of Ascend Comics with Der-shing Helmer, they continue to focus on comics as a medium for their various stories. Their latest work can be found in *ELEMENTS: Earth A Comic Anthology by Creators of Color!*
🌐 **TanekaStotts.com**

Alexis Sudgen is an animator by day and a comic creator by night. She is working on an autobiographical comic, *It's All For The Breast*, about breast reduction, gender, and body image. Previous titles include *The Disappearance of Melody Dean* and *My Sister's Voice*. Originally from Australia, she now lives in Vancouver, Canada.
🌐 **alexissudgen.com**

Scout Tran is a trans*†° mixed-việt goblin "surviving" the hell of late-stage San Francisco by ruining free motorcycles. Ey has two Eisner noms, a Prism Award and some other cool awards, and has been commissioned by the SFMOMA and the Exploratorium for work that has nothing to do with comics.

Josh Trujillo is a writer based in Los Angeles. He is of strong moral fiber and loves his dog, Quinn, very much.
🐦 **@LostHisKeysMan**

Delta Vasquez is a cartoonist and animator based in Portland, OR. He is currently working as an editorial assistant at *The Nib*.
🐦 **@heartseeeker**

Sasha Velour is a gender-fluid drag queen. Velour won Season 9 of the Emmy-winning reality TV competition *RuPaul's Drag Race*. She is the creator and director of the acclaimed drag revue *Nightgowns* which was turned into an 8-part series for new streaming platform Quibi.

249

Sam Wallman is a cartoonist, comics-journalist and labour organiser based in Melbourne, Australia.
🌐 **samwallman.com**

Kendra Wells is an illustrator and comic artist living in Brooklyn, NY. Their debut graphic novel, *Tell No Tales: Pirates of the Southern Seas*, will be published by Abrams in 2020, with their first solo graphic novel, *Real Hero S#!t*, coming in 2022 via Iron Circus Comics.
🐦 **@kendrawcandraw**

Alison Wilgus is a Brooklyn-based bestselling writer and cartoonist. Alison's most recent comics are *The Mars Challenge*, a space book for teens illustrated by Wyeth Yates, and *Chronin*, a queer time travel duology from Tor.
🐦 **@aliwilgus**

Bianca Xunise is an illustrator and cartoonist based in Chicago. Her work primarily focuses on the plight and daily struggles identifying as a young black feminist weirdo in modern society. Her storytelling ranges from simple, relatable slices of life to complex, nuanced narratives about police brutality featured in *The Nib* that have garnered her an Ignatz Award for Promising New Talent.
🐦 **@biancaxunise**

BE GAY DO COMICS!

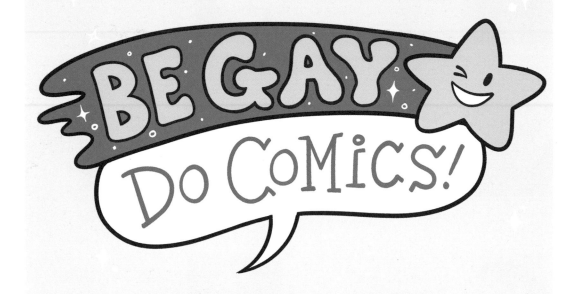

Thanks for Reading!

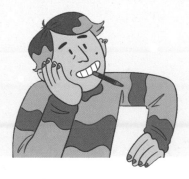